GIRL
ON
FIRE

DANIELLE
BANNISTER

CITY OWL
PRESS

GIRL ON FIRE
By: Danielle Bannister

CITY OWL PRESS
www.cityowlpress.com

Cover Design by MiblArt. All stock photos licensed appropriately.

Edited by Tina Moss.

For information on subsidiary rights, please contact the publisher at info@cityowlpress.com.

Print Edition ISBN: 978-1-64898-093-0

Digital Edition ISBN: 978-1-64898-092-3

Printed in the United States of America

PRAISE FOR DANIELLE BANNISTER

"Bannister weaved a gripping tale with an original concept making *Pulled* a very enjoyable read. I was never quite sure where the author would direct her characters, what the outcome would be which I really liked. And the final outcome was certainly not what I expected, so bravo!"
— *Two Nerds with Words*

"Reading books from authors that you have read before and you think you know their style of writing, and then BAM!!! They go and write something that is completely off the wall for them, you end up loving that author just a little bit more."
— *Kelly's Nerdy Obsession*

"*The ABC's of Dee* was funny and engaging from the first page. I loved being inside Dee's head as she navigated her hilarious dating adventures. She was honest with herself almost to a fault, but her ongoing inner commentary was refreshing and relatable."
— *Avid Reader*

"*The First 100 Kisses* is Bannister's next standalone. I loved every minute of it! The characters are a great match. Complete opposites. The lessons went from sweet to sinful. It was perfect."
— *Two Book Pushers*

"Holy mac and cheese, or should I say burgers and fries *wink* , *The Second 100 Kisses* is just everything to me right now!! A perfect balance of swoon, smexy, comedy, drama, angst, and character building...all while keeping it real. I devoured these books in one sitting and both left me with all the feels."
— *Book Flirts*

To all those struggling to find the light.

Part One

PART ONE

SARAH

WHY

Everyone always wants to know about the first fire I lit. I honestly don't remember it.

I was four.

From what my mom told the media, I stole her cigarette lighter while she was "napping" one day. She recited that story a hundred times to the countless reporters that flocked to our door. She relished the semi-fame that only TV crews could bring to our skanky little trailer park.

Apparently, I'd practically set the whole dump where I used to play on fire. Like I said, though, I don't remember that first time. But I remember every one since.

It was as if something clicked in my brain. Something inside ignited right along with that next blaze. Each fire brought with it a rush, a thrill of excitement, and a profound sense of calmness. Each strike of a match became an extension of who I was—the strong part. The part no one could touch.

My mom never realized the craving that grew inside me after. No shocker there. She never noticed much about me. No one ever dreamed I would play with fire again. I took pride in that. I hid it well for so, so long. Those early years were dark. Darker than you could imagine. Fire was the only brightness to be found.

Let me be clear. There is no forgiveness for what I've done. I deserve what happened to me; of that, I have no doubt.

But where ... how do I even begin to explain?

I guess I'll start with how I ended up here, which is, no doubt, the only beginning you'll care about.

The beginning that ends with the why.

SALVATION

California. That's where I decided I was going to start my life over. It seemed like a good place to disappear into the masses. As good as any, I supposed. I had gotten it into my head that once I turned eighteen, things were going to get better. I'd be an adult. I'd be, I don't know, smarter somehow.

It wasn't the first time I'd run away from home, but it was sure as hell going to be the last. I couldn't stay there. Not anymore. I knew leaving meant I'd have to hitch rides again, something I wasn't looking forward to. But nothing in life is free, especially not a lift from a trucker.

By the time I'd made it to Indiana, my soul was about as low as it could get. That's where Al found me. I was sitting outside a convenience store, sizing up the truckers as they stopped to fuel up, and wondering which one would be the least cruel to a hitcher. It was hard to gauge most of the time. The ones that looked the nicest often were the most sadistic.

Al didn't say anything to me. He just stopped in front of me and handed me a Sprite and a Snickers bar. I looked up at him, my guard raised even though he looked like a hillbilly Santa. He wore a dirty white t-shirt, red suspenders, and a bright neon camo hat.

"Looks like you could use these more than I could," he said.

"Thanks." I hadn't eaten for far too long, and I was hungry. I tore into the bar with the vigor of an animal, which is what I felt like. I had some money on me, but I tried never to spend it——only when starvation seemed imminent.

"You need a lift somewhere, missy?" he asked. I saw what appeared to be genuine kindness. You can tell a lot about a person by the eyes. His were pinched in a smile, not narrowed like a hunter sizing up his prey. That look I knew all too well. Still, he was a stranger, so I didn't answer at first, mostly because I was chewing, but I was also wondering just how safe he'd be.

"You remind me of my daughter," he said. "She would have been eighteen this year." His lips curled inward at an unpleasant memory. He had a dead kid. He struck me as the protective grandpa-type.

"Where you headed?" I asked.

"Mullen, Nebraska."

I stood up. "Well, sure beats the hell out of this place." I met his eye. "What's your price?"

"My price?" he asked, eyebrows shooting toward the sky.

"For the ride?"

His gaze softened, as though understanding what I was asking.

"How about you just help unload the truck when we get there, and we call it square." He hitched his thumb toward his truck.

"What's in it, dead bodies?"

He chuckled. "Well, I guess that's the gamble you'll have to take if you want the lift."

I looked back at the truck again. It had no logos or markings that would give any indication of what was inside. I chewed on my lip and scanned the other lingering truckers before deciding.

"My name's Sarah," I said, holding out my hand.

"I'm Al. Al King. Pleasure to meet you."

Of course, in retrospect, I should have told him, "No, thanks," and taken my chances on another lift, but he seemed like a decent guy, and unknowingly or not, I really needed something decent in my life.

"So what's Mullen known for?" I asked the second day on the road. The breakfast he'd bought for me still weighed heavy in my stomach. I'd forgotten what a real meal had felt like. While he had paid the tab, I had tucked two of the leftover biscuits into my bag to savor later.

"Oh, well, Mullen is a small town, so aside from cattle, probably The Sandhills," Al replied with unmistakable pride.

"What's that? A restaurant?" I asked.

"The Sandhills is more of an area of land than one set place. They're basically grass-covered sand dunes. Awful pretty to look at. A might finer than out there," he said, pointing to the vastness. I followed his gesture and glanced over the static view. We'd been driving for hours without coming across a single bump or curve in the road, not even in the landscape around it. It appeared like we were never making any forward progress but instead, frozen in this part of the world, forever.

"So you have cattle and green sand. Sounds awesome," I muttered.

He laughed a deep, raspy laugh, the kind of laugh you get from years of smoking, although I didn't see the remnants of cigarette butts in his ashtray—only loose change. I frowned, wishing he did smoke. I never smoked, but man, I loved to watch those embers burn.

"We have our fun," he said.

I turned my head and rolled my eyes. "Sure."

"You just wait until you see what you're unloading tomorrow, darlin'."

I let out a breath. "Can't wait."

Al's smile shifted a bit. I got the sense he was going to start fishing for information soon. So far, he hadn't said much, as though knowing I wasn't going to speak until I was ready, if at all. But it was clear he had reached a point where the inquiries would begin.

"Mind if I ask how old you are?" He started with an easy one.

I got that question a lot. Most of the time if I got asked how old I was it was because the guy wanted to know if I was legal or not, which most of the time I hadn't been. With Al, I got the feeling that he was just curious, so I told the truth. "I'll be nineteen this month," I said, picking at my nails. They were caked in filth and never seemed to get clean.

Al glanced over at me. "When?"

"Friday the 13th, of course."

Al laughed. "Aren't you the lucky one?"

I stared at the horizon. "Cursed is more like it."

We didn't talk for a few minutes, which was fine. It was easy riding with Al. Perhaps that's why I didn't ditch him at breakfast that morning. My normal rule was one day. Any more than that and you risked forming an unhealthy bond that even the nice ones had a hard time resisting, but something told me Al wasn't like the others.

"Sarah. You got a last name?" His beady eyes squinted as he smiled.

"Brickle." I realized after I said it that I probably shouldn't have. No one had asked or even cared what my last name was, so it sort of slipped out before I could take it back.

"Brickle? Interesting surname."

I yawned. "Yeah, it's actually dying out. I'm sure my mom was pissed at me for not being a boy so I could carry out the legacy." I scoffed. One hell of a legacy that would be.

He laughed but didn't let the subject drop as I'd hoped. "What about the rest of your family? Got some out this way, do you? Heading for a visit?" I could hear the skepticism in his voice. So far, I had managed to keep our limited conversations away from my past.

"Nope," I said, pulling my knees to my chest. I had already kicked off my shoes, so I flexed my feet a bit, enjoying the coolness of the cab.

He nodded, as though he expected as much.

"Your mom know you're out here?"

I let loose a short breath. I'd better nip this conversation before it escalated. "I had a mom. She was a meth addict. She died. My dad left when I was two. No other family. End of story, okay?"

If he was shocked by my bluntness, he didn't show it.

"Can I ask one last question? And then, I promise, I'll stop pestering you." I could feel Al's eyes flick over to me, waiting, so I rubbed my forehead as permission.

"What are you running from?"

"Honestly?" I asked.

He kept his eyes on the road but nodded.

I laid my head back against the seat and closed my eyes. "Myself."

"Damn hard thing to hide from for long," he said simply.

I stretched my arms back and gave a hearty yawn. "Don't I know it."

I wasn't tired so much as I was bored. I was getting antsy. I dug into my bag on the floor and pulled out a small wad of cash. I'd learned a long time ago to never hold it all in one place. I had forty bucks in my shoe, six in my jeans, and a ten spot in my bra. The backpack I'd lifted from the trash only held a few bills and a bit of loose change. I'm not proud of the services I had to provide to get what little money I had, but at least I wasn't a drug addict throwing it all away. I was being frugal and saving everything I possibly could for that reset button in California.

I fished free six single bills and pressed them as flat as I could on the leg of my pants then placed them in the cup holder next to Al.

"For breakfast, earlier," I said. I'd never eaten in a truck stop diner until that morning. "And for letting me sleep in the cab last night," I added, placing another dollar in with the others.

"Keep your money," he said.

I shook my head. "No, I owe you. It's not much, I know, but take it. Please."

"It seems like you could use that money more than I could."

I glanced over at him. He wasn't saying it to be hurtful, but rather as a way of understanding. I sensed he'd find a way to sneak it back into my bag if I didn't take it, so I relented. Letting out a breath, I grabbed the money and slid it back inside.

"You know, when I was about your age, I stole a car," Al said.

My eyes narrowed in disbelief. He didn't seem the type for grand theft auto.

"My old man's car," he continued.

I frowned. "Well, that's not really the same thing."

"He was the sheriff at the time."

I laughed. "Not smart."

Al was watching the road, but his eyes looked far away, lost in thought. "After he cooled down, he asked me why I stole it. I shrugged and said, 'I needed to get to Annabel's place.'" He smiled. "She's my wife now, see, but back then, I was smitten, and I needed to see her every minute of every day. I told him, 'I needed that car so I could go see her.'" His smile faded a bit. "He said, 'Son, you don't need a car. You need a job. A car is just a thing, but a job gives you the freedom to choose your path.'"

I nodded politely because that seemed like what he wanted me to do.

"Do you have a job? Waiting out there for ya, that is?" he asked.

I snorted. "I don't even have a path." It was meant to sound funny, but instead, it came out terribly sad.

Al pursed up his lips like he was thinking about how he could save my soul. I shook my head, amused.

"Look, I appreciate the lift, but I know what you're trying to do."

He peeked over at me, one bushy white eyebrow lifted high. "What's that, now?"

"I don't need your advice." I blinked. "I don't need anything. Or anyone." I said those words too low for him to hear. "After I unload whatever is on this truck, I'll be out of your hair."

Al surprised me by laughing. "So you want to remain an enigma, huh? Well, that's all fine and good, I suppose." He turned his attention to me for a moment. "I didn't listen to my father when he lectured me either." His expression was kind, but I could tell he was upset. "See, the thing is I have got myself in a bit of a pickle."

"A pickle?" I snickered.

"Of sorts. My oldest son, Brad, well, he just graduated from the police academy." Al smiled. "He takes after his grandpa." The smile faded from his face. "But he's going to be moving to Boston next week to start work and won't be around over the summer to help like he used to. I was hoping I'd be able to help Kyle this year instead, but Annabel's taken ill, the kind of sick you don't just bounce back from..." His eyes began to well up. "She needs me, see, and I can't afford to hire someone to help him."

"Who's Kyle?"

Big Al's eyes cleared as he gave me a proud grin. "He's my youngest. Just turned nineteen. Boy is smart as a tack but stubborn as a mule. He should be in college, making something of himself, but he's insisted on staying on to take after the cattle and his mother when I go on runs." He sighed. "Claims we'd never make it if he left too."

"Would you?" I asked, already sensing his answer.

Al's eyes grew dark. "No. Probably not."

"He's not stubborn then, just smart," I offered. "Like you said."

He gave me a thin smile. "Too smart for his own good." Al took a deep inhalation as he stared down the long road that ran far into the never-ending horizon. "I can't keep on like this much longer. Truckin' is hard on your body, worse on your mind."

"Amen to that," I said, shifting positions for the hundredth time since breakfast.

He was still peering at the horizon. A heavy burden weighed on his mind, so I sat and waited for him to compose himself. It wasn't a time for talking. I had a sneaking suspicion he was gearing up to ask me to help him, and I wasn't sure how I was going to answer.

"Look, Sarah, I'll be straight with you." Al turned on his blinker and slowly eased off the highway, flicking on his hazards before he parked the rig. He turned to face me. "I know we just met, but I have a way of telling a bad seed from a good one," he started.

I held up my hand in protest. "Let me stop you right there, Al." I tucked a chunk of my dark hair around my ear; hair that I relied on in the past to mask my face, but here, it felt like he needed to be clear on who I really was. I needed him to see the real me. "You're sweet and all, but I'm not who you think I am. I'm one of the bad seeds."

He scoffed. "Nah, you just haven't been given the right soil to grow in, that's all."

Such a simple statement, but one that tried to take root in my soul nevertheless. If only that were true... My eyes glazed over with emotion for half a second. I had to swallow the thickness forming in my throat. I'd be damned if he was gonna make me cry.

"Come work for me," he said. "Just for the summer, if you like. I can give you room and board," he said, shifting to face me better, "and a ride to California." At that, I looked up at him. "I go out in late September...I'd be happy to bring you along."

All of my instincts told me to turn him down, to resist the temptation of feeling like I was needed somewhere, if only for a few months. But, of course, I didn't. I told him I would help him, just for the summer. Little did I know that I had effectively set the wheels in motion—wheels that could never be stopped once I had laid eyes on Kyle.

HAY

I'm not sure what I was expecting when I met Kyle. Okay, that's a lie. I had conjured up in my mind exactly what he was going to look like. I had pictured him walking out of some worn-down gray corral, wearing dirtied up jeans, boots covered with dung, the sun shining through the holes in his cowboy hat. There would be a long strand of hay balancing delicately between perfect lips. He'd have broad shoulders about to burst out of a light blue v-neck t-shirt. And then he'd smile, curious-like, at the girl that walked into his life.

Yup. That's where my mind went. Not proud that it went right into the cliché of every stupid girl's dream, but if we're being honest, that's what I imagined meeting Kyle was going to be like. I should have known that fantasy is always better than reality.

The corral was red, not gray, and it was in desperate need of a paint job. The jeans and boots I got right, but that seemed to be what everyone wore out here. Instead of the cowboy hat, there was a baseball cap. The brim of it was curled tight around his face, and the fabric was dirty and lifting at the sides. There was no straw hanging from his lips either. Instead, he spat as he came out of the stall. A big fat gob of it. It made me cringe. His shoulders may have been broad under the muddy flannel over-shirt he wore, but he most definitely did not give me a curious-like smile.

"Who's she?" Kyle grunted. Grunted. Like a goddamn caveman.

Al grinned and clapped his arm around my shoulder, hard enough to make me grimace under the weight.

"Kyle, I want you to meet Sarah Brickle."

Kyle shook his head and frowned, clearly annoyed. "Another runaway, Dad? Really?" He spat again then reached behind him and pulled out a pair of work gloves. He barely looked me in the eye as he approached. "Sure hope you're stronger than the last one." He threw the gloves at me, which I miraculously caught, surprising us both.

"Now, Kyle..." Al began.

"Save it, Dad. You're late as it is. We need to get this hay out before sundown."

Kyle walked off, but he kept peering back at me with an unreadable expression. I stood there, feeling about as big as an ant hill and not sure why until he disappeared behind the truck.

Al took off his hat and scratched the back of his head. Thin strands of white hair covered a nearly bald scalp. "Good to see you too, son," he mumbled, then smiled down at me. "Don't mind him. He's just—"

"Pissed?" I volunteered.

Al's face softened a bit at my bluntness. "Yeah, guess you could say that."

I fiddled a bit with the large worn gloves in my hands. "You got a thing for runaways?" I asked, staring at him through the haze of the afternoon sun.

"Ah, I just have a soft spot for wounded souls, is all," Al said. "I try to give them a chance. A chance the rest of the world saw fit to take away."

"So I am to be a social experiment, then?"

He gave me a sad grin. "No, no. Nothing like that, really." He nodded toward the back of the truck, where I could hear Kyle already inside the bed moving about. "It's just, well, we've not had very good luck with the ones I've brought home. He thinks I'm wasting my time trying to help," he whispered.

"He's not wrong," I replied.

"Why don't you let me be the judge of that."

Together, we walked to the back of the truck, which had been opened and was piled to the ceiling with bales of hay. Kyle had taken off his flannel shirt and tossed it onto the fence beside the truck, revealing those broad shoulders and T-shirt I'd envisioned him having. Perhaps we were both a cliché.

"Kyle, can you show Sarah the ropes? She'll be helping out around here this summer." Kyle paused in mid-movement, as though trying to bite his tongue. After a second, he started tossing the hay from the back towards a long metal conveyor belt. The belt led to a loft area above the barn. Long, hook-like claws dug into the bales as he hoisted them easily down from the tallest row in the truck. Methodically he moved, tossing the bales, then moving to hook another, then tossing again, all with a rehearsed rhythm of a dancer. "Please, Kyle. Let her help. I want to check on your mother."

"Fine," he answered, but he still didn't acknowledge my presence.

Al squeezed my shoulder. "His bark is worse than his bite."

"Awesome," I muttered.

He walked off, leaving me alone with Kyle. I wasn't about to take his shit.

"Look, I happen to agree with you. I *am* a waste of anyone's time, but I owe a debt to your father for the lift and treating me like a human being and not some hooker someone got to use for a few hours." Kyle stopped working and peered down at me, either judging me or pitying me—neither of which I liked. "That sort of kindness doesn't happen in my world very often, so I'm going to pay back that kindness. Like I said I would."

He looked over to the barn, and then back down at me from the bed of the truck. Sweat had already begun to bead along his head and dampen the front of his shirt.

"I'll stay out of your way," I said. "Just tell me what you need me to do, and I'll do it."

He pinched the bridge of his nose, let loose a deep sigh, then stared at me. "Fine." He pointed towards the metal conveyer belt. "Stack the bales as high as you can, near the belt. When this is unloaded, I'll help you get it into the barn."

I nodded like I understood.

"Wear the gloves, and lift with your knees," he advised before going back to his work.

I let free a breath of my own and walked over to the mound of hay that had begun forming. I reached towards the closest one and lifted it up, surprised by the weight. "Jesus," I grunted, dropping it with a thud next to the belt. I swear I heard Kyle snicker, which pissed me off. I vowed not to make any further sounds of complaint.

After a few minutes though, I began panting. My muscles started to burn. The bales kept coming, one after another, and soon they mounted around me like a prison, obscuring both Kyle and the truck from my view.

Sweat drenched my hair, great clumps of it stuck to my face and clung to the back of my neck. The bales were so heavy I had to hug each one to my chest, leveraging them against my body to help ease the weight. As I stacked the start of a fourth pile, I collapsed onto it, needing to catch my breath.

"Sitting down on the job?" I heard Kyle ask. A moment later he appeared around the mountain of hay still waiting to be stacked.

"Just taking a break," I said.

He smiled, a telling grin that conveyed he had pegged me right. I hated it.

Brushing past me, he flicked on the conveyer belt and started taking the hay in the mounds yet to be stacked and tossing them onto the conveyor, completely ignoring the ones I'd piled up as instructed. I watched as each bale rose to the top and fell into the loft above.

He kept grabbing the unstacked bales, completely ignoring the ones I had labored on, all while grinning the whole time.

"You asshole," I said.

He stopped working but only for a second.

"You didn't need these stacked first," I spat.

"Nope. I sure didn't. Stacking them is sort of a waste of time, don't you think?" He tipped his baseball hat at me then started back in again.

I stood up and marched over to him. "You get off on that, do you? Watching people suffer?" I hissed. I'd had my fair share of sick bastards in the world. It looked like Kyle would be no different.

He turned to look at me, first my eyes, then down at my neck. I folded my arms across my chest. Yup. Just like every single guy in the world.

As he walked over to me, I started to shut down. It was really the only way to get through it sometimes. You had to give in to the inevitable, purely for self-preservation. If you let your mind wander, it didn't hurt so much.

He grabbed my head and tilted my neck to the side gently. I closed my eyes and waited for the feel of his lips.

"Hold still," he ordered.

"Or what?" I said on autopilot. Lots of men liked to give orders and consequences. It got them off faster, so I always tried to expedite the role-play with my smart mouth.

"Or this tick is going to bury its head into your flesh."

My head whipped up.

"The what?" My hands flew toward my neck. Panic filled my veins. I was more scared of a bug then being used sexually.

He batted my hands away. "Don't scratch at it. You don't want to detach the tick's head from its body." I swallowed the urge to claw at my neck and instead held my breath. He took his gloves off and tossed them to the ground, then reached into his back pocket, opened a switchblade and held it up to my neck.

"Whoa, what the hell?" I said, stepping back.

Kyle frowned at my retreat. "Stay still. I need to scrape it off."

"Can't you just flick it off with your finger or something?" The hysteria in my voice was embarrassing.

Kyle shook his head at my stupidity. I'd never been bitten by a tick before, but coming at me with a knife seemed a little extreme.

"It's not that easy. How they bite you is far more grotesque than you want to know. Ticks carry toxins that can be transferred when they're squeezed. It's better to just force them off with something sharp...assuming it hasn't buried itself in too deep, that is."

"Oh, God..."

He rolled his eyes. "Just be still. I won't hurt you, but I need to make sure I get its head."

"And if you don't?"

"Then it swims inside your body and can make you really sick. Can I take it out now?" His eyebrows rose in annoyance at my childish behavior.

I swallowed hard, but I made myself be still as I watched him come at me with the blade. I flinched.

"Don't look at the knife. Look at me," he said.

I listened to him, which was a mistake. Up close Kyle was far more striking than he had been from afar. He had those piercing blue eyes that only TV vampires or cowboys in magazine ads have, and his jaw was lined with dark stubble from a day or two of growth. His skin had turned a rich golden brown from years under the sun, with dark locks of hair that peeked out of the edges of his hat.

He clenched his jaw as he worked the knife against my neck. I hated that I'd noticed a small mole that touched the corner of his upper lip. I hated, even more, when I wondered what it might be like to kiss that mark. I knew, in that moment, that this would not end well.

"Got it," he said, which allowed me to breathe again.

I reached for my neck, relieved to find that I wasn't bleeding out. There was just a small bump from where it had been. Then I shivered. "Did you get the head?"

"Yeah." He placed the bug on the fence post before squishing it with the back of the blade.

"Jesus, are there any more?" I spun around, lifting my hair, exposing my neck as I did. I felt so squirmy. I hadn't even felt the one on my neck. They could be anywhere.

"It's a farm. We have bugs," Kyle said, folding his knife back down. "Just check yourself over before you get in the bath tonight. They like hairy spots, so," he fumbled, blushing, "look for those areas, especially."

"Oh my God, gross." I shivered wildly, which made him laugh. It looked good on him. Natural. It was almost as if the façade of the tough guy he had been wearing fell off and the real him came out.

"Let me guess, city girl?"

"New York, but not the city. I lived in the 'less desirable' neighborhoods."

"They don't have bugs in New York?" He frowned.

"Sure we do, I just, ugh, never had one of *those* on me." I squirmed again.

"Well, my advice? Get yourself some boots and tuck your jeans into them. They can crawl up from the ground and then work up the inside of your pant leg pretty easy." He pointed at my head. "You should tie your hair up too, so you can see them if they get on you, wear gloves and...try not to use your chest to carry the hay." He gestured to my shirt that was covered in stray bits of loose straw.

I instantly began to brush them away, terrified more of those suckers were on me.

"You know, I've lived through a lot of shit," I said, scanning the ground. "Leave it to me to die from a tick bite."

Kyle smiled, showing off an adorable crooked grin. "There are worse ways to go, I suppose."

"Gee, thanks."

"You'll be fine. Most of the critters here are harmless, like those ticks, for the most part. They don't all carry sickness, but you want to be cautious. The chickens will eat most of those for you anyway. It's the spiders you want to be careful of."

I jumped onto one of the bales of hay. "Spiders?"

Kyle laughed. "Welcome to Nebraska, Sarah."

"I'm going to die here," I muttered.

"Come on, let's get a drink and get you properly geared up for this kind of work." He walked over to the conveyor belt and switched it off. "I can show you where you'll be staying."

"Great idea," I said, hopping off the hay, not wanting to touch anything in nature ever again.

RUNAWAY

As we walked toward the house, I took my first real look at the place I'd be staying for the next three months. It was a lot smaller than I'd imagined it would be. There looked to be roughly ten or twelve cattle grazing in a nearby field and a small vegetable garden off the porch.

"Is this the whole farm?" I asked, swatting away a fly.

"It's not really a farm in the sense you're probably thinking about. We have a small herd that we eat a few of, sell a few of. The cattle are more of a hobby of Dad's. He drives trucks most of the year and Mom runs a small farm stand. Well, she used to, anyway." His face shifted before he shoved his hands into his jeans which made the muscles in his arms flex. "It's kind of simple out here. We're not rich, by any stretch. We just try to live off the land as best we can."

A chicken ran beside us, bobbing its head aimlessly as though lost. "The ticks are back there," I called after it.

Kyle lowered his head and smirked. It seemed like tough guy image was just that: an image. I'm not sure why that made me so pleased.

He walked up the porch steps, which were worn with age and

disrepair. His cowboy boots echoed loudly across the floorboards. It was an oddly comforting sound.

The screen door screeched as it opened into a modest kitchen area. I noticed the yellow flowered linoleum floor, the pattern of which was worn bare by the sink and around a small table sitting near a half-wall. Beyond the half-wall, it was too dark to see in because of deep brown paneling, but I heard Al's voice and the hum of a TV, so I guessed it must be the living room. White lace curtains billowed gently in the breeze from the kitchen window, making a vase of wildflowers perched on the ledge dance. I couldn't help but smile. It was like something out of a book.

"It's not much," Kyle said, as though ashamed of his humble home.

"It's perfect." I laced my arms around my waist, overwhelmed with wonder that such a place existed. "Growing up I would have killed to have a house that felt like this."

Kyle cocked his head. "Like what?"

I tried my best to smile. "Home."

Kyle started to speak but stopped as his father came in from the living room.

"Oh, good, you've taken a break," Al said. "Come, I want to introduce you to my Annabel."

I followed him into the living room where an older woman sat in a deep maroon recliner that looked like it wanted to swallow her whole. She didn't seem to notice as I came into the room. Her eyes fixed in some faraway place.

"Annabel, I want you to meet Sarah. She's going to be helping around the farm this summer."

I gave a small wave, not sure what else I was supposed to do. She looked at me then, confusion on her face.

"Who?"

"Sarah," Al repeated. "She's gonna help out now that Brad's moving to Boston."

She stared at her husband. "Who?" she asked again.

He sighed, then glanced at me. "She has Alzheimer's and early signs of dementia," he whispered. He sat in the recliner next to her, reached over, and took her hand.

"Some days are better than others, but as you can see, I can't keep leaving her."

I could see him struggling to hold his emotions in check. It was clear that he adored his wife, and to watch as she crumbled in front of his eyes must have been unbearable.

"Where's Molly?" Annabel asked me. "I sent her off to get me some tea and she hasn't come back yet."

I looked to Kyle for help.

"We'll go look for her," Kyle said, taking my elbow and leading me back to the kitchen. He directed me down a small hall off the kitchen. "Molly was my sister. She died three years ago," Kyle told me softly. "She won't remember that conversation in two minutes, so it's better to not upset her by telling her that her daughter is dead, you know?"

"No, right. Of course," I said, as though I understood the full weight of what the burden of living with someone losing their mind was like. I didn't. I had no clue. And yet, it sort of felt that way for me sometimes. Like I was slowly losing who I was, becoming a shell of a person instead of a living, breathing one.

As he led me down the narrow hallway, I noticed it was lined with picture frames and random paintings, some professional looking, others clearly children's keepsakes. I caught glimpses of Kyle and his parents as we walked. I stopped at a large family portrait.

"Was that her?" I asked, pointing to the girl with blond curly hair and a smile that radiated kindness.

Kyle stopped walking and came back to the picture. "Yeah."

He pointed to the other guy standing next to her. "And that's Brad. The pride and joy of the family." I could hear the annoyance in his voice. I glanced back at the picture. Brad looked like a family's pride and joy. Blonde, clean-cut, muscular, square jaw, but fierce too. One look at him and I knew I'd never want to cross paths with him. Something about the glint in his eyes made me squirm in my skin.

I shifted my attention back to the sister. "How did she die?" I asked, but then noticed Kyle's face stiffen at the question. "I'm sorry. It's none of my business," I said, biting the side of my cheek.

"No, no. You should know." He continued walking and opened a door on the left. He had to push a little too as it seemed to stick in the frame. "I'll fix that," he muttered.

I walked into the bedroom. A small twin bed with a white bedspread sat near an open window. Long, white curtains moved gently in the breeze, mirroring the dance in the kitchen. Light hardwood floors that looked like they'd been there for decades filled the room with a warmth the summer sun could never hope to provide.

"This was Molly's room. This is where you'll stay." He sighed. "It's where they all sleep."

"Where all who sleep?" I asked, walking over to the bed and plopping down on top of it.

"The runaways."

I stared up at him.

"Dad's brought home quite a few of them since Molly died." Kyle strode over to the window that had a view of the driveway. "Mom and Molly got into a really big fight one night. Stupid stuff, arguing about chores and boys. Hormones going off the charts and all. She was fifteen. Impulsive." Kyle's eyebrows pinched together. "She ran away."

"Oh," I said.

"We searched for her for a year," Kyle said, walking around the room, touching a few of her belongings that still lingered on every surface as he did. "Brad became obsessed with finding her. He went to the police station every day. He'd graduated by then and just couldn't seem to move on with his life until he found her. I think that's probably why he decided to become a cop. He was convinced she was still out there, just trying to find her way back home, but something in my gut told me she was gone."

He let loose a slow breath, then walked back towards the door and sort of hovered there for a bit.

"About a year after she went missing, a tourist discovered her body dumped at a rest stop in the woods near Toronto." His shoulders slouched and his voice began to break. "The autopsy showed she'd been raped and strangled."

If he was trying to shock me, it didn't. Stuff like that was a very real danger when you lived on your own. I'd had several close calls myself.

I lowered myself further down on the bed until my head was resting on the pillow. It felt nice.

"So that's why my dad picked you up, Sarah. You're the fourth one he's brought home since Molly died. I guess it's his way of trying to protect someone else's little girl."

"He should have picked someone else then," I said. "No one would miss me."

Kyle looked at me. "That's what Molly said too, in a note she left. But we did miss her. We still do."

"Oh, I wasn't trying to be melodramatic or anything. I just mean that I *literally* have no one that would mourn my passing."

"No parents?"

I shook my head. "My dad left when I was little, and my mom passed earlier this year."

"I'm sorry to hear," Kyle said, striding closer to the bed but making sure to leave a good gap between us.

"I'm not. She wasn't exactly Mom of the Year," I said, wishing I'd held my tongue.

"No other family? Friends? Everyone has someone."

I shook my head again. "No, they don't."

Kyle's jaw tensed for a moment, then he broke into an easy grin. "Well, you do now."

I sat up and made sure to meet his gaze directly. "No offense, but I don't want friends. I'm not friend material. I'm the sort of person you try to avoid in life. Trust me on this."

Kyle gave me an unsure look but held out his hand to shake. "Fair enough. Work associates then?"

I reached out and shook his hand, surprised by how his rough, calloused hand engulfed my own. It was oddly comforting holding his hand.

"There should be some boots in the closet; you look about Molly's size. There's probably a hat or two in there as well."

He tipped his head a bit, then left me to my thoughts. The sun was shining through the window, draping me like a blanket. It felt so warm. So utterly perfect. It made me wonder if growing up in a place like this would've made a difference. Then I remembered Molly. I guess some of us were just destined to a life of pain, no matter how we started.

I stretched, trying to get my body motivated to tackle more ticks and spiders when my eyes landed on the set of three pink pillar candles that rested on Molly's dresser. Candles.

I sat up and walked over to them, entranced by their pull. I licked my lips in anticipation. I picked the tallest of the pillars and inhaled their crisp linen scent. My eyes darted around for a match or lighter but found none. I closed my eyes, envisioning the flame flickering gently in the country air. My head rolled back, dizzy with need.

A knock at the door startled me. "Want me to wait for you in the barn?" Kyle asked through the door.

"Um. Hang on. I'll be right there." I placed the candle down, gingerly vowing to find a match, and then I rushed to the closet and pulled on one of the pairs of cowboy boots, surprised that they were comfortable. There was a red baseball hat with a logo I didn't recognize hanging on the edge of a hanger, so I yanked that over my head and fished my hair through the hole in the back. I rushed to the door and opened it, practically running smack into Kyle. He was standing there, my gloves in his hand.

When he saw me, he gave me a sad little smile. It was probably hard seeing your dead sister's clothes on someone else.

"Everything okay?" he asked.

"Yeah. Fine. Let's move some hay."

He gestured in front of him, so I slipped out of the door and down the hall. Men always claimed they let women go first because it was proper manners, when really they just wanted an unapologetic shot of your ass.

His dad was still talking with Annabel. His hand lay on hers as he spewed all the details of his trip, details his wife would never hope to remember, but he didn't seem to care.

Just as I was about to turn away, I noticed that in his left hand, he had a pipe. As he took a drag, I closed my eyes in ecstasy.

Where there were pipes, there were matches.

SPAGHETTI

Kyle and I worked the hay onto the conveyer belt until my stomach roared with hunger. He put three bales up to my one, but we'd made a pretty good dent in it. My hands were all sweaty and gross inside the gloves and growing blisters with each bale I lifted.

When he turned off the belt, I let loose a very audible sigh of relief. I rolled my shoulders back, trying to work out the kinks that had formed.

"Time to eat," Kyle said, taking off his hat and rubbing his arm against his forehead before he placed the hat squarely back onto his sweat soaked head.

"Thank God." I was more than ready to stop for a minute. Eating was a bonus. I'd been days without eating before, but then again, I hadn't ever spent an entire day doing manual labor either. My tank was empty, and the growling of my stomach made no attempt to hide that fact. I was too tired to care how loud it was protesting.

Kyle peeled off his gloves and tucked them into his back pocket, so I did the same. My hands were covered in dirt and grime. As though reading my mind, Kyle walked over to a hose, turned it on, and rinsed off his hands, which were equally as dirty, then held the hose out to me.

The cold water felt so amazing against my filthy hands that I splashed a bit on my arms that had baked themselves in the sun. I resisted the urged to pour it directly over my head.

"After lunch, we'll have to go up to the loft," he said, as we walked toward the house.

I grumbled. I was so sore. I wanted to be done with hay for the rest of my life, but I looked behind me toward the bales of hay that were very clearly piling up in the loft area above. My shoulders slumped.

"We'll need to make room for the rest," he said with a wink. I think he enjoyed seeing me so tired, like it only proved his opinions on runaways were right. I felt determined to prove him wrong. I wasn't some weak little girl. I'd lived through hell and taken the fire back with me.

"Fine. I'll go up to the loft, and you load them onto the belt," I said. Let his ass burn in the sun for the rest of the afternoon. I was going to take the shade of the loft.

A drop of sweat ran down the side of his face. "You'd never be able to keep up with me. Before you know it, you'd be buried in another mountain of hay. Trust me, it will be less painful if we do it together."

I stared up at him. I didn't get the impression that he was trying to be coy or manly, just honest about the task at hand.

"So I'm slowing you down then?" I smirked.

Kyle shrugged. "Let's just say if my brother, Brad, was here, we'd have finished by now." A playful grin danced around his lips.

"Well, I'll try and 'man up' over lunch for ya."

"You're doing fine." He laughed. "You'd never catch up to Brad anyway, especially if he sensed a competition. That guy loves a fight."

"Who says I don't?" I countered, though I wasn't sure why. My type of fighting was based on survival, not entertainment, and yet, for some reason, I wanted to prove I was more than whatever he assumed about me, even if those assumptions were right.

Kyle raised his eyebrows for a moment and then smiled. "I'm

sure you are a sight to be reckoned with, but Brad could take you. He's the sort that always needs to be right and will fight to the death to prove it."

We clomped up the steps in unison. "I guess it's a good thing he's using his powers for good and not evil by becoming a cop then."

"Yeah," Kyle said. There was something off about it though, like he wasn't proud of his brother. A sibling rivalry perhaps?

"You know, Sarah, I may have misjudged you," Kyle said, heaving a bale onto the belt after lunch.

I wiped away the sweat from my forehead that had mounted there with my arm. "Oh? How so?"

"Well," he said, a devilish smirk on his face, "for one thing, you don't give up easily. I haven't exactly been nice to you today. The others would have quit long before now."

I didn't say anything, but my heart swelled with a foolish pride.

"For the record, I'm not normally such a jackass." His shoulders slumped.

"Just to the random strangers that show up at your door who your dad asks you to play nice with?"

He laughed. "Right. Just those." He stopped working and adjusted his hat. The sun blazed behind him. "Truce?" He held out his gloved hand.

"Um, sure," I said, more than eager to take his hand again, even through gloves. That worried me.

We finished that afternoon just as the sun was starting to sink into the horizon. I collapsed onto one of the bales of hay, not caring in the least about any critters that might be crawling on them. I was too beat to care.

Kyle had gone into the house to grab us a drink. I probably could have followed him, but my legs didn't want to budge. I may have even dozed off because the next thing I knew there was a cold bottle pressing against the edge of my arm, waking me from my stupor.

"Oh, thanks," I said, twisting the cap off with the edge of my shirt. I guzzled down the brown fizz before it ran down my cleavage.

"Ah, that's good."

Kyle nodded. "Nothing like an ice-cold pop after a long day."

I laughed.

"What?" he asked.

"Nothing. You said 'pop.' That's funny. We don't call it that. It's soda." I giggled. "Pop. What a silly word."

Kyle gave me a half-smile as he took off his hat and rested it on his knee. His dark brown hair was matted flat from sweat but looked like it would be thick, lush waves when dry.

"So, what was it like living in New York?" he asked.

I sat up a little, understanding we were about to have a chat. I took another long sip before answering.

"Nothing like this," I said, gesturing to the hay around me.

"Was it better or worse?"

I let free a breath and pressed the bottle against my forehead. "Worse," I said honestly.

"How so?"

He was trying to get me to open up and that just wasn't going to happen.

"Nice try, but my past is off limits."

He nodded slowly, as though contemplating his next thought. "I can respect that, I suppose. Is there anything about you that you *can* share? I mean, I don't know anything about you, and you'll be sleeping down the hall from me. I just—"

I laughed. "And you want to know if I'm gonna murder you in your sleep? Is that it?"

He smiled. "Basically."

"Not unless you piss me off."

"Good to know."

I ripped the hat off my head and massaged my matted hair back down my neck. Every muscle in my body hurt; hell, even my hair hurt. "Let's just say I didn't have such an idealistic upbringing," I said, gesturing to the hay loft around me.

He nodded as though understanding, but he hadn't any idea, nor did he need to. No one needed to. Those were my demons to reconcile.

"You know," Kyle said after a moment, "a place like this isn't all it's cracked up to be."

"Uh-huh," I muttered. He had no idea how good he had it.

Kyle sat up a bit. "No, I'm serious. Living out here, in a town of five hundred people? Life can feel—suffocating."

That was an odd word choice. "How so?" I asked. "I would think small town life would be comforting."

He shook his head vehemently. "Nope. There's no way to hide in a place this small. No anonymity. It's like having five hundred mothers."

"Sure, but at least they know you exist," I countered. I would have given anything to have grown up surrounded by people who cared about what happened to me. The fact that I didn't made disappearing from their lives as easy as breathing.

Kyle put down his soda in mid-swig. "Yeah, but if you flunked a test, broke up with a girl, or didn't get into college, everyone knows about it. There are no secrets in a town this small, Sarah. Fair warning. Sooner or later, one of them will discover your secrets." The way he said it was more of a regret than a warning.

"You didn't get into college?" I asked, trying to shift the focus off me.

He smirked, picking up on my deliberate shift in topic. "I may have intentionally written a bad essay or two."

"Why?"

Kyle shrugged. "My dad wanted me to go to college, not me. He harped on me all the time to apply. Brad's future was set in stone because of the academy, so Dad wanted to make sure I 'made something out of myself.'" He took a drink. "So I applied to humor him, but wrote these really incoherent essays on why I wanted to go to college." He laughed. "When I got the rejection letters, I was relieved. He had no choice but to stop bugging me then."

"Not a college-type boy?" I asked, raising my eyebrows. I could see Kyle making quite an impression on girls at a college. I frowned at my arrant jealousy.

"Hell, no," Kyle said, putting his hat back on his head. "I'm a farm boy, through and through." His face went dark. "Brad never fit in here much, but me and Molly...we could have lived off the farm forever." Kyle closed his eyes.

"It must have been fun living with siblings though. Were you all close growing up?"

Kyle nodded. "Yup. Brad and I were fiercely protective of our sister, which, of course, she hated us for." He smiled. "He and Molly had a special bond. I think because she was so much younger than him, he felt almost fatherly with her. Dad was gone a lot in those days. Lots of long hauls where he'd be gone for days, sometimes weeks at a time. Brad was left in charge as 'man of the house.' He sort of became a stand-in father for her, I guess. I didn't mind being excluded, much."

"Middle child syndrome?" I asked, laughing.

"No, nothing like that." He grinned. "I liked being alone. I would lose myself in the work on the farm. It's hard work, but peaceful." His eyes grew distant, as though he was thinking of something unpleasant. "After Molly died, Brad changed. He grew cold. Aloof." He sighed. "I guess tragedy can change people."

"That's for damn sure," I muttered. "So you and Brad aren't close anymore?"

I wasn't sure why I was asking so many questions about his past when I wasn't giving any information about mine away, but it felt so good to talk to him. I was trying to keep the conversation going.

"Um, well. It's different now. When Molly died, he became... darker, somehow. He was there, you know? The day they found her. He'd spent his days with Gramp at the station, listening on the police scanner for any news of her. And one day, they got the call about someone matching her description. Gramp said Brad jumped out of the still-moving squad car and ran over to her pushing his way through the other officers. Despite knowing better, he pulled her into his arms like a child and started crying." Kyle's jaw hardened, as though trying to hold back tears. "He completely contaminated the crime scene. Got his prints all over her. Not that they found any others. The guy that killed her must have worn gloves. There was no other evidence either. He was thorough," Kyle said as he scratched at the back of his neck. It was clear talking about his brother made him uncomfortable. "Man, I'm sorry. You probably didn't want to hear all of that. What about you? What was your childhood like?"

I shook my head. "The day you learn those stories is the day I move on," I said before polishing off the last of the soda. I pointed to my head. "No one gets access to those memories but me." It was a cocky statement, but true.

"Let me guess. You're one of those 'no one gets into my head or heart' chicks, right?"

I smiled at his intuitiveness. "I don't have a heart, so that's easy."

Kyle shook his head and smiled. "So you've never been in love then?"

"Nope," I said, making the sound of the 'p' pop.

"Me either." He spun the bottle in his hands. "But we will. One day, you and I will fall in love."

My head popped up at the unintended phrasing of his words.

His eyes grew wide. "What I mean is that one day, we will both find someone to fall in love with, not—" I could hear the embarrassment in his voice. He pulled his hat over his face. It was ridiculously adorable.

"I knew what you meant, Kyle." I smiled and leaned into the hay. I picked a few strands up and played with them loosely. "So you'll take over the farm when your dad retires?"

"Oh, I don't know," he said. "But for now, this is where I'm needed most." He looked up at me as though that should be all the explanation required.

"Yeah, but what about you?" I countered. "What do you need?"

I leaned closer, genuinely curious to learn what he was passionate about.

"What do you need?" he retorted.

I crossed my arms over my chest. "I asked you first."

He frowned but put his soda on the ground as though thinking of what to say. "I guess I just need to feel needed, ya know?" He glanced up at me. "I'm sure that sounds really simple and boring, but that's the truth. I feel like I have a purpose here on the farm. Like I'd be missed if I left. I want that. I want to have a reason for being." He shook his head. "Pretty stupid, huh?"

"No, that makes perfect sense," I said, and I meant it. I'd never been needed. Ever. I'd always been a thorn in someone's side, another mouth to feed, a vagrant on a street bench. Disposable.

"Your turn," he said. "What do *you* need?"

I closed my eyes and wanted to mirror his answer, but I knew that would reveal too much.

"A bath," I said. "I need a bath."

He laughed. "That's not fair."

"Nothing in life is, Kyle."

He shook his head but didn't press me further. He wouldn't have gotten me to open up anyway.

He stood up and offered his hand out to help me up. "How about some dinner first?"

"That would be divine," I said, taking his outstretched hand. I made sure to let go of it as soon as I stood up, regardless of how nice his hand felt in mine.

As soon as we got inside, I collapsed into one of the kitchen chairs. I was so tired.

Kyle snickered as he downed a glass of water at the sink. "I'm gonna go tend to the chickens."

I groaned, "Okay." I started to get up to help.

"No. Rest while you can," he said, flicking water from his empty cup at me before he placed it in the sink.

I didn't even flinch. I didn't have the energy.

"Don't you worry. You can help tomorrow. That chicken coop isn't going to clean itself, after all," he said with a wink.

I plopped my head into my hands while he headed out of the kitchen. I sat there a moment, resting my body until I reluctantly stood up and stretched. Al and Annabel were still watching TV behind me in the living room. I walked over to the sink and scrubbed away the dirt lodged under my nails. The water pooled brown along the edges of the drain, rimming the white porcelain sink and washing away the evidence of a day's work.

As I washed my hands, a phone rang from behind me. I glanced over my shoulder to see a light green phone mounted on the kitchen wall. I turned off the water when Al came in. He lifted the handle from the receiver and walked over to the table with it, pulling the cord behind him. I didn't even know they still made phones like that.

"Yeah, I got 'em," he said. "Sorry, we didn't get 'em out to you today. It took a little longer to unload the hay than I wagered." He glanced up at me and winked. "I'll get 'em out to you after breakfast tomorrow. That work?" He said his goodbyes then strode over to the fridge, pulling out a can of beer.

"That was Rich Cooper. I got a load in the truck I gotta get to him in the morning."

I cocked my head to the side. "There's more in the truck? What is it? More hay?" It seemed insane to think any more hay could have fit in there, but I had no real knowledge of how trucks were packed.

Al smiled. "Guess you'll find out tomorrow," he said, glancing at his wife as though he missed her, even though he was only one room away. "I should try and make us some supper then, huh?"

"Let me," I offered, knowing he wanted to go back to his wife.

He stared at me, eyes wide. "You can cook?"

"Guess we'll find out," I toyed.

"Well, all right then." He happily went back to sit by his wife, quickly tucking his hand in hers.

Although I was sore, Kyle was right. It felt nice to be needed.

I went over to the fridge and saw it stocked with beer, milk, eggs, and cheese, and some assorted condiments lining the side. There were a hundred things I would have happily eaten, but I felt like Kyle deserved something more filling after the day he'd had. I closed the fridge and opened a few kitchen cabinets until I found some spaghetti and a jar of sauce. That I could make. I used to live on pasta, beans, and Spam as a kid. Mom was never with it enough to cook, and you could only eat so much cereal. I taught myself how to cook a few things. Pasta was one of the staples they gave us at the food pantry, so we always had plenty of it.

I dug around until I found a few pots for the water and sauce and set them on the counter as I filled the larger one with water. I popped the lid of the sauce and dumped it unceremoniously into the smaller pot, splattering a few dots all over myself. Not that it mattered. Nothing I owned was clean anyway.

Lifting the pot from the sink, I placed it on the stove, careful not to slosh it around.

When I went to turn on the stove though, I froze. It was a gas range, not the electric I grew up with. I'd never used a gas range, but I knew how they worked. With a simple flick of a wrist, a beautiful, never-ending fire would rage. Almost drooling, I reached out my hand and gave it an urgent twist. Nothing happened.

The screen door slammed beside me, making me jump.

"Sorry, didn't mean to scare you," Kyle said. "Forgot my gloves." He walked over to the counter and picked them up. "Are you making dinner?"

"I-um. I was trying to, but..." I pointed at the stove, the one that was not burning as I needed it to.

"Oh, yeah, it's an old stove. The starter went out a few years ago. You have to light it with these." He turned off the gas. The propane scent had already reached my nose. It was intoxicating all on its own with the promise of flame. He brushed past me and reached on top of the fridge for a massive box of matches. He held them out to me. I gasped. It was like giving a drug addict a bag of coke. I stared at the box. My fingers ached to snatch them right out of his hands.

Kyle laughed. "I know. It was a little scary the first time I did it too. Let me show you." I blinked at him. *He* wanted to teach *me* how to light a fire. It would have been funny if it hadn't been so hypnotic.

He opened the box, revealing that only a small handful of matches were missing. I watched in reverent awe as he slid the head of the match against the box and almost audibly sighed as it ignited. "Just turn the knob like this, stand back, and carefully place it near the gas."

In a flash and burst of air, the gas was burning. My eyes ignited along with it as the heat from the flames crawled up the pot.

"Pasta, eh? I love pasta," he said, but I didn't really listen, I was too focused on the flame.

His hand landed gently on my shoulder, but my eyes refused to leave the fire. "Don't worry. You'll get the hang of it. Nothing to be scared of."

I smiled softly at the blue flames. "Right."

He laughed and went back outside, having no idea what monster he had just let out of its cage.

LIES

Something happens to me when I watch fire. I check out of reality. I become completely frozen in time, locked in place until it dies out. Only when the embers grew dark would its hold on me slip. It was a brief high that allowed me to feel relatively human. A high I took every chance I got.

This time, however, the fire wasn't ending. It wasn't dying out. It just kept burning, wild and provocative. I watched, riveted by the flame as they emerged from the stove, first as blue-white stubs, then, gradually into long, elegant orange tips. The water boiled down to almost nothing as I stood there, transfixed, watching the flames dance just for me.

"Dinner ready? I'm starving."

I heard his voice from behind me trying to force me back into reality, but I couldn't seem to turn away. I literally could *not* take my eyes off the fire.

"Looks like you're a little low on water," I heard him say. He waved a hand in front of my face, which did little to break its hold on me. When I didn't say anything, he turned off the flame.

Just like that, I was released from my prison. I almost collapsed right there on the floor, but I was able to grab the counter in time before I did. His arm reached out quickly to steady me.

"Whoa, you okay?"

"Yeah, fine," I lied. I took a few deep breaths to clear my head and figure out what I was going to say to him.

He leaned against the counter, facing me with his arms crossed. "What's wrong? Don't know how to cook?"

I frowned. "I know how to make pasta, for God's sake." It came out harsh. I hadn't meant to yell at him, but I didn't know what to say about my behavior. No one knew my secret. Well, at least no one living knew.

He raised his hands up at me in mock surrender.

"Then why you are staring at an almost empty pot of water?" His eyes flicked from the stove then back at me. His brows pinched in concern. "Are you... afraid of fire?"

I opened my mouth to laugh but stopped when I considered how perfect an excuse it would be.

"Yeah," I said, staring at the floor. It was easier to lie when you didn't look at the person. "I didn't know you had a gas range when I offered to make dinner. Sorry."

"Hey, it's okay," he said. He almost looked like he might hug me, so I straightened my posture.

"It was a long time ago. I was just a kid. You'd think I'd be over it by now." I held up my hands, showing off the small burn marks that ran along the insides of my palms. I got those from my early years of 'practice.' "These are a pretty good reminder, though."

"I wondered what happened," he said, almost apologizing for noticing them. I didn't like lying to him. "How old were you?"

I swallowed. "Young."

"Stove fire?" he asked.

I shook my head. Not sure why. It would have been an easy way to end the conversation, but it wasn't dramatic enough. A stovetop fire didn't capture the world-shaking nature of how my obsession came to be.

"Look, can we just not talk about it?" I asked, biting my lip.

"Sure. I just thought it might help, you know," he said, as though he wasn't sure what the right thing to say was.

I laughed softly then walked over to the sink and peered outside, my mind quickly coming up with a pretend back story. "It seems all I've done is talk about it." I played with the edge of my shirt. "Therapists have been trying to get me comfortable with fire for years." I frowned as I thought up the lie. "They kept urging me to light a candle and watch it burn in a safe environment, you know?" I glanced over my shoulder at him, and then back to the window. "They thought if I could do that, it would somehow prove to me that not all fire was bad." I turned around and leaned against the sink. "I was so young when it happened. I've been alone, on the streets for so long, that I guess I thought I was over the fear, but seeing that fire just now, so close...I just couldn't seem to move."

It was a great story. Even I wanted to believe it. It was so much better than the truth. I wrapped my arms around my waist, as though to keep my emotions in check, which probably wasn't a smart move because it made me look vulnerable, in need of protection. Something I didn't want or need.

When he stepped forward and wrapped his arms around me suddenly, I just stood there, not knowing what I should do, but at the same time relishing the feel of his arms around me.

"Everything is going to be okay," he whispered softly into my hair, and I let him. It felt too good to refuse it. And for a second, I almost believed him. For that small blink of an eye, tight in his arms, it would have been so easy to think that maybe the dark days were finally over. Tears started to well up in me at the kindness in his voice. Kindness I hadn't earned or deserved.

"You know what? Just stop. I'm fine." I pushed him away. "You don't need to lie to me." I started busying myself with filling the pot back up with water.

"Lie to you? What are you talking about?" Kyle said, confused.

I set the pot on the stove harder than I should have, sending the water over the edge. I knew my anger wasn't about what he said, it had way more to do with my baggage, but sometimes you lose your mind when you're hurt, and if I was honest, it hurt having someone pretend to care about me.

"It's not all going to be 'okay.'" I had to speak slowly, as though I had to talk to him like a child. "It probably will be for you. You've got a pretty stellar life here, but that's not my truth. Life is going to suck for me, Kyle. It always will, no matter what." I pushed past him to the sink, grabbing plates from the dryer rack.

"Sarah, I was just trying to help—"

I whipped around and glared at him. My face was hot with anger. "I don't need your help. I don't need anyone's help. I'm not a damsel in distress, okay? I don't need you to swoop in and tell me that things are gonna start looking up, because that's not my reality. Not for people with my past," I said, lowering my voice. "We only get to look forward, not up."

I knew that my anger at him was irrational. It was my own bitterness fueling this venom, but he'd opened something in me that needed to come out.

I crossed my arms as I waited for him to get upset, to go on the defensive and shout back at me, but he didn't.

"I think you're wrong. We all need saving, Sarah. Hell, even me. Usually, though, we just need saving from ourselves." He gave me a sad smile and grabbed the box of pasta from the counter. "Why don't you take that bath now?" He nodded to the stove. "I got this."

I ran my hands through my hair and sighed, angry at myself for yelling at him. "No. You worked harder than I did. You go relax."

He shook his head. "I'm used to it though. Go. You can make dinner tomorrow."

"Fine," I said, reacting more out of the muscle spasm that had started in my left arm than anything else. I turned to leave the kitchen when I felt his hand on my arm.

"My mom used to like to light candles when she took a bath, back when she could do it on her own. There should be some on the shelf." He smiled. "In case you wanna give it another go."

Despite my foul mood, I grinned back.

"Thanks. Maybe I will." He had unknowingly just given me his consent to start fires, and I wasn't about to let that opportunity pass itself up.

Using the last of my strength, I made my way to the bathroom. Perhaps a nice soothing bath was exactly what I needed. Well, that and a few candles.

I closed the door and noticed that there was no lock on the knob. Not even a cheap little hook to ensure privacy. Not that it mattered. I was too tired to protest even if a madman tried to beat down the door.

I started the water in the white claw-footed tub that rested along the back wall. A small sink stood across from it. A mirrored vanity lay above it, the toilet just to its side. A small window overlooked a few of the grazing cattle. It was so damned peaceful out here. The entire farm was like a lullaby to my throbbing muscles.

Yawning, I turned on the tub and poured a heavy dose of the bubble bath that lived on the shelf at the foot of it. There was a mixed assortment of hair products and lotions, razor blades and bath sponges. I thought fondly of Annabel as I searched through the frilly assortment. As the hot water foamed to life, I started to peel off the layers of my clothes. I let them flop in a heap onto the floor, enjoying the coolness of the evening breeze as it tickled my bare skin.

The bag of fifty or so tealights and a small box of matches sat on the shelf too. I smiled then sighed, almost drunk with desire.

Normally I had to be careful whenever I lit a fire because I knew the sort of trance it put me in. It left me vulnerable. Matches were practical, quick, and usually easily accessible too. They provided the brief rush that I needed to get through the bad days.

I turned off the faucet and sank into the bubbles, letting the heat of the water work into the ache of all my muscles. I moaned softly as I laid my head back on the tub. I reached over and grabbed the tealight and lit it. I set it down gently on top of the shelf. For several minutes, I watched the candle flicker in the growing darkness around me. It was pure heaven: warm bath, candlelight...

I didn't want to stop watching the flame, but the water felt so warm and relaxing that my lids grew heavy, and I drifted into sleep before my precious flame had even burned out.

BUBBLES

Roosters were loud and slightly terrifying, especially if you'd never heard one in real life before. Trust me, a rooster on TV didn't count. It didn't even begin to bore into your brain the way a live rooster inches from an open window did. I had never been a violent person, but I swear I was fully prepared to climb out the window and kill that thing if he crowed one more time. Seeming to sense the very real threat I made to the universe, he moved himself from under my window.

Unfortunately, there was a knock on my door before I could drift back to sleep.

"Rise and shine, Sarah. Breakfast is on the table." It was Al, and he sounded far too chipper for the butt-crack of dawn.

I groaned a reply and pulled the covers back over my head. Everything hurt, still, even after sleep. I was so tired that I didn't actually remember falling asleep. One minute I was laying in the bath, filled to my nips with bubble bath beside my blessed candle, next thing I knew there was a rooster crowing in my ear.

It was at that point that I scratched my belly—my *naked* belly. I lifted the sheet, and sure enough, I was in the buff, and I didn't sleep in the buff. Ever.

I bolted upright in the bed wondering what had happened. I wracked my brain trying to remember, but all I could recall were hushed whispers for me to stay asleep. I just couldn't remember *who* whispered them.

As fast as I could, I pulled on clothes and rushed into the kitchen, hoping to catch Al and ask him what had happened before Kyle came for breakfast.

When I got to the kitchen, I saw an assortment of cereal boxes, a pile of toast, a jug of milk, and a stack of bowls placed on the table, but no Kyle. I sighed in relief because that's when Al turned from the coffee pot to look at me.

"Good morning," he said, though there was something off about how he said it.

"Morning," I ventured.

"You sleep okay?" His cheeks were burning red with embarrassment.

I blew the hair from my eyes. "I fell asleep in the tub, didn't I?"

"Um, yes," he said, walking over with his steaming mug.

Frowning, I cocked my head. "So did you carry me to my bed? Or did I just wake up and not remember the walk to my room?"

Al flushed about ten shades darker than he already was. "Oh no. I didn't carry you. I don't have the strength for that, even though you only weigh, what, a buck?"

"And a quarter," I said, crossing my arms. "So I walked back myself? Weird. I don't remember that."

Al scratched at his beard. "Well, I didn't say that either."

I closed my eyes, this time turning scarlet myself. Kyle. It had to be. His mom couldn't have lifted a can of soda from her tray without help.

"Ah," was all I said.

Al walked over to me, sort of sheepishly. "I knocked on the door after you'd been in there for an hour, you know, just to make sure you were okay, but you didn't answer, so..."

I covered my face but asked, "So what?"

"I had Kyle check on you."

I gaped at him.

Al shifted his cup in his hand. "I know. I...It just seemed wrong for me to check on you somehow. I'm a married man, and you're just a girl."

I collapsed into one of the kitchen chairs, dropping my head to the table in embarrassment.

"We were worried about you. We thought maybe you'd drowned or something." Al sounded flustered.

"Right. And then?" I moaned through my hair.

"Then I heard you sawing logs," I heard Kyle say.

I lifted my head up and saw him walking into the kitchen.

"I think I'm just gonna go check on your mother," Al said before he gave my shoulder a squeeze and left.

I waited a moment as I composed myself. I lowered my hands to tackle this head on. Kyle had his back to me, busily making his coffee. He had on his work clothes and baseball hat, and his gloves dangled out of the back pocket. His shirt clung just enough to his skin as to not leave any doubt about the muscles that lived underneath it.

"I don't snore," I said, not sure why him saying that I did bothered me so much.

Kyle turned his face and smiled at me. "Yes, you do. It's the only way I could tell you were alive."

I frowned. I'd never slept deeply enough to snore before. Shallow and sporadic sleep was all I ever got. Life on the road or with my mom never provided the most relaxing environment.

"I must have been exhausted," was my pathetic reply.

Kyle came back with two cups of coffee. He slid one over to me and reached to the center of the table for the cream.

"We worked you hard yesterday," he said, stirring the cream in.

I scratched at the back of my neck. "So how did you wake me up?" It felt foolish to ask, but I needed to know how I got to bed.

Heat climbed up Kyle's neck, causing me to blush as well.

"Well, you didn't want to seem to wake up...you just looked so tired... I just carried you to bed."

"Right," I said weakly. "And the bubbles I'd put in?"

"Bubbles? Um, no. There were no bubbles," he said to the floor though his ears grew red.

"Of course not."

Kyle shifted in his chair. "I tried not to look, except to know where to grab onto you, honest. I didn't even towel dry you or anything. I just got you into bed as fast as I could." He winced. "Wait, I got you into your bed. I didn't mean that I got you into bed in a sexual way." His eyes widened. "I'm going to stop talking now."

I smiled. It was fun watching him get all flustered.

"Well, that explains why I woke up in the buff." I sighed. "I'm sorry you had to do that."

Kyle looked up at me with a small grin. "Anytime."

I couldn't help it. I laughed and tossed a sugar packet at him.

"Guess I owe you some help out of *your* next bath then. Be the towel girl or something? After all, you got to see my goods..."

Kyle's eyes almost fell out of his head. I snorted. It was really fun teasing Kyle. "I'm kidding."

There was a mix of relief and maybe some sadness as he nodded in understanding.

"I gather you saw my other scar?" I said, absently running my hand along my side.

"Um. Yeah. That from the fire too?"

I nodded but didn't look at him, just the blackness of my coffee. I'd always hated that scar. Not because of vanity, but more as the constant reminder of what an idiot I was, trying to light a bottle of alcohol on fire.

"Better eat up," Kyle said, saving me from having to change the subject. "We have to take the final shipment in the truck to the Coopers today."

"Oh, okay." I reached for the milk and poured it into my bowl and then reached for the Corn Flakes.

"You put your milk in first?" Kyle asked with arched eyebrows.

"You put your cereal in first?" I countered.

"You're weird," we said at the same time, causing each of us to stumble into a fit of giggles. It was the perfect start to what would end up being a completely messed-up day.

RIVER

After breakfast, Al came into the kitchen with Annabel. She had on a simple flower dress that looked as though Al had just yanked it over her head. Probably the only style she could wear anymore. Her hair had been pulled back into a headband, but her eyes still glazed over, gray and lost.

"Where are we going?" she asked as Al held her by the arm. "Where is Judy?"

I stared at Kyle to get an explanation of who Judy was, but he just shrugged, as though this sort of confusion happened all the time.

Al didn't seem the least bit fazed. He was smiling brightly, just happy to be with his wife. It showed. He loved her. Even though it seemed she didn't know who he was most days, he still loved her. "We are gonna deliver something to our friends—Rich and Martha Cooper. We used to play bridge with them, you remember?"

She gazed up at him with perhaps the vaguest of memory, but then the dullness in her eyes returned. It lasted only a few seconds, but I could tell it was enough for Al. He believed some part of her was still inside the confusion, and he wasn't about to simply let her go. *That* was love. Never giving up on a person.

"We're gonna go pay them a visit. Won't that be nice?" he asked as he slowly led her through the front door.

"He's taking her with us?" I whispered.

"It's not like he could leave her here alone. Even when he goes on a run, I'm at least nearby and can check on her every few minutes. But Cooper's place isn't all that close, and well, it will take a bit to unload his shipment." There was a playful grin on his face.

"It's manure, isn't it? We're moving cow shit, aren't we?"

He busted a gut. "Not just yet, although you'll get your fair share of that when we clean out the chicken coop later. This shipment is a fun one. You'll see." He glanced at my jeans. "You have any shorts?"

"Shorts? No. I don't have shorts."

"How about anything other than a white t-shirt?"

"I own two shirts. Both are covered in sweat and dirt. I grabbed this from Molly's drawer."

The sound of the truck started outside.

"Well, it's too late to change now. Come on." He gestured to the door, and I followed, leaving the empty cereal boxes and half eaten bowls behind. I doubted that sort of thing wouldn't have flown in Annabel's day. I made a mental note to clean up the kitchen when we got back.

By the time we got outside, Al was already backing up the truck.

"Um, he's leaving without us," I said.

Kyle just shook his head, amused by me. "We won't all fit in the cab, not with Mom in there. Tight spaces upset her anyway, so the fewer bodies in the cab, the better."

"So, are we walking?"

He didn't answer but smiled and started to walk towards a beat up, dark blue Ford, but then promptly passed it and continued on to a small shed next to the barn. He went up a small ramp then disappeared inside. The loud roar of something followed a few seconds later. It caused me to jump a bit. A moment later he came out riding a 4-wheeler. A black helmet hid his face. A second one dangled off the edge of the handlebar.

"Get on," he said, pulling up to me.

"No way," I said, horror-stricken. I'd never even been on a motorcycle before, much less something like that.

He pushed the screen of his helmet up so he could look me in the eyes.

"Scared?" He wasn't teasing me. He was concerned, which I didn't like. I didn't want him worrying about me.

I chided myself. I was tough. I slept on the streets and rode with twisted truckers, for Pete's sake. I should be able to handle a stupid ride on what was essentially a toy for big kids.

"Give me that," I said, holding my hand out for the helmet. I shoved it on my head, amazed at how dark and loud my own breath had become. Suddenly I could hear every nuance of it. It was rapid so I tried to calm it.

I stared at the seat before I got on and frowned. There really wasn't enough room for the breadth of my own backside, let alone room for two, but I hitched my leg over and hoped for the best. I sank down into the cushion as the machine vibrated in my bones. The seat was tilted forward so it forced me to slide right up against Kyle's back. I tried to push back, but every time I did, I just slid smack into his back again.

"Hang on," Kyle shouted.

Frantic, I searched for a place to hold onto but, of course, there wasn't anything.

"Grab onto me, silly," he said over his shoulder.

I blew out a breath which echoed in my helmet but did as instructed. My arms looped loose around his waist, and I leaned back as much as I could.

"Hold on tight!" The engine revved, and the 4-wheeler lurched forward, forcing me to grab on much tighter to Kyle than I had bargained for. I swear I heard him laugh as my fingers dug into his chest. I buried my head into his back, terrified by how fast it was going. If I let go, I was sure that I'd fall right off the back and become the roadkill we'd passed.

With each bump and turn, I clung onto him harder, convinced we were going to tip over. I pinched my eyes shut and waited for it to end. After a while, my body got used to the vibrations, but I never released my death-grip on Kyle. I kept my hands locked where they were, clinging to the hope that his sturdy frame would keep me safe. Maybe it felt nice to hold onto him too. Maybe.

"You can let go now," Kyle said some time later. "We're here."

I didn't move. "Sure, the engine sounds off, but it could be a trick," I said, squeezing him tighter.

I felt him shift as he took off his helmet. "Careful, Sarah, or I'll start thinking you actually don't want to let go of me," he whispered.

At that, I opened my eyes and saw we were indeed parked. I ripped my hands from around his waist and quickly stood up. It was one thing to have a little crush on him, but it was another to have him know that.

Kyle slid off the 4-wheeler and rested his helmet on the seat. He ran his fingers through his hair, letting the wind style it however it pleased. I had to look away for fear of being caught gaping.

"That sucked," I said, taking off my helmet. My arms and legs felt numb from the vibrations of the ride.

"The ride back's gonna be worse." Kyle grinned with that knowing look which pissed me off. *What was he not telling me?*

He gestured to where his dad had parked the truck. I suspected they'd been there awhile as it seemed like we'd been riding for hours, even though it had probably only been about twenty minutes.

"Took you two long enough," Al said from the shade of the porch. He sat beside his wife, a glass of what appeared to be iced tea in his hand.

"We got time to try them, Mr. Cooper?" Kyle shouted, hitching his finger to the truck.

"Of course you do, Kyle," another voice came from inside the porch. A tall man, in his early fifties maybe, was standing with his hands draped casually over the worn railing. Just then, a screen door slammed, and a woman in a white dress and apron came out. She looped her arms around the man's waist and smiled down at me. It was a small thing, just a woman embracing her husband, but it hurt to watch. Hurt to see that those sort of relationships. Healthy ones like theirs and Al's with Annabel really did exist. I stared at the ground, not wanting to see the display of affection anymore.

"You know we like to test the tanks before we rent them," said the man.

"The tanks?" I whispered towards Kyle. I just got another damned smirk in reply.

I watched as the adults all went inside, comfortably talking to one another as though Annabel understood everything going on around her. I could relate. I kind of felt like that too. Like everyone was carrying on with their normal lives around me, unaware of the shit that was going on inside my mind.

Kyle headed to the back of the truck. I followed after him, watching as he unlatched the hitch and climbed onto the back, like he'd done it every day of his life. Inside, I could only see stray bits of hay scattered on the floor. Certainly no tanks.

"Come on up," he said, holding out his hand to me.

"Fine, but I won't be as graceful getting up there as you were," I muttered. He smiled, but I took his hand. I placed my foot on the bumper and then Kyle basically lifted me up in one giant tug. "Jesus. You're strong."

"You're not a religious sort of gal, are you?" He snickered.

"God, no!" I said, and then laughed at my own wording. "Are you?" I suddenly worried that I'd offended him.

He adjusted his hat a bit. "Out here, the Bible is about the only thing people seem to read. Turns some people loony."

"But not you?"

He shrugged. "I still go to church most Sundays. Guess it's better to believe in God than the alternative."

"And what's the alternative?"

He dug his hands into his jeans, making his shoulders flex. "That we are just wandering around, aimless with no real purpose."

"That sounds more realistic to me than God," I said.

"So you don't believe in Him?"

I shook my head.

"How can you be so sure?" he asked, not in a preachy sort of way, but with general curiosity, almost as though he needed someone to convince him God wasn't real.

"No God would give me the life I've had. The Devil, perhaps, but not God." I dug my hands in my own pockets and gazed at the worn floorboards of the truck. I didn't like talking about religion, or my past, and here I was mentioning both.

"I know you have a complicated upbringing, Sarah. One you don't care to discuss, so I won't push you to talk about it, but if you ever want to—"

"Thanks. I'll keep these demons to myself. Safer that way," I said, looking him straight in the eye so he'd drop the subject. "Now, where is this tank?"

Taking the hint, Kyle pointed to a large circular piece of metal strapped snugly to the back wall of the truck with yellow straps. As we got closer, I could see that it resembled a giant wash tub from the 1800s. I shit you not.

"What the hell is that?"

"It's a stock tank," Kyle said as he started to undo the ties. "Well, three of them, actually." He gestured to three distinct metal rims, each nested inside the other like mixing bowls stacked on their side.

"Come again?"

He grinned in that way that made you feel comfortable in your own skin; not an easy thing to do. "A stock tank," he repeated. "It's a boat."

"A boat?" I peered at the 'tank.' "I don't see a motor."

"Well, it's more like a paddle boat, but you mostly just float in it down the river."

"So it's a float-boat," I deadpanned.

His laugh echoed off the walls of the truck. "Yes. Yes, it is." He grabbed a hold of the last buckle and nodded his head to the other side of the tub. "Grab onto the other end. They're not all that heavy, but I don't want them rolling over my feet either."

I did as he said by grabbing hold of the thick lip of the tub. When he released the last belt, the weight of it press against me. "Holy shit! You lied. These *are* heavy," I said, straining against them.

"I got 'em. I just need you to balance them as I roll them out of the truck, okay?" Kyle said, shifting the tub so he had much of the weight now.

"Sure, no problem," I grunted.

When we got the boat to the edge of the truck, he told me to hold them steady while he jumped down. Now that they weren't leaning on me, they were far easier to balance.

"Okay, roll 'em down to me." Kyle raised his hands to grab them.

"How do I get them out?" I asked, trying to see how they came unattached from each other.

"They're tied together. Just pass them all down."

"No way! You'll be crushed," I said.

He shook his head at me. "No, I won't. I've done this a few times."

Reluctantly, I eased the boats toward him. With nimble hands, he grabbed each end of the top inner edge of the boats and easily lowered them to the ground. They landed safely on the ground with a small thump. I glared at him.

"Okay, fine, you're a big strong guy," I said, sitting down on the edge of the truck.

He didn't say anything, but the small smirk he gave me indicated that he seemed pleased by my compliment.

I scooted off the truck with an unceremonious leap. "Now

what?" I asked, squinting in the sun. I cursed at myself. I hadn't brought a hat. Clearly, I didn't have this country living thing down yet.

"Now, we go for a test run," he said.

"Test run? In that? Like in the water?"

"Yup." He started rolling the tubs towards an area where a string of kayaks and other tubs were stacked alongside a small ticket booth.

"Shit," I muttered.

When we passed by a small parking lot for tourists, Kyle leaned the tubs against a maroon-colored shed where several other tubs laid. He fished out his blade and easily cut the plastic ties holding the boats together. I helped him remove the boats, marveling that they were taller than me.

A large sign proudly displayed rental fees for the tanks with a separate sign for kayaks. An assortment of kayaks were hung on neat little racks opposite the tanks. So this stock tank boat was a real thing.

Kyle walked over to a large white peg board that held a vast collection of lifejackets. All of them were blue with yellow ribbing and bore a white Sandy River logo on the chest.

"This looks about your size," he said, tossing me one.

I held it in my hands but made no outward movement to put it on.

"What's wrong, too small?" he asked, looping his arms through a vest of his own.

"Um, no, just...I've never worn one. Never been in the water either." I tried to hand it back to him. "Maybe it's better if I wait here."

He blinked a few times at me. "Are you scared of water too?"

I pulled my eyebrows together. "No. Well, at least I don't think so. I don't know how to swim, so I'm not so much scared of the water, just sort of scared of the dying part."

Instead of laughing, he cocked his head. "You never went swimming as a kid?"

I glanced up at him. His face was twisted in disbelief.

Shrugging, I peered over at the water. "No one cared enough to bring me."

His face crumpled for a fraction of a second but recovered so quickly that I might have imagined it. "You don't need to know how to swim to ride down the river." His jaw set firmly in place.

"Yeah, but if I fell out..."

"Then the vest would keep you above water until I got there to pull you to safety." He walked over to me, took the vest, and held it out to me. "Trust me, Sarah. I won't let you get hurt."

"You want me to willingly put my life in your hands?"

"Yes," he said, with no trace of humor.

It would have been romantic if I allowed myself to believe he was interested in me, but I refused to let my mind go there, so I sighed instead. "Okay. It's not a life worth saving, but you seem hell bent, so let's do this."

At that, he grinned. I let the vest slip over my arms and stood motionless as he zipped it up. He buckled me around the waist, sort of pulling me to him as he did. I swallowed the butterflies that arose with the unplanned closeness.

"Thanks," I said, pulling from his grasp. I had to keep my distance from him.

"No problem," he said coyly.

I stared at my vest and noticed a belt. "Hey, there's still a piece dangling. What's that, like an anchor to the boat or something?"

He came closer to me. "Spread your legs," he said.

My gaze whipped up. "Excuse me?"

He blushed. "It's another belt. I need to reach between your legs to get it. It attaches to the front of your vest to make sure it doesn't come off."

"Oh. How very considerate of the vest makers," I said, tentatively opening my legs.

I couldn't deny the rush of excitement I got when his fingers brushed the inside of my thighs, but he was a gentleman and fastened the final belt promptly.

"Ready?" he asked, snapping his own vest in place with ease.

"No, but let's do it anyway."

He handed me two paddles and took one of the boats toward the river's edge.

"Why isn't anyone here?" I asked.

"It's Sunday," he said as though that settled it.

"So?"

"The Coopers don't work on Sunday. That's God's day."

I cocked my head to the side. "That's stupid. It's a good paying tourist day."

He laughed. "He does alright the rest of the week. Everyone needs a day off."

"If you say so."

He rolled the tank onto a small dock area where he eased the tub into the water.

"Well, it's not sinking. I guess that's a good sign," I said.

He smiled and knelt to loop a rope attached to the tank to a post on the dock, keeping it from drifting away.

"Okay, hand me the paddles."

I obliged, and he placed them inside.

"We only need those to push out and to paddle back to the landing at the end of the river. The current will do the rest for us."

"Awesome," I said with no enthusiasm.

He reached his hand toward me. "Okay, now you get in." I glanced at the tank. There was a rim of seating all around the inside, much like a giant hot tub. A large yellow rope laced its way around the edges for handholds; something I was sure to latch onto once inside the boat. Letting out a breath, I took his hand and let him help me in.

Although it made sense that the tub would move under my feet, it still freaked me out. I plunked down as soon as I could and clung onto the rope. Kyle shook his head at me.

He climbed in and the tub bobbled some more, which resulted in a tighter grip on the rope.

"I'm going to push us out now," he said, taking the paddle from off the floor. He unlatched the rope holding us to the dock and the boat began to drift. It only took a few paddles before the boat was coasting quite nicely down the river on its own. Kyle put the paddle back inside the boat then sat across from me in the tank and smiled. The boat rocked a little, but it didn't go fast, so I was able to release my death grip for a bit.

Kyle lay his head back on the boat and closed his eyes against the sun as we floated down the muddy river. All around us were tall green grasses as the river wound around some invisible track. It was relaxing once I let the fear of dying go.

We had been drifting for maybe ten minutes when he glanced over at me.

"How are you doing?" he asked.

"I'm still above the water, so I'm considering that a good thing."

"It is." He laughed. "You brave enough to try something?"

"That depends."

"It's nothing too scary, I promise. I just want to show you how we can make the boat go in circles down the river. It's fun."

"Um, okay. What do I have to do?"

"You don't have to do a thing." He started sliding over the seats, getting closer to me as he scooted.

"Whoa!" I shouted as the boat began to move around in a circle. "Don't you need to be over there to balance this thing out?"

He grinned. "I'm *trying* to throw it off balance. Don't worry. We won't tip over."

As he slid closer, my death grip returned. Although we didn't sink, we did start to spin. Not fast, but enough for me to be slightly wigged out.

"Want me to move back?" he asked as a bit of water splashed on me. I flinched against the coolness of the water as it rolled down my face then onto my neck.

"No, it's okay. I need to learn to let go of control sometimes, right?"

His lips curled into a half smile. "Yup. You do." He slid even closer so that our hips were touching. Letting go of control might not be so bad after all I mused as the tub spun us gently in circles down the river.

"So what's your plan after the summer is over? You gonna leave us high and dry?" He said it in a playful tone, but there was also a layer of hurt there too. I tried not to notice that.

"Um, California."

"California?" Kyle's eyebrows shot up.

"Yeah, your dad's gonna bring me when he goes out in September."

"What's in California?" he asked. "Besides beach babes and palm trees?"

I shrugged but the gesture was lost under the vest. "A new life is out there. A reset button."

"Got something lined up then?"

I shook my head. "No. Just the hope that it's better out there."

"Better than here?" There was no mistaking the hurt this time.

"Better than where I came from."

A slow nod was the only answer I got before a large splash of water doused us both.

"Holy shit!" I screeched. I got covered. I now understood why he asked if I had anything to wear this morning beside a white t-shirt. I was drenched in a split second. My shirt turned translucent in an instant against my skin. Mercifully, my lifejacket covered up my ladies because I didn't have a bra on. I hadn't owned a bra since I'd lived at home. It wasn't something you needed when you were living on the streets. It wasn't like I could borrow one either. Molly's training bras were a bit too small for my modest chest. I prayed that the sun would dry my shirt before the ride was over.

"Maybe I should move back over." He laughed.

"No, I don't mind getting wet," I said, then blushed at my wording.

"Okay." He smiled.

For the next half hour or so, Kyle sat beside me as we talked about the scenery, trying to point out sights as we floated. Both of us completely ignored the fact that we were getting more and more soaked as we went. It felt nice sitting beside him and talking about nothing at all.

I was sad when Kyle pulled out the paddle to bring us to the end point, where another set of tubs and kayaks lived downriver. I didn't want it to be over. It was weird, but I found I liked who I was around Kyle, even forgetting the horrid parts of myself, which was, of course, why things had to go south as soon as we arrived at the landing.

DEAL

In the blink of an eye, the lighthearted air that we had been enjoying all morning seemed to shift as we docked. Gone was the reckless abandon of summer fun, and in its place was something dark and ominous.

A guy, mid-twenties maybe, stared down at us. He was tall with a military style cut of blond hair, giving him the air of authority. He was leaning against the front of a black pick-up truck, arms crossed over his chest, showing off massive biceps. He had a scowl on his face like he was ready to beat the living shit out of the world.

"Brad?" Kyle asked as he paddled toward the dock. I should have been relieved that it was just Kyle's brother, but I couldn't shake the feeling of still being in danger. Kyle docked the boat and helped me to the shore. "What the hell are you doing here?" He grounded the tub and then walked over to his brother and gave him a hug, though it seemed awkward and forced.

"I came to check on you. Dad called me last week, pleading with me again to come down and help this summer until he found some help for Mom. I told him I could manage a week. Imagine my surprise when he called yesterday to tell me he'd found someone to take my place." Brad never took his eyes off me as he spoke. It was as if his brother wasn't even standing in front of him. They weren't kind eyes either but accusatory and full of hate.

Kyle didn't seem put off by his brother's demeanor, so I gathered this was just his lovely personality.

"Brad, I want you to meet Sarah—"

Brad pushed past his brother towards me. "I know who she is."

"You do?" Kyle asked, taking the words out of my own mouth.

At that, Brad looked at his brother for the first time. "I'm a cop. It's my job to know things." He glared at me again. "I ran her name. Not a lot of Brickles in New York."

"Wait, you ran a check on her?" Kyle shoved his brother's shoulder, trying to get him to turn around and look at him, but he was unable to move the sheer mass of his brother.

"I make it my business to know who is sleeping under my parents' roof."

My throat went dry. I had no idea what the cops actually had on me. They'd been to my house plenty as a kid, mostly because of my mom, but they were also around for a few of the fires—all deemed accidents, of course. I got picked up for prostitution when I was sixteen, but they let me off because I was a minor at the time. That stuff wouldn't show on a background check, would it? The way he was eyeing me, one thing was clear: he wasn't thrilled I was here.

"Well, you don't need to worry about Sarah." Kyle said. "She's good people." He stepped in front of me, seeming to purposefully break his brother's sight line of me.

"Good people?" He scoffed. "We'll see about that. Sarah, why don't I give you a ride back to the house so we can talk?"

My eyes grew wide. Kyle's reaction mirrored my own, but then he flexed his fists.

No. I wasn't going to have them fight over something so foolish. I had a feeling Brad would have pummeled Kyle if pressed, and I wasn't going to stand around and watch that. Not if I could put Brad at ease about this situation. The sooner he was satisfied, the sooner he'd leave.

"I'd love to, Brad," I said, trying my best to hide the fear that prickled against my skin. "I wasn't relishing the idea of going back on that 4-wheeler anyway."

Brad smirked. "He brought you out with that piece of shit? Well, I'll take you back to the house in style: leather seats, tinted windows, hell, I even have AC." He was turning on his charm for me. I didn't care for it.

"Sarah," Kyle said, turning to look at me, "you don't have to go with him."

I smiled brighter. "It's okay. He's worried about the stranger in his house. He's just trying to look out for his family. It's fine. Honest. Hopefully, I can put his fears about me to rest."

Kyle's eyes pleaded with me to stay, but then he shook his head in defeat. I got the impression Brad had a way of always getting what he wanted.

I took off my vest, forgetting for a moment about the wet-t-shirt until I looked down. I was mortified by how much skin was showing through my shirt. My nips were clearly visible through the wet fabric. Kyle quickly turned his head away, but Brad held his eyes on my chest. His lip even twitched in amusement until I yanked the shirt away from my skin and crossed my arms over myself.

Kyle quickly took off his own shirt and offered it to me, which I took willingly. I wished I'd had more time to take in his bare chest, but as it was, I probably stole a few too many glances than was polite. The farm had treated his physique well. He was tan and toned in all the right places.

Shaking the thought of him away, I tugged on his shirt, which wasn't as soaked, over my own, and he took my vest for me.

"It will take me a bit longer to make it back to the house since I'm on the 4-wheeler, but I'll check in with you when I get back. Okay?" The gentleness his eyes usually held had shifted into something I could only describe as concern. Almost like he was worried about me. How odd.

"I'll be fine," I said, trying to soothe him. "Don't worry about me." I turned and walked toward Brad. He already had his truck door open, clearly waiting to begin his interrogation.

He offered his hand, but I refused it. He slammed the door behind me, and an irrational panic started to rise in my gut. I had a sneaking suspicion he knew all about me. What if he was going to ask that I leave? I swallowed. It was probably time I left anyway. I was growing...attached, and that was dangerous.

Brad climbed in and gave me a sly grin. He started the truck, blasting the air. The coolness made my damp skin gooseflesh. I tried to position my arms over the nips that had responded to the sudden burst of cold even through Kyle's shirt. Something told me he'd done that on purpose.

As he backed out, he waved once to Kyle. I gave Kyle a weak smile, which he returned, but it was a sad smile. The sort of smile one might give someone they weren't going to see again. It shook me.

A moment later, Brad rolled up the windows, the tinted glass darkening the outside world in an instant.

"So, what do you want to know?" I asked, figuring it was better to just get it over with.

He didn't look at me, just adjusted his mirrors. The auto door locks engaged once he picked up speed, which unnerved me slightly. "For the record," he began, "I already know everything there is to know about you, Sarah. Every last detail."

I set my jaw, refusing to give my hand away in case he was bluffing.

"I know all about your meth loving mom, your troubled youth, your prostitution charge..." He wagged his eyebrows up and down. "You've been a busy girl."

"Well, guess you know it all then," I said, staring ahead. If he had known about the pyromania, he would have mentioned that first, surely. Even so, what he did know was pretty damning. Not that I could do anything about it. He had made up his mind about me, and it wasn't like I was going to change it.

Brad's face twitched with delight. "I also know you are wanted in the questioning of your dear, dead mother."

Shit.

"I didn't kill her," I said quickly.

Brad laughed. "Sure. Because innocent people run."

My eyes locked onto the road, not sure what to say.

"So I'm thinking my dad probably wouldn't be too keen on knowing he was housing a suspected murderer."

Or a pyromaniac. That tidbit must not have been on his search, and I took small comfort in that. After all, that was the biggest of my secrets. Somehow, retaining that part of myself was all that mattered.

"Nope, he probably wouldn't care for that," I said. "I'll leave tonight." I hated thinking how much I was going to miss that farm and the people on it.

"Well, if you did that, I'd have to come after you. You do the crime, you do the time."

I turned to stare at him. There didn't look like any hint of joking on his face. He glanced back in the rearview mirror, and I did too. No one was behind us. A moment later, he took a right onto a dirt road that appeared all but abandoned.

"Is this the right way back?" I hated the sound of fear in my voice.

"It's a shortcut."

A shortcut that led off the main drag and far from view? Doubtful. When he pulled the car over and killed the engine, I braced myself. "Are you going to turn me in?"

Brad ran his hand along the steering wheel. "Well, Sarah, that depends on you." His lips spread into a smile.

"What do you mean?"

He checked his mirrors again before he spoke. "Well, I thought maybe we could strike a deal."

"A deal?"

"I won't turn you in if you do something for me."

I blinked at him. "Isn't it your job to turn me in?"

He smirked. "Like I care that some meth addict bites it?"

"She'd recovered," I said, not that it really made a difference. I let free a breath. "What do you want me to do?"

He slid closer to me and took my chin. "Anything I tell you to do." His hand reached out, grabbed mine and placed it on his crotch. "I like my girls dirty, just like you," he whispered into my ear.

In retrospect, I should have seen it coming. Should have seen the hunter's desire when he first stared at me, but I had let my guard down since being at the farm, and now it was too late.

"So are we agreed?" he asked calmly.

I considered my options: either he turned me in where I would likely get pinned for my mom's death just because of my record, or I allowed him to use me. At least that was something I knew I could endure. I'd been in similar situations before. It was by far the lesser of the two evils, or so I thought.

I nodded once in understanding.

"Good."

Like lightning he grabbed the back of my head, forcing my neck to bend back. I could feel the hair being ripped from my scalp, but I refused to cry out. That's what sick minds like him got off on—fear. I would not satisfy him.

"You'll do as I say," he ordered.

"Yes, Master," I said in my rehearsed tone. The one I reserved for guys like him, the power-trip seekers.

Brad grinned. "Master. I like that." He let my head go. "Now suck my cock, and if you bite me, I swear to God, I will knock out your teeth, understood?" I had no doubt that he would live up to that threat.

Seeing no other choice, I reached down to unfasten his belt.

I'm not proud of what he made me do in that truck...of what he would continue to do to me over the coming days, but it's what happened. At least what I remember of it. The brain has a funny way of protecting you from some things, memories that could unravel your soul. I have no interest in trying to unlock those, even though I can feel them bubbling to the surface as I write this.

It doesn't get any easier from this point on. I'll understand if you don't want to continue.

WARNING

When Kyle found me later that day, I was sitting in the hay loft, mostly hiding from Brad. He didn't say a word to me when we pulled up to the house. He just got out, walked inside, and left me sitting there feeling discarded. I had snuck up into the loft hoping he wouldn't come searching for me.

"Hey," Kyle said. His voice made me jump. "Sorry, didn't mean to scare you." He walked over to where I was sitting, approaching me cautiously. "Brad said he thought you came in here. Everything okay?"

I glanced up at him, blinking my way back into reality. "Yeah, sure. Why wouldn't it be?"

"It's just, my brother—" Kyle began.

"What?"

Kyle sighed. "He likes to give the runaways a hard time."

"Lucky me," I said.

He lowered his head, as though ashamed of his brother. He had no idea how right his gut instinct was. "Yeah, he likes to poke at them, tries to mess with their minds. He's kind of an asshole."

I nodded, not in affirmation but just as a general mark of someone paying attention to a story. In that moment, I had the feeling that he would have believed me if I had told him the truth about that truck ride home. About the deal we'd made, about what I'd agreed to, but I wouldn't do that. He didn't need to know that part of the human mind existed, especially in a family member. Or that his brother had likely made very similar deals with all the other runaways that had graced his farm. Mostly, though, I knew I wouldn't be able to endure how he'd look at me after, the shame that I would feel. No. The deal I'd made was my burden to bear and mine alone.

"He's all bark and no bite," I lied. "He's just looking out for his family, that's all."

Kyle rolled his eyes. "Showing off is more like it. He's always been a bit high and mighty. He loathes it when people break the law, which is why he tormented those poor girls, I guess."

"Tormented? What did he do?" I asked, wondering how much Kyle knew.

Kyle shrugged. "I don't really know. He works them up somehow, but then eventually..."

"Eventually what?"

He peered up at me with unbelievably sad eyes. "Eventually he wins them over."

I raised an eyebrow at him, not sure if I understood what he was implying.

Kyle sat on a bale of hay and stretched at the back of his head. "Let's just say Brad has a way with the ladies."

At that, I scoffed. "I think I can resist his charms."

Kyle smiled, but then his face grew dark. "I was hoping the academy had knocked out some of the cockiness he's grown into these last few years. Guess not."

It probably reinforced it.

"So what did you two talk about?" Kyle asked, tossing a bit of hay at me. It almost sounded like he was jealous I'd talked privately with his brother.

"Mostly about why I was a runaway. If there was a price on my head, that sort of stuff." I laughed to try and cover the truth.

"Is there?" He whispered the question like he wasn't sure if he wanted to know the answer or not.

I shook my head. "I've only committed minor crimes. Things that, if I were rich, would get tossed out of court. Stealing, trespassing, that sort of thing." I stared down at my hands and picked at my nails. "Sometimes when you're on the road, you have to do things you wouldn't normally do... to survive." It was a vague answer at best, but he seemed to relax a bit. "I'm not going to disrupt your family, Kyle. At least, not any more than I already have." Of course, I couldn't help but worry about whether the deal I'd made with Brad would change that.

"You haven't disrupted anything, Sarah. It's actually a lot less dull now that you're here." He gave me a sweet smile that almost made the afternoon drive with his creepy brother worth it.

"Well, 'go me,' for being less than dull."

We laughed and slipped into an easy conversation about the river. It was relaxed, peaceful.

"I thought she was here to work," Brad said, popping his head into the loft. His hands rested on the posts of the ladder. "Or did I misunderstand why you're getting free room and board?"

"Calm down," Kyle said.

Brad scowled at his brother. "There's a storm coming tonight, and we need to get the chores done before it does."

"We're just taking a break," Kyle said, standing up then offering his hand to me. I glanced at Brad, who had climbed into the loft. He shook his head once, but his meaning was clear. It was a command not to take his brother's help.

"I'm fine," I said, rising on my own and swallowing down a throbbing pain in my neck as I pulled myself upright.

"The stable needs to be cleaned, the chickens fed, and I'm guessing the garden hasn't been weeded in ages." He frowned at Kyle.

"It's been a little hard to do it all. On my own." Kyle spat.

"Well, that's what she's for. To be used and abused, isn't it?" Brad laughed, a knowing smirk on his face.

"Don't be an asshole," Kyle said, coming to my aid.

I pushed past him. "No. He's right." I walked over to Brad, making sure to look him dead in the eye. "I owe a debt to your father. And I pay my debts."

Two could play at his twisted game.

"Good," he said, as his lips twitched into a sadistic grin.

Kyle, seeming confused, started to speak, but Brad cut him off. "I think Sarah should shovel the shit. What do you say, Kyle?" He grinned at his brother.

"I can do that," Kyle practically hissed.

"Great," Brad chirped. "Sarah and I will head over to the garden."

My stomach dropped.

"Mind if I pull the weeds?" I asked as sweetly as I could. "I feel like ripping things out by the short hairs today."

Brad just started laughing, so I maneuvered around him and down the ladder. Above me I heard Brad say, "She's a fiery one, isn't she?"

I wanted to laugh. I really did. He had no idea how *fiery* I really was.

"I'm going to the bathroom first. Meet you out there," I said, once I was down the ladder. I deliberately didn't wait for permission from Brad.

My hands were trembling because I needed a release. I needed to light a fire, just a small one, even a match or two would do it. I had to have something to bring my nerves down to normal about being semi-alone with Brad again.

I walked as fast as I could to the house. My limbs were quaking in anticipation, and I wasn't sure how much longer I could hold out. I was thankful that Al and Annabel hadn't made it back yet. I doubted I'd I have been up for small talk.

Once I shut the bathroom door, I rushed over to the medicine cabinet to glance out the window, always paranoid. All that greeted me were the darkening clouds in the distance. I knew I'd need to work fast. I had probably five minutes before they'd start to wonder when I was coming back.

I grabbed at the shelf for the small book of matches that lived there. I closed my eyes and smiled.

Briefly, I debated lighting a candle instead of just a match but knew if I started a candle, I'd need to watch it until it died out, and I didn't have time for that. I was only supposed to be using the bathroom, after all.

My hands began to tremble as I eased myself onto the floor. Letting free a slow breath of anticipation, I reached into the box and picked up a match. Even the feel of the wood made my jaw go slack. With well-practiced fingers, I drew the match across the strike pad. The sound of it igniting was as hypnotic as the first time. That initial burst of color coming to life was the biggest rush. My lips parted in ecstasy.

I waved the match gently from side to side, careful not to blow it out, but eager to watch it flicker longer. I ignored the throb of the heat against my thumb as the match burned lower, the first signal of its pending demise. That was the hardest part, by far. Watching it die.

"Sarah," a voice called suddenly, followed by a loud knock. "Are you in there?" It was Brad.

Cursing under my breath, I blew the fire out, tossed the match into the toilet and flushed.

"I'm in the bathroom. Can, you give me a second?" I asked in my best-annoyed voice. I waved my hands around trying to disperse the smell. I turned on the sink to cover the sound of me opening the window. I wafted the smell outward. The one bad thing about matches was that they left a distinct scent behind. I didn't need Brad getting any suspicions about me. So far, he didn't seem to know about my pyromania, and I wanted to keep it that way.

"Trying to run?" Brad asked, opening the door while my hands were still on the windowsill. He turned off the water I clearly wasn't using. I looked at him, eyes wide, not sure what to say. He sniffed at the air. "Is something burning?"

I had to think fast. I turned around and faced him. "Do the math, Einstein. The smell of a burning match and me opening a window in the bathroom. What do you think I was doing?" I blurted out. The veins in his neck bulged and his eyes narrowed in warning, but I ignored them. "Does watching someone take a shit get you off too?" I whispered. His hand rose up so fast I didn't have time to flinch, but he stopped himself before it made contact with my face.

"You'll pay for that smart tongue of yours," he said. There was no mistaking the very real threat in his words.

"Can't wait," I said, pushing past him. My heart was hammering against my chest as I willed my feet forward and out of the house. I knew I was going to regret upsetting him, but damn, it felt good to piss him off.

RESPITE

Although I'd never been in the garden, it was easy to spot. There was a white trellis overgrown with green twisty vines. Peppered within the vines were a handful of blue, bell-shaped flowers. I dodged a few bees as I ducked through the arch. They swooped in and out of the flowers in a seemingly random pattern.

Once inside the garden, I discovered rows of lettuces, several ripening tomato plants, and a few rows of what looked like some sort of bean that had wrapped themselves around the chicken coop. To the right of that were tall stalks of what I assumed were corn and a few other rows of other veggies I couldn't quite make out based on their stems.

I decided to start weeding the first row. I had no idea what was buried beneath the earth but they sort of looked like carrots. The slight bulge of orange coming out of the dark soil confirmed it.

I sunk to the ground and pulled out my gloves from my back pocket. The gesture reminded me of Kyle, and I couldn't help but smile.

The slam of Brad exiting through the screen door echoed across the farm, so I tried to bury myself in the plants. I looked for green things that didn't have the same wispy tops as the carrots and gave a few tugs. When I saw that they didn't produce a vegetable, just a root, I knew I'd found at least one of the weeds growing on the farm. When Brad came into the garden, I knew I'd discovered another.

I sat back on my knees wondering if Kyle had come out of the barn yet. I would feel safer if I knew he was nearby. I glanced back at the chicken coop to see if he was there, but instead of his kind eyes, I found Brad's. My entire body stiffened.

"You know what I think is funny?"

I wasn't about to engage in a conversation with the bastard, so I turned away from him and saw, to my great relief, Kyle in the distance. He was carrying a bale of hay towards the coop. He nodded his head at me with a wide smile, so I waved at him. At that, Brad laughed.

"*That* is what's funny," he said, gesturing towards his brother with a small flick of his head.

"My waving amuses you?" I said, fully sinking onto my knees and adjusting my gloves. I wiped at the sweat with the back of my hand.

Out of the corner of my eye, I saw Brad wave at his brother, and then he kneeled down to me, a fake grin plastered on his face. "What amuses me, smart ass, is that you seem to have convinced yourself that my brother likes you."

I whipped my head up to look at him. "No, I haven't!"

"Sure you have," he said in a slow lazy tone. "You think he's a good ole cowboy who will look past your city life sins, swoop you off your feet, and ride you off into the sunset."

"I hardly call the trailer trash of New York 'city life'," was my brilliant retort.

He stood up, then walked around me and pretended to inspect the corn behind him. Kyle must have still been watching for him to keep up the pretense of kindness. "Just remember this," he said to the corn. "Your time here is limited, so don't get to thinking this is gonna be your final rest stop."

I stared up at him through the sun.

"I'm not going to let trash like you get your hooks into my family."

Swallowing down the insult, I turned back to the carrots. "I wasn't planning on it."

"Good. Because you're *mine* to play with."

My jaw clenched at the hunger in his voice.

His foot came down beside me, suddenly, kicking dirt over my knees. "Now that's just how I like you, on your knees and dirty."

I bit the inside of my cheek, holding back the anger and humiliation that was mounting.

"After we turn in tonight, I will come for you, and you will be ready for me. Understood?"

My nostrils flared in anger. "Understood," I said, my voice strong, refusing to shake.

He turned and knelt down beside me again and discreetly yanked the hair at the nape of my neck. "Yes, what?" he hissed, careful to look at the top of the fence and not me.

"Yes, Master."

I saw his satisfied look as he got up and went off to tend to the corn.

Disgusted with myself, I finished the weeding as fast as I humanly could, though he never came back to talk to me. There wasn't any need. He'd conveyed his message. There was no longer any reason to speak to the trash.

I didn't eat much for dinner that night. Al made burgers on the grill, and corn on the cob, and I grabbed some greens from the garden. Normally, I would have licked my plate clean over a dinner like that, but my mind was only thinking of what the night would bring.

I started to wonder if I should fake a headache, go to my room, and then just slip out the window. I could use the cover of the approaching night to make my escape. Although I'd have to rethink my plan to go to California, since Al knew that was my endgame. Brad would easily be able to get that information from his father, and I didn't need the cops, or him, looking for me there. I thought maybe I'd venture south. It would be easy enough to live on the road again. It would be as easy as breathing. I had just cleared my throat to mention my "headache" when Al spoke.

"So, how long do we get to have you, Brad?"

Brad peered at me when he replied. "I'll need to leave Wednesday evening. Thursday morning at the latest."

Al nodded but seemed sad. "I have to admit, I did get a bit excited when I saw your truck in the drive. I thought maybe you'd changed your mind, decided to stay here on the farm."

Brad let his fork land on his plate. "Dad, I have a job. I'm a cop now. All my stuff is already waiting for me at my apartment in Boston. I need to unpack before I start Monday. I don't have time to waste out here. This place," he said, gesturing around him, "this was never my dream. It was yours. Besides, you have these two. You don't need me anymore." He picked up his fork and stabbed a cucumber. "And I have criminals to put behind bars," he said as he chewed.

A weight lifted from my heart. *He'd only be here for three more days?* I wouldn't have to leave the farm after all. Come the end of summer, sure, but until then, I could spend the rest of those days here. In that bed. My hands in the dirt and food in my belly. I might even have time to come up with a plan before I left. More importantly, I wouldn't have to leave Kyle yet. My throat tightened at the thought I shouldn't have allowed in.

I had made up my mind. I would stay. I would endure Brad's advances. I could handle an arrogant prick for a few more days.

Hindsight, they say, is everything.

"You feeling okay?" Kyle asked me, putting down his half-eaten corn cob.

"She's fine," Brad said. "She's just not used to working a full day." He reached across the table for more salad as a loud roll of thunder rattled in the distance. I flinched at the noise, but no one else seemed to notice. "You should eat, Sarah. You're gonna need your strength." Brad smirked. "Although, I'm sure you know it's *hard* by now." He glanced quickly at his crotch but everyone else seemed oblivious, which was just how he wanted it.

Big Al forked a bit of corn that he had cut off the cob and fed it to his wife who absently chewed the proffered bite. "Boys, I need to talk to you after dinner." He looked up at me apologetically. "It's a family thing."

"Of course. I'm actually done." I pushed off the table and took my plate to the sink, grateful for the escape. "I'm beat. I'm just going to go lie down anyway."

I saw Brad grin from the corner of my eye and almost ran to the safety of my room. I wanted to lie down, but I couldn't. I felt sick to my stomach. I wasn't sure why. I'd done this sort of thing countless times, just...never when I sort of liked someone else. It felt like I was cheating on Kyle, which was stupid. Kyle and I weren't a thing. And we never would be.

Before I made it to my room, I went into the bathroom to swipe the box of matches. I was going to need to light a few. After about a dozen spent matches, however, I didn't feel any better. Frustrated, I tossed the box under the bed and began to pace the room as the storm clouds rolled in.

There was something *off* about Brad. I wasn't sure why I was so disturbed by him, but from the moment I saw him, my gut told me to run. I'd had other twisted men in my past, ones who liked to give orders or knock me around, but I always could tell where they drew the line. With Brad, I couldn't.

I collapsed onto the floor for quite some time until I heard the light knock on my door. I practically jumped out of my skin. I didn't answer, hoping they'd go away.

"Sarah, it's Kyle. Can I come in?"

I felt my body relax. "Um, okay," I said, sitting up a bit higher to look not so pathetic. He opened the door softly, as though approaching a wounded animal. He wasn't that far off.

"Just checking on you," he said, but then he caught sight of me. I'm not sure what went through his mind, but whatever it was, he seemed to drain of color. "You okay?"

I managed to give him a small nod.

"You don't look okay." He walked slowly across the room and sat down on the floor with me near the dresser a few feet away, seeming to know I needed space.

"Not having a great day." I shrugged.

"Wanna talk about it?"

If only. It's not like I could have said, "Actually, I'm upset because your brother is going to force me to have sex with him in a few hours and I'd rather not." Instead, I chose not to say anything. I'd let him draw his own conclusions and go with that. It's odd how often in life that worked for me. It's easy to let people come to their own conclusions. It's far easier than the truth. At least, for me.

"Thinking about the accident?"

I raised my eyebrows. "The accident?" I asked, genuinely confused.

"Well, the fire. I assume it was an accident." He laughed lightly. *Perfect.* I could work with that.

"I just—I thought I was over it. I mean, I lit that candle the other day in the bath, all by myself, but then I fell asleep in the tub...so I didn't get to do the hardest part..."

Kyle looked up at me. "The hardest part?"

"Putting it out." There was no lie in that. That *was* the hardest part. I never wanted the fire to die.

"So, for you, the fear of fire is not having control of being able to put it out, not the actual fire itself?" he asked, genuinely interested.

"Isn't everything about control? In the end?" I asked, honestly.

"I guess." He shifted his feet a bit, clearly unsure of what he should do now.

Outside, thunder rumbled through the night, making me jump. It also sparked a horrible idea.

I moved away from the window as fast as I could, eyes wide.

"It's just thunder," Kyle said, trying to soothe me.

I continued to stare out the window. "I know. It's just...that's how the fire started. Lightning."

It was the perfect set up for what I was about to ask.

"Oh," Kyle said, standing. He went over to the window and closed it, drawing the thin curtains closed. Through the fabric, you could still see the sky as it illuminated sporadically across the night.

"I remember waking up feeling hot," I said, trying to form the story as I spoke. "When I saw the smoke coming under my door, I just froze." I closed my eyes for effect. "I could hear sirens in the distance. There was a window behind me, but I just couldn't seem to move. I was terrified."

"How did you get out?"

I shrugged and walked over to the bed. "I'm told a fireman broke through the window. I passed out from smoke inhalation. The fire had come into the room by the time they got me free. I almost didn't make it." I looked down at my hands and then touched my side as though remembering. He'd seen those scars. Now he could associate them with a noble fire and not the twisted one they had actually resulted from.

Thunder echoed closer to us, as though excited to be a part of my lie.

"Kyle," I said, "I know this doesn't make any sense, but...could you stay with me tonight? I'm...I'm just afraid to go to sleep...I'm afraid that if there was another fire, I'd freeze again, like with the stupid stove. I don't know. But if you're here...then I think I might be able to relax, knowing someone would save me if a fire broke out."

"There isn't going to be a fire, Sarah."

I let loose an exaggerated sigh. "You're right." I stood up and started to pace again, pretending to wipe away tears for maximum effect. "It was a stupid idea. I'm sorry. I'll be fine."

"No, no. It's okay. I can stay with you. Let me just grab some blankets from my room. I can sleep on the floor."

"Really?" I asked. The relief in my voice was both plain and genuine. If Kyle stayed with me, then Brad wouldn't be able to use me—at least not that night.

Then I did something completely uncharacteristic of me. I hugged him. Just for a second. Just one tiny second I wanted to feel safe.

"Thank you," I whispered. "You have no idea what this means to me." I pulled away quickly, hugging my sides, angry at the weakness I had shown.

Kyle's eyebrows pinched together. "Of course. I'll be right back, okay?"

I swallowed and nodded. When he reached the door, I called out to him. "Hey, Kyle?"

"Yeah?"

"Can you maybe not tell anyone else you're doing this for me? I kind of feel like a big baby."

Kyle smiled. "Mom and Dad are in front of the TV in their room and will most likely pass out there shortly. Brad went to take a shower. I'll leave him a note that I've gone to bed early, not that he cares what I do."

I nodded but kept my mouth shut about how Brad would very much want to know what Kyle was doing tonight and who he was doing it with.

BURN

I changed into some pajamas of Molly's as I waited for Kyle to get back. I was surprised to find that I was shaking while trying to do up the buttons. I was a nervous wreck and terrified that Brad would come in while Kyle was getting his stuff. I kept telling myself Brad wouldn't risk coming to get me while his family was still awake, but I didn't know what he was capable of.

It was only when Kyle returned, pillow balancing on top of blankets, that my heart returned to its normal rhythm. He went right to work at making his bed close to the door.

"You don't have to be that far, you know," I said, laughing in an odd way. I needed him to be closer to me. Hell, if he volunteered to sleep in the bed beside me, I wouldn't have turned him down. That's how scared I was. I was about to deliberately disobey Brad, and I had no idea how he'd react to that defiance.

Once Kyle had settled down onto the floor next to my bed, I noticed his mind seemed a little far off. That's when I remembered what his dad said at dinner about a "family matter."

"Everything okay with the family meeting?" I asked.

"Huh? Oh, right," he said, as though remembering he was in a conversation with me. "Um, Dad's bringing Ma to visit a nursing home tomorrow."

"Oh. Is that a good thing?" I asked.

Kyle let free a deep breath, which confirmed that it was, at the very least, a complicated thing.

"The place sounds great. She'd have her own living space and round the clock care…"

"But," I said for him.

"But it's like four hours away."

"Oh."

"Yeah," Kyle said.

"Isn't there anything closer?"

He shook his head. "Not that he can afford."

"Oh," I said again.

"It would kill him to be that far from her. He spends every second he can with her when he's not on runs. He told us after his run to California, he's not gonna make the long hauls anymore. He has another six-day haul early next week." Kyle rubbed his hands down his face. "The thing is, he can't afford to retire and take care of Mom because he owes so much on the farm that, even if he sold it, he would take a loss. I just don't know what we're going to do. Either he stays here and the bank forecloses on him when he can't pay the mortgage anymore, or he wins the lottery and moves with Mom out of town to the new facility."

"Are there no other options?" I asked, knowing they'd probably exhausted all avenues.

"Nothing comes to mind. He'll start selling off the cattle, I suppose, scale back on the farm needs and then, I guess, I'll find a job, try to help as best I can."

"Wow. You must really love your folks."

He looked up at me.

"I do. They are everything to me," he said with no trace of lying.

"That must be nice. Having people you care about so much."

"Have you never had that?" he asked.

I tugged the sheets up to my chin. "No."

He frowned. I could tell he was going to start questions so I reached over to turn off the side lamp, but hesitated.

"Do you mind if I leave the light on?"

"Sure," he said, shifting on the floor. While leaving the light on played nicely into the fear story I'd created, it also ensured that Brad would see his brother on the floor when he came in. That was something I didn't want Brad to risk missing in the dark.

We both sat still for a bit. Neither one falling asleep, but not needing to speak either. It was comforting. "Thanks again for staying with me tonight, Kyle."

"Anytime, Sarah."

I closed my eyes as tight as I could and prayed I'd be asleep when Brad came knocking on my door. With Kyle sleeping right beside my bed, he'd be hard pressed not to notice his brother there, keeping watch. I tried my best not to imagine the fury that might rouse in him when he saw what I'd done.

As much as I wanted to sleep through the night, I didn't. I heard the second Brad's feet started down the hall toward my room. I wanted to squeeze my eyes tight together, but I had to force them to stay lightly closed so it would appear as though I were sleeping. Every muscle in my body tensed when I heard the door open.

"You better be awake, because I'm—" I heard him whisper but then he stopped cold. My heart was racing, bracing for him to shout, or at least, wake his brother up to ask him what he was doing, but he didn't.

I opened my eyes a fraction to see what was happening. Brad just stood there in the doorway, hovering, as though weighing his choices. I could hear his breathing go from labored anger to a stealthy calm. After a few tortuous minutes, he closed the door behind him softly. I listened carefully to the weight of his body as it drifted back down the hall.

I let out a slow breath, trying to calm my heart rate. I didn't move, though, my muscles were still seized in fear.

I needed to focus on something that wasn't Brad, but I

couldn't relax. I tried to listen to the rain outside, normally a calming sound, but the way it pelted the windows left me on edge.

After about an hour, when I felt confident that Brad wasn't going to return, I eased myself out of the bed and walked over to the window.

Despite the story I'd made up to Kyle, I actually loved thunderstorms, when I was inside, that was. Sleeping outside in one wasn't as pleasant.

I pushed back the drapes and leaned against the sill, watching the sky as it lit up the night. It was fascinating. Not like fire, but close. I leaned my nose onto the glass. It felt cool against my hot skin. It was rather warm in here, so I opted to open the window to let a little of the chilled night air in. As my fingers touched the sill, however, I noticed the hairs on my arms rise. A second later, the largest bolt of lightning I'd ever seen shot across the sky. The resounding clap of thunder shook the ground and caused me to shriek.

Kyle woke with a start at the sound of my scream. A few more bursts of light and some smaller rumbles tore through the dark clouds. I stepped back from the window slowly, as though I had been struck myself. The hairs on my arm were still standing up. I started shaking. It was one of the closest strikes I'd ever seen. It felt like it hit right in front of me.

"Sarah?" he asked, rushing over to me. "Are you okay?"

I couldn't speak. I was too stunned.

He seemed to sense I was having issues because of the storm. He instantly tried to soothe me. "Hey, shhh. It's okay, it's okay." He put his arms around me like a mother might do with a scared child, and I let him. It felt calming to have him that close.

That's when I saw it.

I pushed him away and walked to the window as though stuck in some terrible nightmare.

"Fire," I whispered.

"No, it's okay, there is no fire, I promise," he tried to calm me down, but I raised my hand like a robot and pointed. "Fire," I whispered again.

He came up beside me and saw what I was seeing—the hay barn. On fire.

"Holy shit!" Kyle rushed out of the room, leaving me standing there. Alone.

I was transfixed, frozen in place, as I watched the fire rage. I was locked not in the normal ecstasy that I felt when I watched things burn, but in legitimate fear. I was becoming the lie I had told. The irony was fitting. In my mind I knew that I was going to die here, watching the fire that I grew up with inch its way to my paralyzed form.

That's when I felt his hands on me.

"I'm so sorry, Sarah. I didn't mean to leave you. I thought you were behind me, come on. Let's get you safe."

I had to blink several times to see him through my watery eyes. Kyle was there, lifting me into his arms.

"You came back," I said. The shock was clear in my tone.

"Of course I did. I would never leave you behind."

I clung to his shoulder, holding tight to his lie. I knew full well that he would abandon me. In the end, they all did. But for now, I allowed myself to believe him.

When we got into the kitchen, he put me down.

"I have to wake up the others. Will you be okay for a second?"

I nodded and watched as he raced down the hall to Brad's room. Kyle pounded on his door until Brad ripped it open.

"What the hell, man?" Brad shouted.

"The barn's on fire. Come on, we got to try and stop it before it gets to the house."

"Jesus," he replied.

A second later they came rushing out of the hall. Brad either didn't see me or didn't care that I was in the room. He ran outside and stood there for a second. His hands went up to his head in disbelief as he watched the fire burn.

Kyle spoke beside me. "Go wake up Dad. Get them out of the

house. Can you do that?" I blinked at him. "Sarah, can you do that?"

"Yes. I'll get them out," I said though my voice was shaking.

"It's going to be okay." He leaned over and kissed the top of my head, and then he was gone.

"What's going on?" Al asked behind me, walking into the living room and rubbing his eyes.

"The barn's on fire," I said. "They went out to stop it, but we have to get out of the house."

Al's eyes widen, instantly awake. "You get Annabel," he said dashing through the kitchen to help his boys.

"But," I tried. We needed to leave.

"Go. Get Annabel," he yelled at the door. "Call the fire department!"

A second later the sound of the screen door shutting echoed off the walls of the empty house, leaving me in the darkness of the shouts of the men trying to calm the beast outside.

My breathing grew shallow in my panic. My heart rate was climbing. I was scared. Me...scared of a fire. I had no idea how to process that.

I had to focus, though. I had to get Annabel out of the house. As quickly as I could I rushed to her room, flicked on the light, and began shaking her awake when Al came in. He rushed over to his wife, taking her hand from mine.

"What's going on?" Annabel asked him.

"It's all right. We can go back to bed. False alarm." He put his arm around his wife and looked back at me. "It's out," was all he said before he returned his attention to his now very confused wife.

I left their room, rushed to the porch, and watched through the downpour as Brad and Kyle walked around the barn a good ten times. I thanked God for the rain. Yes, God. I knew the rain was probably the only thing that kept that entire farm from going up.

As they headed back to the house, I stood there, unsure what to do.

Brad came in first, cursing under his breath before he stormed past me and went to his room.

"I haven't called the fire department yet," I confessed to Kyle. "I wanted to make sure your folks were out first, then Al came in and told me it was out."

"No, it's okay. It's out. We don't need them now. Their sirens would have terrified the cattle even more. We got them out to pasture until the smoke clears in the morning. Wasn't much damage, from what I could see. Contained itself mostly to the loft," he said, pulling his wet shirt off and flopping it on the floor. I looked away as he grabbed a dish towel hanging from the stove handle to dry his face off. "There's a hole in the roof that will need mending, and we'll need a new weathervane, but aside from that, I think the rest of the barn is fine. I'll have a good look in the morning." He rubbed his hands over his face, clearly exhausted.

I am ashamed to admit it, but I started to cry. The fire had scared me. It had shaken me to my very core. Fire, the one thing in my life that I could count on to ease my mind, was now something I didn't even want to think about. To poor Kyle, though, it must have looked like I was reliving my worst nightmare, and in a way, I was. How would I ever be able to light another fire without being reminded of tonight? If I couldn't light my precious fires, then what was left? What could ever possibly hope to fill that void?

"It's out," he said. "We triple-checked every inch of that barn and the area around it. It's out. There is nothing dry in the barn. Nothing will reignite tonight."

I sniffled a bit but clung tight to my sides.

"Hey, Sarah, it's okay. Really. It's out."

"The whole house could have caught on fire," I whimpered.

He came over and took me into his arms, where I went willingly.

"But it didn't, thanks to you. If you hadn't spotted it when you did—"

I felt ashamed. I could always find fire.

"I'm scared," I said. And I was. Everything about who I was

and what I loved now felt dirty and horrific. I felt sick over ever liking fire in the first place. My stomach rolled, and I started shaking hard.

"It's okay now, Sarah. I'm here. You're safe."

But I wasn't. I would never be safe again.

HELL

I'm not going to lie. This memory is a hard one to repeat, especially on paper where you can read it over and over. Putting these memories onto the page ensures I'll never be able to forget them...which is actually why the words have to come out. I don't deserve to forget what happened. I deserve to relive this hell for the pain I've caused.

When I woke up the next morning, Kyle was gone. The sun was flooding Molly's room, making me squint. It was far brighter than it should be for the morning. I must have slept in. I stretched but stopped when I heard the air brakes of Al's semi.

Confused, I rushed out of bed in time to see his truck pulling away. "Why is he leaving so early?" I heard myself ask.

Their appointment to see the facility wasn't until later in the afternoon. I glanced at the clock on the bedside table and gasped. It was almost noon. I'd slept half the day away.

Fumbling around the room, I searched for my pants. I'd kicked them off last night at some point after the fire debacle but I couldn't seem to find them. I bent over to check under the bed.

"Now that's exactly how you should have been last night when I came to see you," Brad's deep voice said from behind me.

I froze for a second and then forced myself upright. "Ever heard of knocking?"

His hand was in my hair, pulling my neck back faster than I could even flinch.

"You really shouldn't test me today. You're already going to be punished for what you did to me last night. Don't make me add to that list."

"Wha—at about Kyle?" I squeaked. Surely, he wouldn't try something with his brother here.

He yanked my head back harder and ran the back of his other hand down my throat.

"Oh, you mean your guard dog? He just went into town to get new roofing supplies. He wanted to take you with him, but I convinced him you needed your rest." He pressed his lips close to my ear and whispered, "He'll be gone for hours."

I deflated under him; his grasp on my hair was the only thing holding me up.

"Come on, I want to show you where we'll be playing today." He shoved me out the door and led me down the hall to his room, his hand still firmly holding my hair. He kicked the door open with his foot, sending the door flying. Pushing me inside his bedroom, he threw me on his bed, like a rag doll, before he locked the door. I scrambled off the bed searching for a window to crawl out of, but he snatched me by the wrist before I could get far.

"Oh, no, you don't. You don't get to dodge this bullet. You've earned this."

I screamed, though I knew it would do little good. The closest neighbor to the farm was miles away, and with everyone gone, there would be no one to hear my screams. It was just how he wanted it.

From his back pocket, he took out a pair of handcuffs, probably the same ones issued to him as part of his uniform.

"The first thing we need to do is restrain you. Wouldn't want you to pull a muscle or anything now, would we? You still have chores to do and a roof to fix."

"Let go of me!" I screamed, trying to pry his hand off my wrist. He swatted my face away like a fly. My skin prickled with heat as the first cuff closed around the hand he held. Quickly, he reached for the other one. I tried to break free, hitting him with any part of my body that I could, but he easily ensnared my other hand and locked the cuff closed.

"You're gonna pay for your breach of contract." He laughed, clearly enjoying himself. I squirmed, using my legs to try and kick him.

"Hold still!" he shouted as he kneed me in the gut. The force of the hit dropped me to my knees. He let go of the cuffs, and I crumpled to the floor trying to find a breath. I wanted to run, but the pain was intense. He'd knocked the wind out of me. I couldn't seem to get air to enter my lungs.

As I gasped, I saw him remove a massive boxing bag that was hanging from his ceiling. It landed next to my head with a violent thump.

"Get up," he muttered, dragging me by the cuffs to my feet. I was still struggling to breathe normally as he pulled me upright. The metal dug into my flesh as he yanked the cuffs over my head.

"This should hold you." He lifted my hands so the chain from the cuffs rested on the hook of the boxing bag. My feet barely touched the ground, so I couldn't get the leverage to free the chain from the hook.

"Now, what to do about those pesky feet?" At that, I tried kicking at him, first with one leg, then with both, but the pressure of the metal cutting into my wrists tore my skin and took the fight out of me.

He didn't seem concerned by my attempts to get free. He casually walked over to his dresser, moved away some socks then held up plastic ties. "These should work nicely."

Pushing the drawer back with his hand, he turned and waved

the ties back and forth slowly in the air. The smile on his face confirmed just how much fun he was having.

As he got closer I started to kick at him again. He sighed, as though disappointed, then pulled his hand back and slapped me across the face. My head bounced off the back of the door, which made my head spin. Stars formed around my eyes as I hung like a dead weight on the hook. I tried to regain consciousness as he worked on securing my ankles. Helpless I watched him loop the ties through two metal eye hooks that were drilled into the bottom of each side of where the boxing bag had been. He'd planned this all out.

After each foot was trapped, I hung there completely vulnerable. My legs were spread apart and my arms caged over my head. I could do nothing to prevent what was about to happen.

I watched, emotionless as he cocked his head and smirked.

"Now...to remove those clothes," he practically sang.

Ever so slowly he started to unbutton the pajama top that I had borrowed from his dead sister's bureau. I wanted to tell him that, but something told me he might get off on that morbid tidbit, so I just watched, deflated, as he tired of his slow speed and ripped away each remaining button. Tiny white circles flew across the room with reckless abandon. Because my arms were over my head he couldn't take the top off. I felt some small victory in that until he reached behind me and simply tied the tails of the shirt together. He'd thought of everything.

His fingers trailed from my back to my stomach, inching their way up my torso, but he stopped. He saw the angry burn mark that covered my side. His face fell into a frown.

"Not so attractive now, am I," I hissed.

He stared at me, eyebrows drawn tight together in aggravation. "We all have scars." He lifted up his shirt, exposing a thin but long scar near his heart. "You should see the other guy." He grinned. "No, what has me upset is...further up here." His hands traced over the burn to the breast above it.

"Not aroused I see," he said to my nipples which hadn't

snapped to attention under his touch. A wave of pride rushed through me, until he slapped my right one so hard that it couldn't resist shriveling in fear. I braced myself against the smack to the left one.

"Much better."

He grabbed one of my breasts in his hands, then gently began sucking on my nipple. His teeth dragged roughly across them when he switched sides.

"Now, for the pesky pants," he said, licking his lips. He walked over to his nightstand, opened a drawer, and extracted a pair of scissors. He sauntered back to me. "I hate to admit it, but you do taste good, for a whore."

I spit in his face. He closed his eyes as he hardened his jaw. He tucked the scissors back into his pocket and then wiped his face. A second later his hands were around my throat, his fingers squeezing away my attempt at a scream.

"Do that again, and you will regret it."

I yanked at my restraints, but it was useless.

"You're just like the others. You don't know how to take orders. That's why I hurt you. I do it to teach you," he said, taking his hand away. I gasped for breath as he reached behind him and snagged the scissors again. "Now, where were we?" he purred.

I closed my eyes, trying to hold back the tears, as I felt the elastic band in my pants give way. A few rips and I was left in only my underwear.

Instead of cutting them off, though, he traced his hand over my nipples again. The flesh around them was still red from his blows. From there he trailed his finger down my belly button, and then under the fabric of my underwear. I whimpered as his fingers played gently with the hairs. "Please stop," I cried.

"Oh, we're just getting started, Sarah."

A second later his fingers slid inside me. I couldn't contain my tears anymore. I let them spill freely down my face.

He was relentless in his assault. "You see, the reason I started to finger the girls is because a dry screw is not nearly as fun as a wet one, and since we have nothing but time today, I'm going to go nice and slow with you." His face buried into my neck as he drug his teeth along my skin. I hated the feel of his body touching mine. He felt like acid that would never wash away. I turned my face from him when he tried to kiss me.

"Try as you might to resist the urge to get wet for me, but you will eventually lose." He massaged his fingers inside me. "I'm rather persistent." He lowered his head to my ear and whispered, "When I'm through with you, you will *want* me inside you. You will *beg* for me to screw you."

"Never!" I hissed.

My muscles clenched around his fingers at the intrusion, but he just laughed.

"Stop resisting me, Sarah. Your body will betray you with enough stimulation, no matter how hard you try to fight me. I will win, so if you want this over faster, just relax and let it happen."

"I hate you," I said with all the energy I had.

His fingers pulled out of me. He sighed. "You need to learn to watch your tongue." He looked disappointed.

I didn't care.

He walked away as I struggled in vain again to get free. I could feel the bottoms of my wrists opening up against the restraints as I thrashed. My voice pleaded for anyone to help.

At his dresser, he dug around a bit and produced a strip of black leather that encased a red ball. My eyes widened.

He pointed to a bookshelf above his bed. "Oh, and don't forget to smile for the camera."

My eyes flicked to the shelf where I saw his cell phone propped. The red dot indicated it was recording.

"This is going to be so much fun to watch again and again and again..." He walked over to me and cupped my ass.

"Don't touch me, you sick shit!" I shouted.

He laughed. "Oh, I *am* going to touch you, and you won't be able to say a word."

With his other hand, he pinched his fingers down on my nipple so hard that I screamed in pain. My scream allowed him to easily force the gag into my mouth. He buckled the leather belt behind my head, and I could do nothing to stop him.

With the gag firmly in place, all I could do was let out a muffled scream. When it sounded more like an aroused moan than a plea for help, I just stopped making any noise at all.

"Well, I can see this isn't working." For a moment, I thought he may have tired of me and was going to let me go, but when he reached into his front pocket and pulled out a lighter, my heart almost stopped. He smiled at my reaction as he pulled back the switch. I flinched at the sight of it and turned my head away.

"What? Don't like fire, Sarah?" He grabbed my chin and held it still, holding the flame close to my face. I whimpered, but it did nothing to deter him. "That's not what I heard."

I started to cry as he held the flame near my nipples. The heat rose in the air, wanting to melt away more of my flesh.

"Didn't think I knew about your fetish with flames, did you? Well, up until this morning, you held your secret very well. I'll give you that."

He took the lighter away from my chest and held it up to my face again.

"Maybe watching this burn will get you wet." His fingers dug back into me, and I sobbed into the gag, wondering when this nightmare would be over. I just wanted to shut down. I was trying so hard to get out of my head, but he wasn't letting me get there.

After a moment, he let go of the lighter and tossed it onto his bed. He stood back and stared at my helpless body.

"You know, it's really a pity that the rain smothered the fire last night. Having this place go up in smoke would have saved a lot of problems for Dad. With the insurance money, he could have moved out of state to that facility to be with Mom."

I looked down at him, even more disgusted with his train of thought.

"Oh, don't look at me like that. People do it all the time." Then, as though bored, he slid my underwear down to my ankles and cut those off too. "It's a hard one to make convincing, though, because of so much insurance fraud. Lightning would have been an act of God." He started to unbutton his pants. His erection was pressed firmly against his jeans as he worked them off. "But if an arsonist got carried away one day, well, that would be covered too." His pants fell to the floor. He kicked himself free of them then took off his t-shirt with one swift move. I closed my eyes when he started to remove his boxers. I wanted to fast forward over this part of my life and never relive it again.

"Oh, this is perfect," he said with boyish glee. I opened my eyes and saw his naked butt at the window. He looked back at me, a twinkle in his eye. "Kyle's home. Must have forgotten something." He wiggled his eyebrows up and down. "Let's give him a show, shall we?"

My eyes bulged out of my head, and I started to buck and scream in protest. There was no way in hell I wanted Kyle to hear or see any of this. Even if it meant I might be saved from Brad's attack, I wouldn't be able to bear Kyle seeing me so...vulnerable.

"No, don't you see?" he purred. "This is how it *should* be. He'll finally understand what a dirty little whore you are and will stop wasting his time on the trash." He reached into his drawer and pulled out a condom. "No offense. Not risking my dick getting exposed to your filth." He tore off the wrapper and rolled it over his cock.

At the sound of the screen door slamming in the kitchen, he walked over to me and jammed his dick inside me before I could even register what was happening. I tried to scream through the gag as he pushed further.

"That's it. That's how I like my girls. Helpless. Weak. And needing to be punished for disobeying orders," he whispered. The walls rattled as he thrust into me.

"Brad?" The sound of Kyle's voice had me pleading with him to stop. Instead, Brad's eyes grew wide with delight seeing my inner torment.

"Yeah, baby, that's it. Scream for me, Sarah! Ride my cock. Ride me, bitch, ride me!"

Tears blurred my vision as he continued his thrusts in a more frantic way. I wanted to die. I wanted him to just cover my mouth and take all my breath away.

Kyle seemed to hover at his brother's door, listening to my betrayal. Tears streamed down my face until I heard Kyle's slow, but deliberate, steps walk back down the hall.

When the screen door slammed behind him, every ounce of happiness I'd had ever felt at the farm drained out of me. Kyle was gone. Not that he had ever been mine to begin with, but the feeling was just as strong. There would be no recovering from this.

Brad climaxed inside of me as the squeal of tires echoed across the farm. He yanked my hair hard as he came, but I didn't feel it. I didn't feel his hands on me anymore either. There was literally no feeling.

Brad let out a guttural noise with his release, but there was no relief to be found now that it was over. The worst thing he could have done to me had already happened. He had taken Kyle away.

After he pulled out, he took off the spent condom, threw it in the trash, and flopped on his bed. "*That* was perfection, Sarah. Simple and pure perfection."

My face was covered with dried up tears. After a moment, I mumbled a request to him through the gag, but, of course, he didn't understand me. As though humoring me, he got off the bed and ungagged me.

"Was that a 'thank you?'" he asked, smiling.

"No," I said. "I asked you to kill me." My voice was scratchy from screaming, but it didn't lessen the weight of the request. I needed him to know how serious I was.

"Kill you?" His eyebrows rose. "No, precious, we have far too much fun together. Besides, I'm a cop. Killing people is against the law."

"So you're above murder, but not rape? How convenient," I

said, ready to get hit for the comment, ready to feel something other than this shame, but he only shook his head at me.

"I'm not a rapist. We had a mutual agreement. You agreed to this, Sarah, like it or not. It's not my fault you had so much dirt to blackmail you with."

"I never agreed to *this!*" I screamed, though my voice came out raspy.

"Ah, but you did. You agreed to do whatever I wanted. So what if my tastes are a bit more extreme than others?"

"They can lock you up for what you did to me," I said.

"For consensual sex? No, I don't think so." He sat up. "Besides, they'd never take a street rat's word over mine anyway."

As much as I hated to admit it, he was right. No one would believe my side. Not even Kyle.

"Please," I begged, "Just kill me. Leave me in a ditch somewhere. I'll leave a note saying I left, just, please?"

Brad's eyes grew dark. "You want me to leave you in a ditch? Like some sicko did to my sister?"

I cried harder, not that he wouldn't kill me, but knowing full well that I wouldn't have the courage to do it myself. If I had been that strong, I would have done it years ago.

I vaguely felt him cut the ties free at my feet. The muscles in my legs throbbed when I was able to put my weight on my own two feet again. Even so, I could barely stand up as he took the cuffs off.

I should have killed him for what he'd done to me right then and there. I should have sunk my teeth into his jugular and watched him bleed out, but that would have meant that I cared about what happened to me next, and I just didn't. Instead, my knees gave out and my body slid to the floor.

I was done. Done with everything.

REPAIRS

I'm not sure how long I stayed there on the floor, crumpled and bleeding, with the pink pajama top still tied behind my back. It could have been days for all I knew. I kept trying to will myself to stop breathing, to let the pain go, but with each inhalation, the stab of my reality intensified.

I watched Brad's feet as they slithered their way back into his jeans. His dresser opened, then shut, followed by the sounds of a shirt being tugged over his head. As his bare feet came closer to my head I imagined him drop kicking my skull like a football, but to my dismay, he picked my limp body up in his arms instead.

He didn't say a word but simply carried me into the bathroom where he propped me gently on the floor. Kneeling by the tub, he turned on the water and checked the temperature before he turned around.

"I won't put soap in," he said. "That would sting too much." He gestured to my hands. "When you're out, I'll get those bandaged."

His voice was kind, perhaps even remorseful, the pattern of abuse at its finest.

I didn't say anything. I'm not sure I could have even if I wanted to. I let him pick me up and ease me into the tub. The warmth did feel good, although the pain along my wrists was still there, regardless of missing soap. I swallowed the pain, not wanting to let him know how badly he'd hurt me. Although the bruises all over my body were beginning to show, betraying my mock strength.

He stood and walked to the cabinet to retrieve a washcloth. As much as I wanted to sink into the water and let it consume me, I sat there, still the victim in his twisted game.

"It hurts," he said, coming back with the washcloth. "I know. Let me bathe you."

Clearly he meant to stay, and I didn't have the strength to protest, so I let him wet the cloth and run it along my back and legs. He used great delicacy when washing my lower half, almost apologetic in his strokes. After a few minutes, I glanced down at the water, noting that the bath had become tinged pink with my blood.

He must have noticed too because he pulled the drain out of the tub and held up a towel for me. I rose, biting my lip against the pain that seemed to radiate from every pore of my body. He held my arm as I stepped out of the tub then began to dry me off, being ever so careful with his movements.

"You did well today, Sarah," he said while working the towel over my body. "You did very well. I admit I was a bit harsher with you than I normally am so early on in my grooming, but you just have such a smart mouth." His hands grew firm on my skin, causing me to tense, but then he relaxed and smiled. The beast had been contained for the present. "I'll give you the night off to rest."

My eyes closed, fully understanding that our time together was not over.

I continued my mannequin-like stance as he led me back into his sister's room. Methodically, he dressed me, his fingers gentle, like a child might dress their doll. I couldn't help but wonder if that's how he thought of us—the girls he broke into submission as nothing more than a plaything.

When he was finished with me, I'm sure I looked like a normal girl getting ready for her day, so long as you didn't look at my wrists. Those were still red and raw; the true symbol of what I felt like.

I held still as he worked on the cuts. He carefully dabbed ointment on them. The areas just below the thumbs were the worst. The skin had broken through there. The bleeding had stopped and the dried blood had been washed away, but the flesh was still angry and deep red. I had no doubt that bruises would arise around the entire length of my wrists from the way they throbbed. Not that it mattered.

After they were wrapped gently in gauze, he led me out into the kitchen. There, he pulled out a drawer and gave me some work gloves. They had small green flowers on them, his mother's, no doubt.

"You will stay in your room for the rest of the day. I'll make up an excuse for you. I'll bring you something to your room to eat tonight, but wear these when you come out in the morning. I'll make sure you work in the garden." I took the proffered gloves and stared at them. "Understood?"

I could only nod my agreement and tried to turn away, but he held my shoulder.

"When I leave the farm, you'll leave too."

I looked up at him, confused.

"Not with me," he clarified. "On your own. Your time is up here."

I hated myself for crying. Hated that I cared that I would be forced to leave the farm, hated that there wasn't anything here for me anyway. Not anymore.

"It's for the best. Kyle won't want you around now that I've had you."

"I can go now," I whimpered, trying to steel my resolve. Although I was beyond sore, leaving would be better than having to look Kyle in the eye after what he heard today.

"No. You're mine until I leave." The softness his voice once had suddenly wore off. "If you try to run or speak about our agreement with my family, I will turn your ass in. I will handcuff you to my own hand until they drag you away. Make no mistake, Sarah, I can come up with a hundred different felonies I could falsely pin on you that would leave you with no chance of parole. I'll make sure you are locked away for the rest of your life if you breathe one word of this or run before I'm done with you. Are we clear?"

"Crystal," I said, allowing only one last tear to fall.

"Good. Follow my lead, and everything will be just fine."

How wrong he was.

"Before I let you rest, I want to show you something." He grinned. He gestured to the door, so I followed after him. Like the good dog I'd become.

It hurt to walk down the porch steps, but I didn't complain. I think it pleased him that I couldn't keep up with his uninjured gait.

As he got closer to the barn, I froze. It was the first time I'd seen it after the fire. I couldn't walk any closer. I started shaking, staring up at the blackened embers that licked the roof of the barn.

"Oh, don't tell me you're scared?" Brad said, sauntering over to me.

I took a step back.

"Oh, this is rich. The pyromaniac is now terrified of fire?" Brad started laughing as I closed my eyes and hugged myself. I was having a hard time processing the shift as well. I hated how scared I was and could only pray that the fear would go away. I needed the fire more than Brad could ever comprehend.

"I have to say I'm a little disappointed at your reaction. I was actually looking forward to showing you this. I thought you, of all people, might appreciate it."

"Appreciate what?"

His twisted smile returned.

He pointed to a single wire that ran down the barn. "See that?" He walked over to the edge of the barn while I took a few tentative steps with him. He held up the wire that had become dislodged from its place underground and was now just dangling from somewhere on the roof. I followed the wire up to the top of the weathervane...or what remained of it. A charred rooster lay tipped on its side.

"This is a grounding wire," he said. "It runs from up there all the way down to the ground, so that if lightning strikes the weathervane, it travels down the wire and into the ground so you don't get a fire."

"But you did get a fire," I said. My voice was still hoarse but a bit stronger.

He nodded. "That's because technically you're supposed to install two wires. One isn't enough. One is actually more dangerous than not grounding at all."

I looked at him, and my confusion was clear.

"Most people don't know that, you see, but I did my homework." The twinkle in his eye revealed the truth. He had wired it wrong on purpose.

"You wanted the barn to burn?"

"Oh, not just the barn but the whole house too. They're practically attached, so it would have been easy."

My eyes must have bugged out.

He shook his head. "Don't look at me like that. I made sure we had working fire alarms before I installed this last summer. Sure, I wanted the house to burn, but not those inside it." He frowned at the wire before tossing it to the ground. "Pity Kyle got to the bulk of the blaze so fast. If it had burned a few minutes longer, it would have caught the hay bales inside on fire. After that, even the rain wouldn't have been able to stop it."

I stared at him. It was one thing to think about it, but a whole different thing to attempt it.

"You probably think I'm a monster, huh?" he asked, though it was clear he didn't want an answer. "Mom needs better treatment than Dad or Kyle can give them. When Molly died..." His face broke for a fraction of a second, revealing a glimpse of something secret he held there. "When Molly died, my mom died with her.

Her mind started to slip not a week after my sister was found dead. We chalked it up to a lack of sleep from worry, but that was the beginning of the end." His eyes hardened. "Now that I'm going to be gone...I just needed to see them safe."

In a warp, twisted sort of way, it sort of made sense. For one, brief moment I saw the boy Kyle had loved before his sister died. The brother that he'd grown up with.

Just then a cloud of dust started coming down the road. It was a truck. Kyle's truck.

Brad's sadistic mask slid back into place. "Not a word of this to Kyle. Put your gloves on," he said, slinking his arm around me.

My insides turned to stone. I didn't want to see Kyle. Not now, not so broken. Not ever. My hands shook as I worked the rough fabric over my hands. The edge of the glove just barely covered the bandages. I tried to stop shaking as his fingers dug into my side.

"Take my lead," he hissed.

Kyle's truck slowed as it came down the drive. The truck-bed was weighed down with a load of shingles that had been tied to the back. I couldn't look up from the ground as I heard the truck stop and his feet hit the ground.

"Hey, brother," Brad said. "Welcome back. I caught myself a filly while you were out." Brad shook my shoulders a bit, forcing my eyes upright.

I grimaced as I watched Kyle's jaw harden.

"So I heard." His eyes darted down, his hands dug deep into his pockets.

"You did?" Brad asked innocently.

"Yeah. I forgot my wallet. Got to hear the final act."

Brad's hand grabbed my ass. I held back the flinch. "Well, she was a feisty one, but nothing I couldn't break. Isn't that right?" He peered at me, the threat clear in his eyes.

"Right," I whispered, with a small fake smile.

Kyle took a few steps back. "I'm just gonna start work on the roof."

"I'll help ya," Brad volunteered. "I told Sarah she could have the rest of the day off. I reckon she's a tad sore, if you know what I mean." He smacked my ass hard again then headed for the truck.

Kyle's face seemed to mirror my own. Disgust.

When he turned toward the back of the truck, he didn't look at me. The message was clear; he had shut me out. My eyes flooded with tears.

To Kyle I had become someone to overlook, someone to not waste their time with. It was my fate. I would always be a mystery no one cared enough to try and solve. In the blink of an eye, I had become the garbage yet again.

NUMB

Numb, I walked into the house. I didn't register my surroundings as I passed by them. Nothing mattered now. Not the chickens needing to be fed, not the dishes piled high in the sink, and least of all my self-pity.

I turned into my room, desperate to find some comfort from the pain that had begun welling inside of me. I felt sick and heavy with guilt. They were feelings I'd never allowed myself before and I wanted nothing more than to turn them off. Fire was the one thing that always helped me shut down thoughts of worthlessness in the past, and now I couldn't even do that.

I ripped my gloves from my hands and threw them to the floor. I wanted to rip the bandages off as well but worried seeing the marks that remained would make the whole thing that more real.

Once inside the bedroom, I thought I'd feel better, somehow comforted by the warmth of the late afternoon sun, but there was so much sunlight that it made me feel vulnerable somehow. Like I was being watched, or judged, by someone up above. I needed it to be dark. I needed to be somewhere that I could hide away from the world. I needed to disappear from view.

My eyes fell on Molly's closet. I stepped in it and pulled the accordion doors behind me. Small slivers of light shone through the slits, but it was better somehow. I curled up tightly into a ball, just wanting the pain to stop. I wanted someone to hold me and tell me that everything would be okay. I wanted Kyle's arms around me.

That's when I started to shake. It was a cross between sobbing and an official mental meltdown. I couldn't stop. Even as my head banged against the wall and Molly's shoes dug into my thighs, I couldn't stop shaking. I was afraid that if I stopped, my mind would start thinking about Brad, about what had happened, about his future plans for me, and I couldn't let my mind go there, so I just shook until I was in so much pain that I must have passed out.

When the knock came at my door, I screamed, at least in my mind I did, though no sound came from my lips.

"Leaving you some food," I heard Brad say, but he didn't open the door.

I honestly didn't recall getting out of the closet or even eating the food, but I must have because when I awoke the next day, I was in bed and the food on the tray was gone.

The sun had yet to rise, but a quick glance at the clock told me it would soon enough.

I flicked on the light and let my eyes adjust, sore as they were from being cried dry yesterday. I sat up, cracking my neck.

"Enough," I said to myself. "Enough of this shit. You are stronger than this. Pull yourself together."

I was stronger than that. I had to be.

It was time to stop being a baby and focus on living through these next two days under Brad's supervision. I could take two more days of whatever he had to dish out. Then I could leave this place and never think of anything about it again. I would be the one girl that bastard wouldn't break, even if it killed me.

I flung the sheets off the bed, ready to start planning for my eventual departure. It was good knowing I had time to prep. I'd have time to collect some things, maybe even get some food, because God knew I'd lived off less.

Once my eyes adjusted to the brightness of the lamp, I rummaged through Molly's closet. I would need a backpack or some sort of bag, mostly to carry food and layers of clothes. You'd never carry anything of real value on the road. Not if you wanted to keep it. My fingers flicked absently to the place where the necklace I used to wear was ripped off my neck many years ago. It had been my mother's. The first time I'd ran I'd swiped it, wanting some reason to remember her. I took nothing the second time I left, needing to forget.

I forced my attention back to the clothes. I didn't want to walk down that memory lane ever again.

In full planning mode, I picked a few T-shirts from the back and a nice large knit sweater that seemed warm yet thin enough to cram in a bag. Bulky things were cumbersome on the road, but the sweater looked perfect for the nighttime chill. I would need something to keep me warm, especially now that I couldn't rely on my precious fires anymore. My heart stung at the loss, but I shoved the thought aside. "It will be warm where I'm going. I won't need fire then," I chanted to myself. I wasn't sure exactly where I was headed now that California was out. Didn't matter. Anywhere would be better than here.

Finding a beach bag on a top shelf, I pulled it down and examined it for size. Not too big, not too small. It had a zipper which looked fairly strong, although, given enough time that too would break. It would do the trick.

I crammed in the clothes, a pair of sneakers, and a pair of jeans, and sighed. Not a bad start. Now it needed some food.

Since it was still dark, it seemed like as good a time as any to sneak in the rest of the supplies. I'd spied some EZ open canned food in the pantry. There was nothing more frustrating than being hungry with only a can of food that you couldn't open. I contemplated swiping their can opener too. They could always get another one easy enough, after I was gone.

Because I'd slept in my clothes, I was saved the trouble of

trying to get dressed. The way my muscles hurt, I wasn't sure I would have been able to get them on alone anyway.

Quietly, I opened the door into the darkness. I padded down the hall, pausing with each creak of the floorboard. I did not want to wake up Brad, and I held my breath until I got into the kitchen.

Mercifully, the floors were much quieter on the linoleum. It was still dark in the kitchen, though my eyes had adjusted enough to see the outline of the fridge.

Carefully, I opened the pantry door and began feeling around.

"Looking for something?"

I shrieked quietly, knocking a box of something onto the ground. Something fell from the box and onto the floor.

"Shit," I hissed, bending to scoop whatever it had been back into the box.

A light flicked on, and there was Kyle. His hand still on the kitchen light switch, a blue bathrobe closed loosely around his waist. His brown hair was wild and curly, jutting out in all directions from what must have been a fitful sleep.

"Sorry. I was hungry," I lied.

He looked down at the spilled crackers then bent down to help pick them up, but his eyes froze on me in mid-bend. I followed to where his eyes landed—my wrists.

The bandages were still covering the cuff lines, but I knew exactly what it looked like to him.

Instead of acting surprised or upset, he slumped back onto his feet, as though all the air had been let out of him.

"Why?" he asked simply.

I tried to think of a reason to give him aside from the one he'd come up with when he said something else.

"Why do they all try to kill themselves?"

I sunk into the ground with him, curious. "Who?" I asked. I had the burning feeling that my question was more important than the one he'd asked me.

His beautiful eyes dug deep into mine and latched on, almost as though they were looking for something to stop the world from spinning.

"The runaways. You make number four, and each one of them has tried to kill themselves." The sorrow was deep in his gut. "That day in the tub? I thought you had drowned yourself," he said, though unable to look at me. "Why do you all want to die?"

Guilt lodged in my throat, trying to form the right words. I could end his suffering if I just told him the truth. None of them had tried to kill themselves. Each one of us had fallen prey to one form or another of his brother's twisted sex games, but I couldn't do that. I just couldn't. If I could spare him that burden of knowing what his brother was capable of, I was going to try.

"I didn't try to kill myself," I said. I removed each bandage, the clear red cuff ring was still there, slightly healed, but enough to prove that they hadn't been sliced open with a blade.

He leaned forward and took my hands in his, turning them over a few times. I felt so utterly ashamed. He looked up at me, waiting for an explanation.

I swallowed the lump that had formed in my throat. "It's from handcuffs," I said, burying the shame. He gave me an unbelieving look. "I...like it rough," I said as calmly as I could, fighting back the urge to cry. I had to lock my eyes on the floor, afraid I'd be sick otherwise.

"As for the others," I said, needing to get the focus off me, "I don't know what their story was, but I can tell you being on your own changes you, and not for the better." I closed my eyes for a moment. "Maybe being here made them start to feel normal again. Loved, cared for. Maybe the idea of going back on the road after feeling important to somebody was just too terrifying to contemplate, and suicide seemed like an easier way." It made perfect sense to me.

Neither one of us spoke for a long time. My eyes turned glassy. Tears begged to fall, but I forced them back. I wanted to protect him. I needed to. I could take the pain. I was built for it.

"I'm sorry," he said after a bit.

"For what?"

He stood up. "For not being the kind of guy you wanted." My eyes pricked with emotion. "I could never do that," he said, looking at my wrists. "Not to someone I cared about."

With that, he walked out of the kitchen, leaving me alone with his empty glass of milk and the tears that were now allowed to fall.

GAMBLE

I couldn't go back to bed after Kyle ripped my heart out and tossed it aside. I tried to convince myself it was for the best. After all, I wouldn't be seeing him soon anyway. It was better for him to hate me. It would make leaving that much easier.

Back in my room, I switched my brain to auto pilot. I'd live whatever hollow life there could be here until I was allowed to leave. I'd wake every day, breathe in and out, and follow all the orders Brad wanted to dish out. Then I would be free.

Pulling on my gloves, I went outside before the others awoke, fed the chickens, and collected about dozen eggs. It was good to be outside. Peaceful.

The air still felt heavy though. Dark clouds lingered in the sky, ready to let loose another storm. I worked quickly to pick some of the strawberries that had fattened up and placed them in the small basket that held the eggs.

Back inside, the kitchen was still quiet, so I tucked my gloves into my back pocket and washed the strawberries. In one of the cabinets, I found a cute bowl and placed them in the center of the table. I kept busy making coffee, getting a bowl for the eggs, and setting out the bread for toasting; domestic things I wouldn't be allowed to do soon.

Remember this. Remember it all. I knew it was what I'd miss the most, the semblance of a family—even if it was temporary and fleeting. I clung to it with every ounce of strength I had left in me.

Shortly after I came inside, the sky turned dark, and it started to rain. It didn't look like it would let up soon, so I couldn't very well go out and garden to hide my wrists in work gloves. I frowned, wondering what I should do. My wrists were still pretty red, though far better than yesterday.

I rushed to my room and found an oversized hoodie of Molly's that hung long on my arms and covered my wrists nicely. It even had those little thumb holes. It was perfect. I could still use my hands while keeping my wrists fully covered. I couldn't help but wonder if the person who invented these had ever tried to slit their own wrists.

When I came back out, Al was there, smiling and filling his cup.

"Morning, Sunshine. You make this?" he said, lifting the cup.

I nodded. It felt so good to have made him happy. It didn't last.

Brad came in, yawning, still in his pajama pants and little else. He took one look at me, then the rain outside. I glanced at the hoodie. His silent nod of approval confirmed that I had been relieved of punishment for not wearing those damned gloves.

Kyle came in shortly after. I tried to apologize with my eyes, but he just gave me a small nod and said nothing while he made his coffee. That was fine. I could deal with silence. It's what I was raised on.

When everyone had woken up, I set to the task of cracking the eggs, careful to keep the shells out of the sunny yokes swimming happily in the silver mixing bowl. It was soul-soothing work, the kind of work I could die happily doing the rest of my days, after, of course, I had learned how to cook more than the basic stuff a kid could learn on her own.

Grabbing a fork, I scrambled the yolks in a bowl with some milk. I poured a bit of olive oil into the pan, almost humming as I worked, but then I stopped.

The stove. How had I forgotten about that damn gas stove?

I stood there, hands stiff against the bowl as though hanging onto it as an anchor. I had no idea what I was going to do.

"Here, let me light that," Kyle said, putting his empty coffee cup on the table. "Your hands are full." He knew damn well why I was just standing there and had come to help, though he didn't look at me. He pulled down the matchbox from atop the fridge and slid one quickly against the side. The flame shot out of the match, making me jump backward, and sloshing some of the egg onto my hands.

"It's okay," he soothed quietly, as though not wanting to alert the others to my distress. I glanced over at the table and saw Brad smirking at my reaction. Bastard.

Kyle stepped in front of me and lit the burner so I wouldn't have to see the ball of blue as it burst into flame. "I got this. Why don't you start on the toast?"

I nodded as I let him take the bowl of eggs from my hands. My breath was a bit unsteady as I placed a few slices of bread into the toaster.

Closing my eyes to calm down, I pushed down the toaster and took some deep breaths. I placed my hands on the edge of the sink to steady myself.

"Feeling okay?" The voice suddenly beside me made me flinch.

"Oh, sorry, Al. You scared me."

He placed his hand on mine. I pulled away on the off chance he'd feel the bandages on my wrists. "Well, you scared me with that migraine of yours last night. Wasn't sure I'd see you this morning." The look in his eyes told me that he was scared of the same thing Kyle had been.

I smiled at him and whispered, "Just that time of the month." That line always worked to change subjects.

"Oh." He blushed and went back to the table, taking Annabel's hand as he did. Although she had a lost look in her eyes, her body seemed content as he leaned in to kiss her cheek. I smiled. He would always come back for her, no matter where her mind had sent her. It was raining hard outside, but the sun seemed to be shining on the two of them. Seeing Al so happy somehow made everything okay. I was surprised by how much I would miss them.

After breakfast, the boys went out to re-secure the tarp that had blown off. The repairs on the roof weren't finished and would likely need to be held off for another day. While they worked outside, I cleaned up the mountain of dishes that had been piling up. It was simple, mind-numbing work. Just the thing I needed. The soapy water also hid my wrists from Al after I'd rolled up my sleeves. It stung a bit, but the reminder of the pain was a good thing.

Once the cattle and chickens had been fed and the tarp placed, I discovered what happened on the King farm on rainy days: poker, of course.

Al came into the kitchen with me after Annabel had drifted off in her chair. He drank his coffee quietly as the sound of the gentle rain surrounded us.

After the boys got back inside and dried off, Kyle set down a worn stack of cards and a small bowl of sunflower seeds next to his father.

"Are you still hungry?" I asked, marveling at how many eggs they had all packed in at breakfast.

"This is what we use for chips," Brad said, glaring at me as though I asked too many questions.

"Wanna play?" Al asked, patting the chair beside me.

"I don't know how," I said. I didn't know how to play any games, really. I never had anyone to teach me games they didn't have in grade-school.

"I'll show you," Kyle offered.

My eyes flicked toward Brad who gave a swift, but subtle 'no' gesture.

"I think I'll sit this one out," I suggested.

Al nodded. "You could sit with Annabel. She's drifting in and out, but I think she might like the company."

Brad blinked his consent, so I gladly left the room to sit with Annabel.

Her 'shows' were on when I walked in, and her eyes were half open. Her 'shows' consisted of re-runs of *Looney Tunes*. I couldn't help but smile. They were re-runs back when I was a kid. I had no idea they still aired. That's when I noticed the large tape case of *The Best of Looney Tunes* sitting propped open on a VCR. I knew they didn't make those anymore.

As Annabel watched the show, she seemed transfixed. She didn't laugh at it, but she did seem entertained. Perhaps they reminded her of a time when she was young, or perhaps it just served as an anchor in a place where her mind roamed in and out of consciousness. Maybe it was something familiar to hang onto. Fire had been that for me. Without it, I felt lost. Adrift.

"Molly, can you turn it up?" Annabel asked, taking my hand in hers. Her hand was remarkably smooth, yet thin and cool. "Those boys make too much noise playing with their trucks." I happily obliged her, wondering which memory she was reliving now. How old was Molly in her mind? Did Brad and Kyle ever play with their sister? What had it been like growing up in a place where your parents loved each other? With a runaway, a sadomasochist, and a gentleman, apparently. How we turned out had nothing to do with good parenting. It was all dumb luck, as I had suspected all along.

The darkening sky, along with the sound of the rain on the roof and the soft shuffle of the cards, caused my eyes to slowly close. I jerked awake every few minutes to check on Annabel, who seemed as tempted by sleep as I was. Eventually, we each succumbed to the urge to rest a bit.

It was only when I heard Brad shout, "This is bullshit!" that my eyes popped open fully. Beside me, Annabel woke too, instantly distressed.

I tried to soothe her, but Al came rushing in, taking her shaking hands and helping her off the couch.

"It's okay, darling, Brad just lost his cool again. You know he doesn't like to lose. He gets that from you, you know." Annabel blinked at Al a few times. "Come on, my love, let's go sit out on the porch and watch the rain like we used to when we were kids."

"I don't like the rain," she said, although her voice seemed unsure if that statement was true or not.

"Well, let's have a sit outside to get some fresh air then until he cools off," Al said, leading her quietly past a still fuming Brad. He was glaring at his brother. A chair was on the floor, tipped there in seeming anger.

I knew a heated discussion was brewing, and I wanted no part of it. Of course, the only way to get to the safety of my room was through the kitchen, so I stood in front of the recliner I had been in, not sure what to do.

"You shouldn't have made the bet if you weren't willing to stick to it," Kyle said in an oddly calm manner.

I couldn't help but wonder what the bet had been about. When Brad pointed at me a moment later, though, I found out.

"Sarah belongs to me until Thursday," he was fuming quietly. "When I leave, you can do whatever the hell you want with her."

I gaped at him, both embarrassed and mortified that he spoke those words aloud.

Kyle pushed his chair back slowly and stood up. He was an inch or two shorter than his brother but didn't look it in that moment. All I could see was Kyle's back through the half wall that separated the kitchen from the living room. His shoulders were tight, as though standing his ground.

"She's not some cattle that you keep," Kyle said.

Brad scoffed but didn't say anything, probably angry with himself for revealing so much about his character already.

"That's not how I meant that to come out," Brad said. "It's just...I was going to leave Thursday. That only leaves one more day left with her. It's not fair."

Kyle's shoulders relaxed, though only a touch. "Then you shouldn't have been so eager to bet her."

"Fine," Brad said. He walked over to his brother and stood

beside him. He placed his hand hard on Kyle's shoulder. "Whatever. Take her to your stupid carnival tomorrow." He lowered his head to whisper in his brother's ear, but his gaze was fixed on mine. "But when you get home, she'll come crawling back to me. Guaranteed." In his glare, I saw the very clear order he was giving.

Without another word, he walked out of the kitchen and down the hall into his room. The resounding slam of a door only hinted at the rage that was boiling in his veins. A rage I knew I'd feel the full effect of sooner or later.

I swallowed the fear of his anger as Kyle stepped into the living room.

"Sorry you had to hear that," he said. He really did look apologetic.

"What was that all about?" I asked.

"I guess I sort of won you as a date to the Mullen Carnival tomorrow." A blush creeped into his cheeks. "It comes into town once a year for a few nights. There's a Ferris wheel, cotton candy, that sort of thing." He gave me a boyish grin, which I couldn't understand. Why was he trying to be nice to me? He hated me. "Only if you want to go, that is. I won't force you to have fun if you'd rather stay here and be dark and dramatic some more." His eyes were kind, but the expression he wore told me he didn't know what my answer would be. Neither did I.

"A carnival?" I said, stalling.

"Yeah, it's about the only amusing thing this town ever sees. It's good for a few hours of fun. Usually, anyway. Brad loathes it. He never goes. He thinks it's small-town hick stuff."

"Is it?"

He smiled. "Absolutely."

"And you bet who would take me to it?" I asked.

Kyle scrunched up his nose a bit. "Well, I suggested we bet on who would take you, but Brad amended it to, if I won, I'd take you. If he won, I had to fix the roof by myself." Kyle sighed.

"I've never been to a carnival before," I said, honestly.

"Really?" Kyle asked, seemingly shocked.

"No. I really didn't do anything as a kid." My eyebrows pinched together in shame.

Kyle shoved his hands into his jeans. "Ah yes, your elusive past you always hint about but never expand upon."

My hackles raised in defense until I saw that it was just a passing thought for him and he wasn't going to press me for more details.

"So will you go? I mean, it should be fun, assuming the rain stops by then," he asked, looking up at me.

I stared at him, confused. "Why? Why would you want to go to a carnival with me? You hate me."

His eyes softened around the edges. "Because you slept with my brother?" His words were like a punch to the gut. He stared at the ground for a second. "Yeah, I guess I was upset at first, but then I realized that's just the way the world works for Brad. He always gets the girl. I *did* warn you about his charms."

"Yeah, you did," I whispered.

"It doesn't mean we still can't be friends, does it?"

"I didn't intend to—" I started to say, but stupid tears came instead of the words. I felt horrible for my actions. I hated that I had upset him.

"Hey, it's okay," Kyle said, walking over to me and placing a tentative arm on my shoulder. "I'm not angry at you, honest. I know he has a way with girls that I don't have. He's always been like that, ever since we were kids. Hell, sometimes I wish I were more like him."

"No." My head snapped up, my tears stopping cold in their tracks. "Don't say that. Don't ever wish to be like him. Ever."

His expression shifted to confusion, and I knew I'd said too much.

"I'll go with you to the carnival, okay?" I said to change the topic.

"Great."

I felt awkward all of a sudden, so I excused myself to go take a nap.

That's what I would have done too, if Brad hadn't been lying on my bed waiting for me when I got there.

Sometimes when you gamble, even if you win, you lose.

PAYMENT

He was lying on my bed. His hands tucked under his head, muscles relaxed, eyes closed. I had hoped for a half a second that he'd fallen asleep and that I could sneak out without waking him, but of course, he was just waiting to pounce.

"Your day of rest is over, my dear, and since I don't get to have you the whole day tomorrow, I have to make up for some lost time right now."

A familiar fear danced over my skin, causing me to gooseflesh. He wanted to scare me. He wouldn't really try anything with his family so close.

"Oh, I thought you should know," he said with a calmness that unnerved me, "I got an interesting alert today. It seems that the NYPD is very interested in your whereabouts, Sarah."

I stiffened. He'd already told me that I was wanted for questioning concerning my mother's death, but I could tell the stakes had been raised.

He propped himself onto his elbows. "Did you know a church burned to the ground on the *very same day* you skipped town? The same day your mother was found dead."

My eyes widened, wondering what he was insinuating, and yet knowing at the same time.

"Three people died in that fire," he said, slowly sitting up. "A janitor, some homeless man in the alley too drunk to move when the fire broke the walls, and a nun." He stood up and walked over to me, peering into my eyes the whole time. "A *nun*."

"It wasn't me," I said, quickly, hating how guilty it sounded. I hadn't lit anything other than small bits of kindling and never near buildings.

He gave me an exaggerated sympathy nod.

"I'm sure it wasn't, or maybe it was." He smirked. "I could give a rat's ass." He reached out and twirled a few strands of my hair, gentle, yet ominous. His eyes tracked as his finger curled my hair around it. "Here's the thing that *will* matter." He gave the strand a hard tug. "You like to start fires. You have a history of it. There's a fire, not two blocks from your house, the same day your mother winds up dead. And you?" He let the hair go. "Are nowhere to be found. Odd. Don't you think?" He brushed his thumb along the edge of my jaw before he bent down and gently kissed my neck.

"The dots are there, Sarah. The 'truth' doesn't matter." He pulled his lips off my neck to look me in the eyes. "In the end, people just want someone to blame, and you fit the profile. I doubt you have an alibi for the time of the fire. Am I right?"

My silence was the only answer he needed.

He nodded. "So you see, you'll be guilty until proven innocent. Which we both know won't happen."

The expression on his face was clear. His little speech was a reiteration of the rules. Follow his orders or be turned in. I wasn't sure which choice was worse.

"What do you want from me?" I hissed, though careful to keep my voice low. "You want to gag me again, or should we go out in the living room this time so the rest of the family can watch?" My nostrils flared with rage.

Brad smiled and got close to my ear then grabbed my hand and placed it on his erect cock. "Oh, don't be so vulgar. I can be as silent as a church mouse. And so will you."

I closed my eyes, resigning myself to another round with Brad.

Fine. Whatever. I just wanted to get it over with. I walked like a robot to the bed, but he grabbed my wrist.

"Springs are too noisy, don't you think?"

He put his hands on my hips and herded me over to the window sill.

"Pull your pants down," he ordered.

I looked up at him, angry beyond words, which pleased him.

"Now, Sarah," he whispered.

I clenched my teeth together as my fingers struggled to unbutton my jeans. I let out a breath then slid the fabric down my hips, letting my underwear fall to my ankles along with my jeans. I tried to focus on the light drops of rain as they fell on the window. I wanted to lose myself in the storm outside, to be swept away with the rain, washed clean by its touch, but behind me, I heard his pants fall to the ground as well. The sound of the belt hitting the floorboards forced me into the present.

"Now bend over and put your hands on the sill."

I obeyed, my eyes closing against the world as I did.

His hands molded slowly along my back, snaking themselves up and inside my shirt. Expert hands easily shoved inside my tank top as his fingers closed around my breasts.

"I want you to think about him," he said, leaning over me.

"What?"

"Kyle. I want you to think of my brother as I screw you." My stomach turned. Brad's breath was hot against my back. "I want you to imagine his hands are the ones cupping your breasts right now."

"No," I whispered, refusing to let Kyle enter my mind. No way in hell would he taint Kyle's memory for me.

"Don't tell me you haven't dreamed about his hands running across your body? Haven't wished it was his fingers moving inside of you instead of mine?"

Without warning, his fingers dug inside me, making me bite my lip. I knew what he was doing. He wanted me to think of his brother so I would enjoy his assault, but I wouldn't give him the pleasure. I wasn't going to confuse my memories of Kyle with him.

"Fine, suit yourself," Brad said, and like lightning, he was inside of me, the shock of him filling me up burned, and I started to cry out in pain.

"Shhh," he said, covering my mouth.

I swallowed my cries as he thrust slowly at first but then faster.

As he grabbed onto my hips, a soft knock came to the door. Brad froze inside of me.

I turned my head towards the door.

He shook his head slowly.

"Sarah?" It was Kyle.

I sighed with relief at the thought of temporary respite, but when Brad's rhythm began to pick up his pace again, I knew that his brother being outside the door had become a turn on—the risk of getting caught.

"Sarah?" he asked again.

"Answer him." Came Brad's barely audible reply. The sound of his hips as they smacked into my ass must be audible from where Kyle was standing, but if it was, he made no mention of it.

"I'm f-i-i-ne." My voice wobbled as my body shook under Brad's control. "Mi-graine." I forced out. Faster and faster he pounded into me, the sound of skin on skin seemed to thunder in my ears. I didn't want him to hear this. I needed him to go away.

"Okay, feel better," Kyle said weakly. Brad gave one last grunt with his last thrust and nearly put my head through the window. His whole body tensed as he released into me, small pants of satisfaction cut through the evening air.

He pulled out of me after a few moments, tossing a spent condom at my feet.

"Take care of that," he said, slapping my ass. I sank to the floor under the window and stared across the room. A single tear rolled down my face.

Brad yanked up his pants and sighed. "My job's not finished 'til I make 'em cry." He grinned. "You have fun at that carnival tomorrow, providing you can walk. I'll be waiting for you when you get back."

He left at some point. I heard the door shut softly behind him, but I didn't move. I tugged a sheet from off the bed, curled into a ball against the sound of the rain outside, and cried myself to sleep.

CARNIVAL

I'm not sure why the depression kicked in on that particular morning as opposed to the first encounter with Brad, but something snapped in me during the night as I shivered in the cold. I realized what my life had become, and I didn't want to exist in it anymore. My life had been one shit situation after another. I wasn't meant to bring happiness or be happy. Of that much, I knew for certain.

As I lay on the floor, mulling over my life, I heard the sound of voices outside of my room. I dragged myself up to peer through the window. The windows were thin, so I could hear the conversation.

"Now, we'll be at Ruth Ann's for most of the day," Al was saying. "I've got to build up the courage to ask her to help with Annabel's care. I don't reckon she'll be happy about giving us money as those two never got on, but I'm running out of options." He sighed. "We'll be back before dinner." Al stopped. "You sure you don't want me to stay and help with the roof?"

"No, Dad," Brad said. "It's a couple of shingles. No big deal."

Kyle spoke next. "If you need me to stay and help..."

"I don't need my little brother's help. Go to your stupid carnival. I've got this under control."

I heard footsteps walking away and could practically taste the venom in Brad's voice. He was pissed. No surprise there.

After a moment, the sound of Al's truck door shut and the semi's engine roared to life.

Kyle had said money was tight, but I didn't know it was begging tight. I felt guilty. I wish I had been able to be more helpful in my time here. Found a job or something...then again, I had no qualifications. I'd never held a single job, and I highly doubted there was much to be had here anyway. The entire time I'd been here I had been little more than a useless mouth to feed. The only thing I had ever been good at was setting fires.

Fire...

My eyes darted to the candles on Molly's dresser as a slow smile spread across my face.

I stood up, feeling a sense of purpose I had never felt before. I tossed the sheet aside, kicked the condom under the bed, and bee-lined for the shower. I needed to wash Brad's touch off of me, but then I could do one decent thing with my life before I either ended it myself, or it was taken from me by way of a life behind bars.

I dressed cheerfully in the quiet silence of the early morning. I was finally going to do something important with my life.

"Soon, Molly. Soon. I'll make things right for your family," I whispered to the room.

Kyle was waiting in the kitchen when I came out. He was holding a bowl of cereal in his hands. A small dab of milk dribbled down his chin as he lifted the full spoon into his mouth.

I had no desire to eat, but I knew I needed to keep up appearances. I grabbed an apple from the bowl that sat on the table and bit into it, not tasting it as I chewed. I adjusted the brim of my hat low to cover my eyes, hoping to hide the redness that lay there from a night of tears.

"After I tend to the chickens, we can go if you're okay with that?" Kyle asked. "Brad's already out in the field mending a fence. He probably won't start the roof till we're long gone. Stubborn as an ox, he is." Kyle shook his head in frustration. "He was pretty grumpy this morning so I thought it might be better to leave before he got back."

"Great idea," I said. "What needs to be done? I'll help."

"I'm just gonna put out some fresh hay for the layers and toss down some feed," Kyle said, as I put down my half-eaten apple on the counter. "You feed the chickens. I'll grab the hay."

"I can do the hay. I just have to run to the bathroom first."

"Nonsense, the hay is heavy. I can do it."

"It may be heavy but at least it doesn't bite. Besides, I'm way stronger now," I said and turned to leave the kitchen.

I heard his reluctant footsteps as he headed to the chicken coop. It was the opportunity I needed. Somehow, I knew that the universe had given me this window, and I was not about to let it close on me. I ran back to the bedroom, reached into the closet and grabbed my bag. I'd be leaving after the carnival, one way or another. I just had one thing to check off my list first.

Outside, I rushed toward the barn, hiding the bag in front of me in case Kyle was watching. I disappeared through the barn doors, dropped the bag, then took my hat off and laid it on a bale, purposefully. From there I picked up the bale beside it and carried it back to the chicken coop. I was slightly amused at how it really was easier to carry even after only a few days of farm work.

Back in the chicken coop, Kyle and I pulled at the bale and lined the chicken beds.

"Not worried about ticks anymore?" Kyle asked, watching me put hay down.

"I'm not worried about anything anymore," I said, smiling. And I wasn't. My path had been laid out for me. All I had to do was follow it. Nothing else mattered.

"Well, that's good. You'll need that attitude for some of the rides at the carnival." He laughed, but I could feel him looking me over, seeming to sense the shift in me but not able to understand the reason for it.

"So, do I have to ride on that 4-wheeler again?" I asked as we left the chicken coop.

Kyle laughed again. "No, we'll take my truck. Unless you wanted to ride it?"

"No. You're truck will be fine," I said.

My mind was focused on what I was about to do, but I tried to smile so Kyle wouldn't think something was wrong as we walked toward the truck. Nothing was wrong. Everything was finally right.

His truck was an old, beat down, fixed a thousand times sort of vehicle, but it suited Kyle. He was the type of guy who didn't throw something away just because it was broken.

He walked around and opened the door for me, but I didn't get in.

"My hat! Shit, I must have dropped it in the barn. Hang on, I'll just go snatch it," I lied as I began running towards the barn before he could offer to do it for me. "Start the truck. I'll be right there."

As soon as I cleared his line of sight, I raced up the loft ladder. Time was ticking. The roof still had a blackened area that climbed down the wall mere inches from where the perfect kindling hay would have ignited if Kyle hadn't watered it all down during the fire. It was nice and dry now.

Although I was in a rush, I also needed to do it properly. Bending, I retrieved the match that I'd tucked into my sock when I grabbed my bag. I struck the match on the edge of my teeth and it burst into life.

It was odd. I hadn't hesitated even for a second. Lighting the match didn't make me flinch, nor did I become mesmerized by it. The flame had become the means to an end. The thing I was put on this earth to do. No longer was the match a vehicle to a high. It had become a tool it was designed for.

I let the match burn bright for a moment then gently blew on it until only glowing embers remained. I placed it on the floor and delicately put a few fistfuls of dry hay on top like a small house around the smoking matchstick. If I did it right, the hay wouldn't smother the flame, but provide the fuel for the slower burn I was after. I couldn't drop a match into the hay. It would ignite too fast, and I needed to be long gone before anyone found out I'd set it. It had to burn slow so that we'd be out of view when it went up. I knew that Brad wouldn't do anything to stop it once it began, but Kyle would have, so my plan had to work.

I was going to do what Brad had failed to do. I was going to give his dad the insurance money he so desperately needed. If anyone deserved a happy ending, it was Al and Annabel. I had convinced myself that it was a good thing for everyone involved. What happened to me didn't matter.

The light smoke that drifted upward was a good sign that it would work. Satisfied, I practically flew down the loft stairs. I grabbed my bag and tossed it discreetly into the back and was in Kyle's truck in less than a few minutes.

"Where's your hat?" Kyle asked.

"I couldn't find it," I said, completely forgetting to snatch it on the way out. "It doesn't matter. Let's go. I'm excited!"

Kyle put the truck into drive as I watched the farm fade into the distance in the rearview mirror.

I turned the radio on, pretending to enjoy the country music that blared from the speakers when, in reality, I was sneaking a peek out of the rearview mirror. I kept waiting for the dark line of smoke to appear, for my plan to crumble, but it never came.

After a few minutes, we were far enough along the road that his entire farm disappeared from view. I bit my lip, suddenly sad. Today would be the last time anyone would see the barn.

I shook the thought away. No. This was a good thing. Think about all the good that would happen with this fire. Helping more than hurting. I had to remember that.

Kyle and I slipped into easy banter as we drove down the road towards the carnival. I was about to ask how far away it was when a Ferris wheel loomed large in the skyline. Small lights blinked their hellos, and soon after, the traffic began to thicken. Everyone and their brother seemed to be pulling into the parking lot.

"Wow," I said.

Kyle smiled, seemingly pleased that he'd impressed me with his tiny little town.

I didn't talk much as we walked the strip. My eyes danced around to the flashing lights. I was having a bit of a hard time concentrating as greasy carnies yelled at us to play their rigged games. Mix that with the smell of fried food and the sickening sweetness of cotton candy and my insides feel like it was on one of the rides that whizzed above our heads.

I'm sure Kyle took my silence as shock and awe, and it was. Just not over the carnival. I couldn't shake the feeling that I'd made the wrong choice. On the one hand, I had done this for him, but at the same time, I was taking away his family's home...their memories, their way of life. It was the most conflicted a person could be, and here I was, trying to act like I was enjoying myself.

Kyle seemed oblivious to my inner turmoil as he tugged at my hand to go on a ride. My feet moved forward along with him, but everything around me blurred as I wrestled with what I had done. I had never technically committed real arson before with the full intention to hurt someone or something. That was the difference between arsonists and pyromaniacs. I just wanted to watch it burn. That was the only high I needed, but now I'd sunk to a whole new level of sickness.

Had I become a monster?

Around me, sounds became muffled like I was hearing everything from underwater. I could feel my limbs moving, but my mind was far away...on a house up in flames.

I was vaguely aware as Kyle led me up some stairs. I barely felt the bar that locked into place over my shoulders.

Had I made a huge mistake?

Beside me, I could hear Kyle's muffled words. I didn't understand what they were, but he sounded excited. I think I managed a smile. It was hard to remember that he remained oblivious to the fact that his house was most likely now nothing more than ash. A sudden panic hit. I'd hoped that the ground was moist enough around the house from the rain the night before as not to spread the fire to his neighbor's farms. My goal had been only their house, not the surrounding ones. I said a final prayer that it remained contained. God owed me at least one favor for the hell he had made me live through.

When the ride lurched forward, and the summer air hit my face, a fog began to lift. The sound of a soft clicking entered my mind as my body pressed back in its seat. My vision cleared, and I realized where we were—a roller coaster.

"Shit," I said, grabbing at the bars that strapped me firmly in place. "I don't want to be on this." My eyes darted up to the sky where the track vanished. While I'd never been on a rollercoaster, I'd seen them on TV and had no desire to fall off the face of the world.

"It's okay, Sarah," Kyle yelled over the sound of other scared riders. "It will be fun!"

No. It wouldn't. I didn't want to be in this. I didn't want to be pinned down. Trapped. No. Not again. I couldn't move under the restraints. My legs pressed hard against the floor trying to get free from Brad's hold.

"If you want this over faster, just relax and let it happen." It was Kyle mouth moving, but Brad's orders replaced whatever Kyle was trying to communicate to me. I bucked against the bar harder. Brad's face was everywhere I looked. I pinched my eyes closed. I knew he wasn't there. I knew it wasn't his hands forcing me into submission. I knew this was just a silly ride and yet... I was being held down. Forced to do something against my will. Again.

I started beating my hands against the padded red leather that held me prisoner. I was trapped, and even if I did manage to break free of the harness, I wouldn't be any safer than where I was. But I didn't want to feel any of that. I didn't want to endure the fall.

As we crested the top I realized that the rollercoaster had become the giant metaphor for my life: an inescapable hell that no one could save me from.

I started to scream. Not the exuberant wail of terrified joy, but the deep, guttural release of pain from all the years of torment I'd tucked so neatly away inside the dark recesses of my mind. I tried to close my mind against the fear, but instead, sense memory flooded in. Deeply suppressed memories haunted me. Hands pinned me down while I cried at seven years old. A faceless man hovered over me at nine as mother's latest boyfriend forced himself inside me. At fourteen, a man with a beard and blackened teeth forced my mouth open for his cock. Ever changing faces of men were shouting at me to "hold still" and "be quiet." Screams, begging, pain. As my body thrashed around in the cart with the turns, all I could feel was their collective weight on top of me. I screamed for it to be over, for the pain to stop, but I was slammed against another wall, another bed, another fist.

"Get her out!" I heard a voice yell as the flood of memories receded from where they came. "She needs to get out, please!" I felt hands on my shoulders as my body shook out of the nightmare.

I opened my eyes slowly, and Kyle come into view. His eyes were wide as he shouted for workers to free us. When the bar lifted off my shoulders the worker tried to get me out, but Kyle shoved him aside, insisting on helping me instead.

Everyone was watching us as we made our way down the stairs, which made me extremely uncomfortable, but we were quickly forgotten when Kyle placed me in the shade of a nearby tree.

I had never been so happy to lean against a tree in all my life. Just feeling its strength behind me was enough to help pull myself back together. This was the first time I'd ever lost my shit so horrifically, and I wasn't sure I knew how to cover for it.

Kyle's face had paled beside me. "I think we need to get you to a doctor," he said, digging out his phone.

"No. I'm fine. I guess, I just don't like roller coasters," I said. No hospitals for me. Hospitals would ask for information. They'd put things on record. My name would be in a system. No. No hospitals.

I forced myself upright and rubbed my hands over my face. "See? I'm fine." I said, trying to keep my voice from shaking.

Kyle lowered his phone but not the level of concern. "Sarah, you're not fine. You were screaming."

"I know. I was scared," I said, wiping the tears from my face.

"You were screaming, 'Get off me'." His eyes wrinkled in concern. "Who, Sarah? Who did you want to get off you?"

I felt my face drain of color. I hadn't realized I'd said anything during the screams. I looked up at Kyle. He was waiting for a name. A single person to place his anger, problem was, there wasn't just one.

"There are too many to count," I said, tearing up. I had to sit back down.

He sunk to the ground beside me and took my hand in his. I was too drained to pull away. Too tired to keep up the lies anymore.

"What do you mean?"

I glanced at the tree branches, trying to sap them of strength. I'd never said any of this aloud before.

"What happened to you?" There was such worry in his voice that it would have been cruel to let him simply use his imagination. I had to tell him...at least some of it.

"My mom—she had a bit of a meth problem when I was young. I told you that my dad took off when I was like two, so I don't remember him. I think my mom started using after he left, kind of as a way to cope with the loss or something. Maybe it was before." I sighed. "Hell, maybe she's the reason he left. I never found out." Getting that answer would have meant talking with my mom, and that was one thing we never did. "She didn't work. She was on state aid. Once that ran out at the end of each month, she couldn't pay for her drugs anymore so..." I closed my eyes. "I was used as payment."

"Payment?" The horror in his voice carried over the sound of giggling children as they walked near us, desperately tugging at their parent's arms to go faster.

"Yeah."

His face looked ashen.

"How old were you?"

I shrugged. "The first time I remember I was like seven, I think, but it was probably before that. She'd been using for a few years by then."

"Jesus," he whispered.

I laughed bitterly. "Nope, Jesus was of no help, trust me. I tried asking Him for help so many times. Either He never heard me, or He just didn't care." I opened my eyes but stared over at the riders merrily climbing aboard the rollercoaster, oblivious to the hell I was reliving in my mind.

"It went in phases with my mom. We'd have a few decent years. She'd clean up, but then she'd fall off the wagon, and well, the older I got, the more men in her life were willing to take the trade." I rubbed my hands over my face a few times. "It would have been so easy to disappear into the fog meth, you know? Make it all go away? But I didn't. I felt like I deserved the pain. Somehow, in my stupid mind, I'd convinced myself that I was the reason my dad left and the reason my mom was so unhappy, so I never once complained. I just took it." I laughed weakly. "Pretty pathetic, huh?" I wiped away a tear then stood up, brushing the grass off me as I rose. "The first time I ran away I was fourteen, never even finished school."

"Nobody came to look for you?" he asked.

"Who? Who would come? My mom didn't give a rat's ass about me. Hell, my teachers didn't even know my name. They called me Sally. I was a ghost in my town. The nameless kid no one saw." I swallowed the pain of that statement. "While I was on the road, though, I got sick. Like really sick. Pneumonia. I was walking the streets, delusional." I sighed at the sky. "I have no idea how, but I found my way back home. I remember knocking on her door, then lying down on the steps waiting for her to answer."

I couldn't look at Kyle as I talked. I didn't want to see the pity in his eyes, so I peered at our interlaced hands instead. It gave me the strength to keep talking.

"Apparently, during the time I was away," I continued, "she'd managed to get her act together. She went through rehab or some shit, found God, and all that jazz. She wanted to 'save my soul', black as it was. She said God had led me to her door, and she was going to save me as He had saved her." I shook my head. "I was too out of it to care what she did with me."

I rubbed the bridge of my nose a few times to clear my vision. It was so hard saying all of this, but I couldn't seem to hold back. The truth kept pouring forth like a pot that had been left to boil over.

"I spent a few weeks in the hospital recovering from pneumonia, then she brought me home. I had been 'reborn,' as my mom called it. She sent me to therapy for my many issues. I started gaining some weight. I even considered getting my GED."

I glanced at the crowds again.

"Then she died. No warning. No long-standing illness. She just fell asleep and didn't wake up."

"Oh, Sarah." I could hear the agony in his voice, and I didn't want him to have to feel it, so I pushed on.

"So I did what I had to. I ran. Again."

"But why run? You didn't do anything. It was just her time," Kyle said.

He didn't understand how the world worked. How could he, in his perfect, sheltered environment? "I was scared," I said simply. He could never understand the complexity of the situation, so I didn't bother to explain it.

Kyle's forehead wrinkled with concern.

"Before I left town, though, I called in an anonymous tip to 911 from my mom's cell. As much as a huge part of me hated her for my childhood, I also couldn't let her sit there and rot."

"You did the right thing," Kyle whispered. I frowned. It didn't feel like it. Nothing I ever did felt right." What happened after you left?"

I shrugged my shoulders. "I went back to life on the road. It wasn't hard after you've dealt with the guys I grew up with. In fact, each time I left, it was easier because now I was the one in charge.

I got to determine how much of myself I got to give away. I got to decide if the ride was worth the price." My hands had begun to clench without my knowing it.

I felt Kyle's hand squeeze back, as though trying to absorb some of the pain for me. I pulled my hand away and tucked my hands under my legs.

"Is that why you let my brother handcuff you? To be the one with the control?" He asked it so honestly, it made my breath catch. I could hear how much it hurt him to ask, but also how much he needed to know.

I couldn't tell him the truth, so I pushed away the tears building. "Sex is always about control."

"Funny, I thought it was about love."

I smiled a sad little smile.

"That's never been true for me." I didn't look at his face as I said that. I was overwhelmed. I began walking through the crowd, wanting desperately to be swallowed up in the confusion.

He found me, of course, as I knew he would. He didn't try to get me to talk, though; instead, he walked beside me. His gaze fixed on me from time to time, though I didn't return it. I was ashamed. I had let him see a part of me no one else had been allowed, and I wasn't sure how I felt about that.

We must have walked like that for about twenty minutes when Kyle asked if I was hungry.

"Actually, I am," I admitted.

He smiled at me, and together, we went to a hot dog stand and ordered up a mountain of fries and four dogs, all loaded down with chili and melted cheese.

As we inhaled our second hot dog, Kyle's face grew serious.

"Can I ask you a question?" He squinted at me through the afternoon sun.

"Um. Sure." I wiped my mouth with my napkin, bracing for whatever question he might have, and if I'd be willing to be truthful in answering it.

"Have you ever been properly kissed?" he asked.

I frowned. "What do you mean by 'properly'?"

He leaned in, slowly, cupped my face gently with his hand, and traced his thumb over my bottom lip. I shivered. "Have you ever been kissed by someone who loved you? By someone who asked your permission?"

He was mere inches from my lips. I became very aware of the sound of my heart in my ears.

"No," I whispered, our lips barely touching.

He pulled back a bit to look at me. "May I kiss you, Sarah?"

I blinked at him, not sure what to say. Before I let the moment slip away, my heart answered for me.

"Yes."

His eyes softened, as though drunk on something. Then he closed his eyes and leaned in again.

That's when his phone went off. Naturally.

Cursing, he moved away to dig it out of his pocket. I swallowed the breathlessness of that near-kiss. The one that would never happen now because I knew who had called him, even before he answered it. It would be Brad, calling to tell him about the fire.

"Hey, Brad, can I call you back? I'm a little busy here."

I started to sweat. My hands went cold. My breathing came faster, and I could hear the blood racing in my ears. I should have left by now. I should have followed my plan. I was going to let him go on a ride while I watched, and while he was on it, I was going to slip away. I had completely lost track of my plan.

Nausea rose. This was it, when Kyle would find out what I'd done. This was when he'd hate me forever.

Kyle held the phone to me. "He wants to talk to you." He seemed as confused as I was.

My eyes widened. I hadn't planned on this. I wasn't sure what to do, so I steadied my hand and reached for the phone. I walked away from the bench we'd been sitting on and out of earshot before I answered.

"Hello?" I said, barely audible.

"I don't know if I should be proud of you, or if I should punish you," he growled. "I'm thinking the latter."

The line went dead in my hands. Fear prickled along my spine. He knew. I had to run. Now.

"Sarah, what is it?" Kyle came up behind me. I handed him back his phone.

"I'm so sorry," I said, and then I ran. I broke into a full sprint down the midway, dodging kids with balloons, people snapping pictures, and teenage boys trying to play cool as they looked for girls. I couldn't help but feel a pang of jealousy as I ran past them, jealous of their safe and uncomplicated lives.

I could hear Kyle behind me, yelling at me, which only made me run faster. I had to get to his truck, get my bag, and get the hell out of this town. After a few minutes at full speed, however, my lungs burned and my sides cramped. I wasn't physically fit enough to outrun him. Knowing I wouldn't be able to go on much longer, I gave up the effort. I slowed to a walk, headed over to a fence, crumpled onto the ground beside it and waited for Kyle to catch up to me. Apparently, this was going to have to get ugly before I could leave.

"Sarah!" he panted, racing up behind me. He stopped next to me and took a few gulps of air before he spoke. I took that time to figure out what I was going to tell him.

"You have to stop following me. You have to let me go," I said. It was a pathetic request.

He sank down next to me. "Let you go? Sarah, what's going on?" Kyle's face shifted. "What did Brad say to you?"

I let free a deep breath. I needed to hurt him. I needed to convince him I wasn't some "thing" he could save. I was a monster, and he needed to know it.

"He found out about my past."

Kyle was quiet for a moment. "So? There's nothing to be ashamed about—"

I held out my hand to stop him. "Not that past. That's a pretty easy one to peg together." I curled my arms around my waist for support. "Brad found about my dark secret. The kind of secret no person with a soul should have."

He looked at me, waiting.

"I'm a pyromaniac."

His eyebrows shot up, disbelieving.

"I like to watch stuff burn," I said, making sure he understood.

"But...no, you're scared of fire. I mean, the stove..." I could see his mind trying to piece it all together. "The barn?" His face paled.

"No! I didn't start that!"

He cocked his head as though wondering if he could believe me.

"Honest!" I said, pleading with him. "In fact, that fire scared the shit out of me. I haven't wanted to light one since that day." I felt his eyes drilling into me, searching for a lie that wasn't there.

"I'm trying to understand here. Help me understand." I hated how upset his voice sounded. I fiddled with my hands. My eyes focused on my fingers as they twitched.

"When you saw me at the stove the other day, it wasn't fear that held me in place." I looked him in the eye. I needed him to understand. "It was intoxication. I got lost in watching the flames —I couldn't pull myself away from it. It's a sickness, Kyle. I'm messed up."

I held up my hands, showcasing the burn areas along some of my fingers. "I got these when I was seven, trying to put out a blaze. I wasn't very good at it back then."

I lifted my shirt, showing the melted flesh on my side. "This one was an accident. I had lit a bottle of booze on fire when I was ten. It exploded." I swallowed.

He didn't say anything so I lowered my shirt. He leaned against the fence and asked the one question I knew was coming.

"Why?" he asked.

I walked over to the fence and stared at the sky.

"Everyone wants to know that. I guess people think if they know why they can come to terms with it. Without the 'why', people live in fear that it will happen to them or something.

Understanding the 'why' helps remind them that they aren't the crazy ones."

"I didn't say you were crazy."

I shook my head but didn't look at him. "You'd be wrong." I turned. "I'm broken, Kyle. Whether that's from my messed-up childhood, or bad DNA, the fact is, I'm a psychopath. I'm not a safe person to be around. I told you that from day one. I'm better alone, where I can't hurt anyone."

"Sarah, you aren't better alone. No one is. There must be treatments for this, medicine or therapy."

I nodded. "There is, and I've been on them all." It was just like him to try to fix me. "The thing with pyromaniacs is that most who have it are young boys, and they usually grow out of it. If you still have it as an adult, well, you're screwed." I kicked at the ground. "Story of my life. I don't know why I light the fires, I just do. I will always need them in my life. Always." I sincerely hoped that were true. I wasn't sure how I'd function on the road if I didn't get back my love of fire.

"I think you're wrong," Kyle said softly. "It's pretty clear why you light fires."

I couldn't help it. I laughed. "Oh, really? Please, enlighten me. Why do I light fires?"

"Well, given your past, I'd say that you've made fire your friend."

"My friend?" I scoffed.

He walked over and stood beside me. His arms draped the edges of the chipped white fence. "It probably wasn't at first. It was probably more of an escape from your life. But I think, over time, it became your friend. I mean, think about it. Lighting fires was something you could count on to cheer you up, make you feel less alone, right? Hell, it was probably the one reliable thing in your life." He shrugged. "I would think fire became a symbol of consistency...of safety for you in a world that was so hostile."

Such a simple answer. So basic and pathetic. Had I turned fires into my friend? Thinking back on how they made me feel, it was disturbingly accurate. It took me a moment to find my words to speak.

"So what's the cure then?"

"Simple. You just need someone to care about you, someone to listen when you need to be heard, someone to lean on when you're hurt, someone to laugh with when you're happy. Someone like me."

He reached out and took my hand.

"You?" I raised my eyebrows at him.

"If you'd let me."

My eyes began to tear over. If only it could be that simple.

"It's too late for me, Kyle. Trust me. By the end of this day, you are gonna hate me." I buried the thought of the loathing he was about to have for me. "Please don't follow me," I said.

Kyle started to speak, but I put my hand up in protest.

"I'm not giving up on you," he said. His jaw tensed.

I nodded. "I know." Tears stung my eyes. "That's why *I'm* giving up on *you*." I took a step back. "Thanks for trying. It's more than anyone in my life has ever done, but some things aren't able to be fixed."

I turned and made my way toward the exit. I knew that Kyle would follow after me, but I had to keep moving. Once he learned what I did, there would be nothing left here for me. Better to leave now, before he learned the truth. If I didn't lose him by the time I made it to his truck, I would start without my bag. I'd started with far less before.

What little cash I had on me would have to be enough. My mind grew heavy thinking about starting over.

You knew this day was coming. You were foolish to let yourself get attached.

"Sarah." Kyle hooked my elbow from behind me, not hard, but enough to get my attention, "Tell me what's going on. There's something you aren't telling me. Everything was going fine until Brad called. What did he say to you?"

I sighed and dropped my shoulders. "Nothing. He just wants me gone."

"What? That's crazy. Look, he's angry he lost the bet. I'll talk to Brad. It will be okay." Kyle was spinning, and I couldn't blame him. I was mucking the whole thing up.

"There's a warrant out for my arrest, Kyle."

That stopped him.

"There was a fire in my town. A church, I guess. People died. I didn't do it, though Brad didn't seem to think that would matter." My shoulders slumped. "He's right. I don't have an alibi, no one to vouch for me, and well, I *am* a pyromaniac." I blew a bit of air out of my mouth. "They'll lock me up in a heartbeat. I can't go to prison. I can't be caged like that. I just can't. So I'm running. It's the only choice for me."

"But if you didn't do it..." Kyle started.

I turned to look at him, resting an arm on his shoulder hoping he'd understand. "It won't matter. Not with my history."

"This doesn't make any sense! He's not going to turn you in. You're his girlfriend."

I laughed a loud deep laugh. "I'm not his girlfriend. I'm just something to amuse him. But now I am a threat to his family's safety. I don't blame him, Kyle. He should be scared of me." My hand slipped off his shoulder. "And so should you."

I walked a few feet away. "Now, as I said before, please don't follow me." I closed my eyes for a moment, trying to find the strength I'd need to walk away from Kyle, but then forced my feet toward the exit as fast as they would carry me.

I'd like to think that he called for me. That he begged me to turn around, but I don't know if he did or not because all I could focus on was the black truck that had pulled into the parking lot.

Brad's truck.

ASHES

Billows of dust cascaded around his truck as he sped into the lot. The entirety of it was lost in the cloud of smoke as it came to a halt.

I whipped around and saw Kyle behind me. "Oh, God. Please don't let him take me."

"Take you where? Jail? No, Sarah, this ends right now. You don't have to be scared. He's not going to hurt you."

I had lost all pretense of being strong. I was terrified of what Brad might do to me. I hid behind Kyle, and I hated how weak I must appear.

"Sarah, it's okay."

I heard Brad's door slam and the sound of his feet fast against the dry earth. I buried my head in Kyle's back. My fingers dug into his arms.

"Step away, Kyle., She's mine," he said.

"Brad, calm down. She—"

I saw his fist fly through the air and make contact with the side of Kyle's face before I had time to scream. Kyle hit the ground with a thump, leaving me frozen and exposed.

In a flash, his hand gripped my wrist and forced me toward the truck. I kicked and screamed, but he didn't let go or slow his pace. He simply took hold of my hair as he opened the passenger door.

"Get in!"

"Let go of me!" I kicked against him, hitting his calf. I was hoping he'd release my hold so I could squirm out, but all it managed to do was piss him off.

"Why, you cunt," he spat, smacking my face so that it hit the edge of the open door. Hard. My head spun. My muscles went slack. The sounds around me was muffled, but I thought I heard the click of metal. When the coolness clasped around my wrists I knew he'd cuffed me to the door. A second later, I felt his hands around my waist as he forced me into the cab of his truck, cursing and huffing as he shoved me into place.

I felt blood run down from the corner of my forehead, but I was too dizzy to move. The pain hadn't registered yet, but I knew that it would, all too soon. I blinked, trying to clear my vision.

Craning my neck, I strained to look out the window. Kyle was starting to stand up.

"Stay back!" I managed to get out before Brad turned his attention off me and back to his brother. He thrust me down into the seat and shut the door behind him, blocking my view, but the grunts and blows that echoed outside indicated that they were fighting. I was cuffed so there was little I could do to stop the fight, but I had to do something.

"Stop!" I shouted. "Somebody, please stop him!"

I heard one final grunt, someone panting, and then uneven staggered steps towards the car. I screamed when the door flung open.

"It's okay," Kyle said. Blood was running down his nose. His left eye was dark and swelling shut. He stared at me, the side of my face now caked with blood. Tears streaked down my face. "Jesus. What did he do to you?" he asked.

So many things.

"I'm gonna get you out of here," he said, placing his arms under me.

I held up my hand. "I'm cuffed." I started to cry as the metal brushed once more against the still healing skin.

"Okay. It's okay. I'll get the keys off Brad." Kyle pushed the door open wide and turned back to where he had left Brad, except, he wasn't there.

"I'll ask you to close the door now, little brother," Brad said, opening the driver's side door with a gun pointed at his brother's head. Kyle stepped back, his hands in the air.

"Brad, what are you doing?" Kyle asked. His face was completely confused.

By now a crowd had begun to gather around the edges of the parking lot. Raised voices in alarm started buzzing.

"It's alright!" Brad called to them. "I'm a cop. This woman has a warrant for her arrest. I'm taking her in."

This news did little to quiet the crowd, but they did seem to take a few cautious steps back.

"Brad, you can't do this. She didn't do anything!" Kyle pleaded, hands still raised.

Brad laughed. "She didn't do anything? She set the goddamn house on fire, Kyle."

"No, she didn't. That was lightning. She couldn't—"

Brad pulled back the hammer of the gun, causing me to gasp. "The farm is on fire as we speak."

"What?" Kyle asked.

"The little bitch here decided to torch my room."

I peered at Brad. "Your room?"

"Yeah. Thought I would be too busy out in the field not to notice? I'm smarter than that. I saw it as soon as the smoke reached the sky." He glared at Kyle now. "I tried to put it out. I tried to contain it before it got the rest of the farm, but there was too much of it. I had to crawl out of a window to save my own neck."

"I didn't—"

"Liar!" he screamed. "You've been lying about who you were from the start. You were just waiting for the right moment, weren't you? You waited until I was the only one left in the house. You wanted me to die, didn't you?" His face was red with anger. "You knew I was suspicious of you. Thought I'd take away your perfect little life, right? Well, the joke is on you. Your ass is going to jail."

"Brad, put down the gun. Let's talk this through," Kyle said, taking a step closer.

"No! No talking. Our house is gone. Do you understand that, Kyle? Gone! And she did it. She's going in, so shut the door and step away from the truck." When Kyle didn't budge, he shifted the gun towards my head instead. "Now."

My eyes bugged out of my head as the gun inched closer to my face. I closed my eyes, ready for him to pull the trigger. Ready for this nightmare to be over.

Although I couldn't see him, I knew Kyle had obeyed when I heard the door shut behind me. My skin drained of color.

Brad shifted the truck into drive and sped out of the lot, leaving the crowd and my will to live far behind.

He didn't say a word as he turned onto the main drag. My vision was still blurry, and my head throbbed, but there was one thing I knew with absolute certainty.

"I didn't start a fire in your room."

Brad smirked, checked his rear view mirror, then put the gun back in his holster. "Oh, I know. You *tried* to start it in the barn, but your failed attempt gave me the idea."

I stared up at him.

He shook his head at me, clearly annoyed by my stupidity. "I saw you scoot into the barn this morning from the field. When you all sped off, I went in and looked around. Saw your hat near the ladder. That's when I smelled smoke. It was barely smoking. It would never have done the job. You did, however, leave me a nice bit of evidence: a match with your prints. It was just too perfect to leave behind, so I left that baby right outside my window, safe from the blaze but easy enough for investigators to find. Now, I know what you're thinking: why not let your little-fire-that-could try to catch? Well, I guess I was afraid it would look fishy if a fire started in the same place. Lighting never strikes twice, right? Nah, it was better to have it start in my room. There was far more motivation to go after the cop's room. I'll admit, it also did a pretty damn fine job of destroying any evidence you may have had on me and our little 'adventures' too. So win, win, really."

I felt my body go slack. It made perfect sense. He had my prints, a logical motivation, and my record to seal the deal. Everything he wanted.

"What happens now?"

Brad hissed. "Now you rot in prison, like the scum that you are. If you see a gal named Claire Winslow, you tell her 'hi' for me, would ya?"

My stomach twisted in knots.

"Good old Claire stayed with us last spring. Seems she was a wicked thief. Caught her red-handed with Dad's wallet one day. Can't trust the runaways. I keep telling Dad this, but he always brings them home to me. It seems wrong not to play with them a bit first, don't you think?"

The grin he wore made him look like the Devil himself.

He pulled into a parking lot. I looked around, noticing a few local shops, people milling around and catching up on local gossip on the sidewalk, blissfully unaware of the madman among them.

He parked the truck and killed the engine.

"I'm ready," I said simply.

He laughed at me. "Well, you may be, but I'm not quite done with you."

I looked up at him. There was a demented glint in his eye. He was enjoying himself. He wanted to see my fear. My panic. I vowed to refuse him that despite the acceleration of my heart.

"I must admit, of all the girls I've had the pleasure of experimenting on, you have been my favorite, by far." He took out his gun and traced it along my cheek, clearly not worried because of his tinted windows. Not that it would have mattered if they weren't. I had learned from experience that people tended not to look for trouble. They kept their eyes straight ahead, never acknowledging the bum on the bench or the cries of rape in the alley. Brad must have learned this too.

"Screw you," I said. He had no power over me. Nothing to hold over my head anymore.

He cocked the gun and forced it into my mouth.

"I will screw you one last time, and this time, it won't be part of our arrangement. I'll do it without your consent. This time, it *will* be rape," he growled into my ear. "I don't know what it is about you, but you seem to make me want to satisfy my darkest fantasies, Sarah. You should feel honored."

I mumbled something around the gun.

Frowning, he took it out, placing the barrel at my temple. "You're mumbling, Sarah. Didn't your mother teach you not to talk with your mouth full?" He smirked.

"Pull the trigger," I said. "If you're going to screw me, it's going to be with my dead body." I sat up as tall as I could, fully meaning every word.

"Brave little shit, aren't you? But you will be taken. Alive. I'm not a monster, after all." He wiggled his eyebrows then thrust himself on top of me, one hand on the gun, the other madly trying to undo his pants.

Using all my strength, I gripped the hand with the gun, trying to pull the trigger for him. I was ready. Ready to end it, ready to be done with suffering. He wasn't going to lay another finger on me, not while I had life in my body. I grabbed his hand to force it to my scalp. He sensed what I was doing and shifted the gun.

When it went off, I smiled, waiting for the darkness to take me.

It was only when I felt Brad go limp on top of me that I knew I'd failed. Somehow, during the struggle, I'd pulled the trigger and managed to shoot him instead of me.

That's when the screaming and panic started outside.

I let myself go limp as well, the fight now gone from me as his warm blood pooled around me. I couldn't kill myself now. I deserved what was coming. I had to pay for my crime. I closed my eyes and waited for them to find me, to charge me. I was ready for them to send me away where I finally couldn't hurt anyone anymore.

And they did.

So that's it. That's my story. That's the mystery of how I ended up here. Even though Brad's death was an accident, even though I didn't start the fire that ended up taking down your farm, I am still guilty. Guilty of allowing it all to happen in the first place.

I'm sure you're probably pretty angry that I only spent a few days in prison. But the docs decided I needed to go to a mental rehabilitation center before completing my sentence. I didn't make that call. In fact, I begged them to let me stay and rot there.

I was shipped off to the looney bin so I could be mentally with it when I served my time; so in the end, it's a more fitting sentence. The place I'm at isn't all that bad, I guess. It's not the stereotypical white padded walls, syringes full of medicine, each patient madder than the last sort of place. It feels more like a hospital. There are no visible bars on the windows, although they do have alarms in place and a fence around the complex. But we don't see them. It's designed to feel like a home, instead of what it really is. I guess it sort of does. I mean, it's nothing like the farm, but it's a far cry from the cell I was in.

They've got me in therapy. My shrink is nice, though, ironically, she's scared of fire. She doesn't worry. I haven't wanted to start a fire since that last day...

I need you to know I'm not proud of what I did. I feel horrible for killing Brad. No matter what he did to me, he didn't deserve to die like that.

It was important for me to write this. Not just for the therapeutic value, but I also knew I needed to tell you what really happened, even if you didn't believe me. Even if you hated me more now. I needed to do this, for me.

I've got a long way to go in this rehabilitation cycle, but I'm not going to give up. I think I can finally see a bit of hope returning to my life, and I'm going to fight for it.

They said that they are going to mail this to you. I gave them the only address I had for you on the farm. I know it's no longer there, thanks to me, but I'm hoping that one day, it might get forwarded to you, wherever you are. One day, you may get to read about my side of the story.

The romantic in me hopes you get this, read it, and come rushing to tell me that you forgive me. But the realist in me knows that even if this somehow makes it to you, you'll never bother to read it, and maybe that's how it should be.

If you take away anything from this, please let it be this: Kyle, you were the one bright spot for me in a world that was otherwise filled with nothing but darkness. For that, I shall always be grateful.

I am so sorry for everything I have done to you and your family, Kyle. I want you to know that I wish nothing but the very best for you.

-Sarah

Part Two

PART TWO

KYLE

BOXES

When you grow up as a middle child with a sister and a brother on either end of you, you get used to being surrounded by family. Someone is always teasing you, or there to talk to, a hand ready to help when needed, but now... now I'm an only child. The thought leaves me more alone that I thought I could ever feel. Sure, I still have my parents, but for how long? Soon, I'd have no one.

Maybe that's how Sarah felt. Alone in the world.

No. I won't think about her. She's the reason you're here in the first place. She's the one who killed Brad.

I walked around the unopened boxes that littered his Boston apartment. The apartment was bare, save what the movers had brought in three months ago. He'd had his belongings shipped here before coming to the farm, but he'd never gotten the chance to unpack. Fortunately, he'd paid the first six months' rent in advance. That's the type of guy Brad was: a planner.

He didn't like surprises.

A thin layer of dust and stale air lingered around me. It had taken me this long to build up enough courage to come and sort his belongings. The last few weeks had been spent moving into the new place, doing all the funeral planning and insurance paperwork with Dad. The last thing I wanted to do was sort through Brad's belongings, even though I knew it needed to be done.

It would have been so easy to hire a company to just haul all of his things away, but that would have felt too cold. He wouldn't have wanted some stranger going through his stuff. So it was with a sense of family obligation that I drove to Boston to take care of this last loose end before trying to move past the nightmare. It would have been quicker to fly, but I had no intention of breaking my air travel virginity. The road suited me fine.

My phone rang as I was about to open the first box. I recognized Dad's ringtone. I placed the box cutter on the kitchen counter, eager for the distraction. I wasn't sure I was ready to do this yet.

"Hey, Dad! How's Mom? You get her all settled?" I asked, hopping onto the counter.

"The last of the papers were signed today, so I guess she's officially a resident now." I could hear in his voice that he was about to cry.

"Yeah, but you get to visit her all the time, right?" We both knew this was the best fit for Mom, but it also was the formal admittance that she wasn't ever going to get better.

"Yep. Seven to seven. Told them to count on seeing me for all those hours," Dad said. I smiled, knowing how true that statement would end up being.

"Did you call back the insurance guy?" I asked, pushing the box cutter blade up and down as I talked.

Dad sighed. "They're gonna transfer the funds to the bank on Monday. Stop worrying about us. Tell me how your trip was. Any problems?"

Neither one of us liked to talk about the insurance money. While it was a relief, it was also heartbreaking to think about why we got it in the first place. The fire had taken everything. Burned it right down to the slab. The only thing left were the cattle that had run off into the far pasture during the blaze. We sold those off to a neighboring farm for next to nothing.

I still remembered walking around the ashes and thinking there was no way she could have done it. That it had to be a mistake. When they found a match with her prints a few feet from where the blaze started, however, I lost it. I was fuming at her for weeks. All during the trial, I wanted her to look at me. I wanted her to know how much hatred I had for what she'd done, but she never picked her gaze up from off the floor. She never denied any of the charges. She knew she was guilty. I hated myself for being fooled, for trusting her. She destroyed my life, and she knew it. That's why she couldn't look at us.

Don't think about her.

"I'm not."

"You're not what, son?" Dad asked.

"Um, not worrying about you," I said, forgetting for a moment that I was talking to him. "Trip was fine. No problems." I left out the fact that the check engine light had come on in Ohio, but I was able to fix it quick enough. Good Old Bessie might have her fair share of problems, but there was still a lot of life left in her yet. I wasn't ready to send her out to pasture.

"Are you okay, son? I mean, doing this on your own? Should I have come out there with you?" The regret of him not being able to be in two places at once was clear.

"I'm fine. Mom needs you there way more than I do. Besides, I haven't started yet. I just crashed when I got here yesterday. Two days on the road wears a person out. I was about to open the first box when you called."

"Oh, well, don't let me keep you. I just wanted to let you know that I got a package here for you." Something was off about his tone.

"A package?" I asked. "Who is it from?" I never got any mail. It must have been a mistake.

"It was sent from some rehab place in Lincoln. It's from Sarah."

My jaw hardened. "Throw it away."

"Kyle—"

"I said to throw it out. I don't want anything to do with her."

My anger bubbled to the surface again. I didn't want to hear how sorry she was for killing my brother and burning down my house. I didn't care that she was in rehab. None of it mattered now. She had ruined my life. She did warn me from the beginning not to get close to her, but I ignored her. Fool me once, shame on me...I was damn sure not about to be fooled twice.

"It's a pretty thick package. Don't you think you should see what it is first?" Dad asked.

"No. I don't want to see anything from her." My resolve was firm. It took everything I could to believe the ugly truth. She had been lying about who she was the whole time. She was the monster she claimed to be. I shook my head. I had been so sure that was a mask she wore to protect herself... How wrong I had been. I couldn't forgive myself for falling for her act. I hated that I defended her when Brad showed up at the carnival to take her in. His instincts were always right. She was a liar and a murderer, and I didn't want her lingering in my head anymore.

"Well, okay." Dad sighed. "I guess I'll leave you to it, then. Call me if you need anything."

I jumped off the counter, shoving Sarah firmly out of my mind once more. "Will do. Give Mom a kiss for me."

"Of course." He hesitated before he hung up. "I love you, Kyle."

My throat closed with sudden emotion. "Love you too, Dad."

I tossed the phone down and grabbed the cutter, ready to busy my mind. I snagged the top box that had the word "kitchen" written on it. I slit the top open to sort out what I'd take back for sentimental reasons, what would be donated, and what could be trashed. Looking back up at the boxes, I knew this would take a while. Not that it mattered how long it took. There were still three months left on his lease, and it wasn't like it this was holding me back from anything.

Without the farm, I sort of lost my purpose. The insurance money would cover most things, but that took time. Until then, I was aimless. I'd need to get a job and find a place to live when this was all over, I just wasn't sure *where* I wanted that new life to be. It never occurred to me that I might live outside of Nebraska, but after all the bad memories there, I thought it might be a good idea to start fresh.

Before I could figure out my plans, though, I needed to take care of this last bit of business.

I knew the vast majority of his things would be donated or trashed. Brad was never a very sentimental guy, but I promised Dad I'd look for some reminders of the son he'd lost. Of the brother I'd never see again. I shook off the tears that were starting to form and got back to work.

The first box proved to be nothing more than shot glasses and a few coffee mugs. I repacked them, taped the box and wrote "donate" on the outside and placed it near the door.

"One down. About a gazillion to go," I said to the mountain before me.

I worked the entire day, sorting clothes and books. Many of them were academy issued so I would call them to give those back. *He would have been a great cop.* Sure, he was cocky and arrogant and held a massive chip on his shoulder since Molly passed, but I thought once he was an officer for a few years, it might bring out the good in him again. Hunting down bad guys, helping civilians in need...it was going to be just what he needed to turn himself around. My shoulders slumped. He was never given the chance.

Sighing, I tossed another box to the donate pile.

"Time for a break," I said, stretching. It was almost dinner time. I was getting hungry. I'd worked straight through lunch and was now regretting it.

I found my cell and placed a pizza delivery. I could have gone out, but I was gross and sweaty, and it felt important to get this done. I needed this to be taken care of before I could come to terms with his passing. Well, that was the hope anyway. There hadn't been nearly enough time to make my peace with it. I'm not sure if there ever could be peace with losing a sibling. I hadn't found it yet with Molly. I still missed her every damned day.

I flopped down on his mattress that I tossed on the floor last night and closed my eyes for a moment. My muscles were stiff and my mind felt like a wet sponge, saturated with emotion. Maybe Dad was right. Maybe I shouldn't have tried to do this alone.

Outside a siren went by, forcing my lids open. It was the sixth siren I'd heard today. City life sure was noisy. It was no wonder the people here always seemed on edge. I found myself missing the quiet of the farm. The farm that was no more.

I rolled onto my elbows to check the remaining stack of boxes. Only about a dozen or so more to go, surprisingly: a few "clothes boxes," two marked "bedroom," a "bathroom," and one labeled "basement." I would be done by tomorrow at the latest. Hell, maybe I'd finish it tonight.

I closed my eyes again. "After dinner," I muttered.

My eyes popped open.

"Basement?" This apartment didn't have a basement that I could tell. Huh. The farm didn't have a basement either, and I highly doubt the academy dorms had one. So why label a box basement?

Dragging myself off the bed, I went over to the boxes and shoved things out of the way to access it. I had to admit, my curiosity had gotten the better of me. I cut through the tape and opened the flaps.

The first thing that caught my eye was the glint of something metal. The light wasn't very good in that corner of his apartment, so I pushed it further into the living room, where a pile of empty boxes lived. It wasn't very heavy, just awkward to get around all the garbage.

Looking inside again, I saw the thing that had caught my eye and pulled it out: Handcuffs. I tossed them over to the police return pile. "You belong there," I said before digging back into the box.

I grabbed the next item. "That's a lot of cable ties, bro," I said, shaking my head, and I tossed those into the keep pile. Those were always handy for repairs.

The next thing in the box, however, I had to question. I pulled out what looked like a noose. I turned it over in my hands a few times in confusion before I placed it down and shifted through the rest of the box. I was unsure what a few things were, but I had a sinking feeling that they were sex toys.

"What the hell is all this shit?"

I dug around the wads of crumpled newspaper until my fingers found something smooth —a box of some kind. As I lifted it free, I smelled cedar waft up to my nose. I froze, recognizing the ornately carved jewelry box at once. It was my mother's, the one that had been stolen when Claire lived with us at the farm. The one Brad said she stole before he kicked her out.

"Why does he have this?"

Slowly, I opened the box and let out a shaky breath. It was all of Mom's jewelry. Her large silver and jade necklace, her diamond earrings Dad gave her on their twentieth anniversary, and so much more. She cried for weeks after it went missing.

Instinctively, I lifted the inner tray to check the compartment below, and among her pearls were three numbered memory sticks. I frowned. Those were definitely not my mom's. She didn't even own a computer. No one at the farm did. So why were there memory sticks in Mom's jewelry box, and more importantly, why did Brad have it?

I glanced around Brad's apartment.

"Where did I put his laptop?"

I had to shift through the "donate pile" for a bit before I found it. I hadn't wanted it. I had no use for computers when we'd lived on the farm. If I needed one, our local library had three that I was well versed on.

Once it was plugged in and awake, I grabbed the memory stick labeled one and plugged it into the USB port. My face contorted in impatience as I waited for the files to load. Whatever was on it was massive. Maybe pictures?

After a few minutes, several videos loaded into a folder labeled: The Runaways. My heart raced. That was Brad's pet names for all the girls Dad took in. Was this proof of their crimes, maybe? Confessions?

Confused, I clicked the first video open.

"Are you ready to have some fun, Beth?" Brad was saying from behind a black screen.

Beth? That was the name of the first girl Dad took in like three years ago.

Suddenly, the blackness on the screen came into view as what looked like a lens cap was removed. It was the digital camera he'd gotten for Christmas a few years back. He'd loved that thing.

Brad's face took over the entire shot just then. He wore a big grin. He positioned the camera a bit until his bed came into view.

My eyes bugged out of my head when the camera focused on Beth, who was completely nude and anchored to his bed with cable ties. She was struggling against the restraints as Brad walked over to her.

"Oh, hush now. Remember, you can't scream. It gives me an awful headache. Besides, you wouldn't want me to call your daddy and tell him where you are, would you?" He pulled off his shirt as Beth whimpered. "Does your daddy touch you like this too, you dirty girl?"

Brad cupped her breasts as he straddled her.

"Jesus Christ," I heard myself say.

She said something I didn't understand, which only made Brad laugh. He reached under his bed and came back up with a noose in his hands. A noose. The one I had just held in the box.

"Oh, such a naughty girl. I told you to be quiet. Why can't you girls ever listen to me? I guess I'll have to shut you up myself." He slipped the rope over her neck as she tried to scream. He smacked her hard across the face. "Scream again, and I tighten it harder." I could see the fear in her eyes as she struggled against him.

"Oh my God..." My eyes bulged in horror as he pulled off her underwear and began to shove his fingers inside her. Beth's tears streamed down her face as he held one hand tight on the noose and kept the other hand inside of her.

"Brad, let her go!" I screamed at the screen. She cried out in pain, and he made good on his threat by pulling the noose so tight she started to turn blue.

"You make another sound, we do that again. Got it?"

Beth nodded weakly before he finally let her go. She stifled a few coughs as Brad got undressed, the rope still caged around her neck like a dog.

His naked body straddled her. I thought I would be sick. "Just enjoy the ride, you naughty, naughty girl." His hand wound around the rope as he thrust himself into her.

I closed the laptop.

"No. No, he couldn't have," I said, pacing around the living room. "That must have been some weird sex thing they had together, that's all. Role playing. He wasn't really hurting her," I whispered. "Was he?"

My head was revolting against the idea just as fast as my gut seemed to confirm it. There was no doubt that Brad's demeanor had changed after Molly died. He would have admitted that too. He had grown distant, more hostile, but that was just stages of grief some went through, wasn't it? But to do this? It didn't make any sense. He'd seen what had happened to his own sister. She'd died because some sicko strangled her, and here he was, using a noose on someone not that much older than Molly had been.

That's when I had a sinking thought that maybe he had killed Molly. Had their bond been more than sibling affection? Had Brad gone too far one day? They never did find the killer because the crime scene was corrupted...because of him... They only found his prints on her body. They assumed it was from when he rushed over to hold her in his agony, but had he done that merely to cover his tracks?

No. No. He couldn't have done that. Not to our sister.

Maybe I had this all wrong. Maybe one of the other videos could prove that. As much as I didn't want to watch anymore, I clicked onto the next one. I had to know if my brother was a monster, or just severely kinky.

My face paled as I watched more of the same. In all subsequent videos Beth never once looked happy to be there. A sudden thought hit me.

Oh my God. *Sarah.* My eyes flicked back to the other two memory sticks remaining. "No, no, no," I said, grabbing one of them. My hands shook. "Please, not Sarah. Brad, please say you didn't do this to her too."

I tried to calm down and think rationally. After all, there was no way he had videos of her on these sticks. He had shipped his stuff out before he had even met Sarah. Still my mind refused to accept that fact until I had made certain.

I was only slightly relieved to find Michelle, our second runaway, where I had imagined Sarah would be.

Michelle was nineteen. She had stayed with us two years ago for a few weeks, until Brad discovered that she was a prostitute and threw her out despite Dad's protest to let her stay. Dad had said that she could change, given the right environment, but the next day, she packed up and left on her own.

Reluctantly, I played the first of Michelle's videos.

"Hold still!" Brad hissed at her. Through the duct tape over her mouth, I could see the line of tears etched onto her face. His hand came down across her cheek and knocked her off her feet.

"Get up," he ordered as he kicked her in the gut. She whimpered on the floor, naked, her dark skin making the silver tape around her hands and feet practically glow. "Listen to me when I speak!"

I stopped the playback and stared at the monitor. It was clear from the thumbnails of the videos that all four videos were of Michelle. I refused to watch any more of them.

I assumed that the memory stick labeled three would be of Claire, our third runaway. She stayed with us last year. She was eighteen, and according to Brad, a heroin addict. That's why she stole things. He kicked her out. I couldn't help but wonder if perhaps he was just done with her. His needs had been met.

As much as I didn't want to, I hit play on the first video. It took only four seconds to recognize the blonde curls of Claire. She was the one from Florida. She was making her way to Canada to escape an abusive boyfriend, she'd said.

When the video came on, I watched in utter disappointment. She was naked and bent over. Her hands had been cuffed to her feet. When Brad came up behind her, I turned it off. She had escaped nothing by coming to the farm.

As I sat, stunned, on the couch, the three memory sticks revealing their ugly secrets, I couldn't help but wonder why there wasn't a fourth one. Had he not filmed Sarah? Had she been strong enough to resist him? Had he changed? My heart leapt a moment. Perhaps she had been spared...or perhaps anything he made had burned in the fire?

The image on the screen lay frozen as I tried to figure out how to process all of it. The first videos had been poor quality, so I could have probably convinced myself that I didn't really see what was there. But the last one of Claire, that was taken on what looked like his cell phone, and the quality there proved, without a shadow of a doubt, that it was Brad.

My head whipped up. "Where did I put his phone?" I got up and started searching the "keep" pile for the Ziploc bag of Brad's belongings that we got from the funeral home. His phone had been in it, along with his wallet and a pack of gum.

If he had used his cell on Claire, maybe that's what he'd used with Sarah, and if so, it wouldn't have burned in the fire.

Naturally, the phone was dead. It had been without a charge for three months, so I had to fish out my charger, hoping it would work. I had no idea where his charger was in all the mess.

I paced around the room waiting for the phone to be charged enough for me to be able to turn it on. As I did, I kept trying to tell myself there was no way he could have done that under our noses. My room was right beside his! I would have heard something.

Wracking my brain, I tried to remember back during each of the runaways stay...was he ever alone with them?

I stopped pacing. Of course he was. Now that I thought about it, Brad was always the first to volunteer to watch over Mom when Dad and I went out of town to sell cattle, get hay, feed...anything. Brad was always more than happy to stay back with Mom. Our runs would take hours, sometimes half a day.

My stomach rolled. He must have set Mom up with her shows and then went to work.

At that moment, his cell burst into life. His smiling eyes greeted me in the wallpaper. Before today, looking at pictures of him hurt. It reminded me that he was gone. But now, seeing his face hurt for an entirely different reason. I didn't know the person smiling back at me.

I swiped the phone and saw it was password protected.

"Damn it."

I sat there forever trying anything I could think of for a password: Runaways, Garbage, Fetish.

I tried each name of his victims. Yes. Victims. That's what they were. It made me sick each time I keyed in a name, wondering how much shame and pain they carried with them thanks to my brother. Of course, none of those names worked.

Disgusted, I tried a new password: BRAD. I was in. Of course he'd chosen his own name.

I clicked on the app that read "Videos." At first glance, all I saw were a bunch of self-made ones he'd taken solo in the mirror or with someone goofing off around the academy campus, but nothing damning. His photos held nothing either, save for more vanity. There were over fifty posed shots of just him.

Flipping through his screens, I began looking, for what I wasn't sure. There were games, a tip calculator, maps, a weather app... nothing that seemed out of the ordinary. I swiped until there were no more screens, just his smug looking face as his wallpaper. Angry, I collapsed back against the couch, ready to admit defeat. The phone proved to be a dead end. I swiped one last time to bring me back to the homepage, but instead of bringing me to his landing page, there was another screen. With a single folder named: Garbage.

Sitting up, I tapped the folder.

My stomach rolled. Video thumbnails. Five of them. What they contained was concealed by the large white play arrow, but somehow I knew exactly what I would see. They would be of Sarah. I just knew it.

I didn't want to watch. I didn't want to know what he did to her, and yet at the same time, I had to know. I *had* to see what sort of hell she had to live through right under my nose. With my heart in my throat, I hit play on the first video.

To my surprise, it was a shot of only Brad in his truck. The phone seemed to be recording from a dashboard mount.

"Today I get to take my first look at runaway number four. Sarah Brickle." He wore a huge grin as he turned down the Coopers' road. I saw the back of their sign in the background. "Let's see if she proves to be stronger than the others, shall we?" His eyebrows wiggled up and down, and I wanted to punch him. My own brother.

He pulled into the dock where we first saw him at the start of the summer. He got out of the car, and for a few minutes, you couldn't hear anything, but then Sarah got in. My throat tightened. She looked so scared, so utterly terrified—right up until Brad got in. After that, it was like a mask had slid over her face, protecting her from the monster that I now knew him to be. It was heartbreaking to watch her transformation.

I watched in shocked horror as he toyed with her by revealing how much he knew about her past and how he was threatening to turn her in.

"What do you want me to do?" Sarah asked. Her voice was strong as she sat, looking straight ahead, as though she knew what he wanted, even expected it.

"Anything I tell you to do," Brad said a second before he took her hand and shoved it onto his pants. "I like my girls dirty, just like you."

It was so surreal. That wasn't my brother. The brother I knew would never talk like that to a woman, but then again, that's probably not how he saw Sarah. He didn't see her as a woman, but like the file he'd labeled her in the videos: garbage.

"Now suck my cock, and if you bite me, I swear to God, I will knock out your teeth, understood?"

Sarah's eyes seemed to glaze over as she lowered herself onto him. I looked away at first, but mercifully, the camera only captured Brad's enjoyment from the waist up. Neither of them spoke when he'd finished with her. I couldn't either. I was at an utter loss for words after what I had seen.

The video played on as they sat there in silence, him with a smug look on his face, and hers with a long far away gaze. It was like she wasn't even there. She was off in some alternate universe where no one could hurt her.

Why did I let her go with him? I knew something wasn't right, and I still let her go.

There was a knock on my door which made me jump. I glanced up from the phone and cursed. The pizza guy. I put the phone face down on a box in front of me and went to pay the guy.

As soon as I shut the door, I shoved the pizza aside. There was no way I was hungry now. Not knowing the hell I was no doubt about to go through watching the rest of these videos. And I *had* to watch them. I had to know what he'd done to her.

DISGUST

My finger hovered over the second video. I wasn't sure I'd be strong enough to watch them. I swallowed the lump in my throat as the next video loaded.

It was dark, but there was a dim light behind him. It was Brad. He was in his room, talking to his camera.

"It's just past midnight and life here on the farm is about to get a little dirty. I gave Sarah instructions in the garden earlier today to be ready for me when I came to her room." His lips pinched into a smile. "If she isn't, well, I'll just have to punish her, won't I?"

The phone shifted and the screen went dark as I heard his feet creep down the hallway. The audio muffled as he opened the door and repositioned the camera: "You better be awake because I'm —"

The camera lowered suddenly, as though he was shocked by something. The camera landed right onto my sleeping body. The hair on my neck lifted. It was the night she had claimed to be too scared of the lighting to sleep alone. She hadn't been scared of the lightning. She had been scared of him.

For a moment he just stood there, his quick breathing the only thing that could be heard. Then, he left. and the screen went dark again. Once he got to his room, Brad's face came into view. Even though it was dark, I could see the red blotches on his cheeks from his building anger.

"Oh, that dirty bitch," he hissed into the phone. "She'll pay for this betrayal. She'll pay." With that, the video ended.

I sat there, stunned for a moment. Had he taken his revenge on her? What had he done?

The next video in the queue was just over forty-five minutes long. All the other videos had been four minutes max. I went pale at why it was so much longer.

With shaking hands, I tapped on the video and waited for it to buffer.

I watched, sickened for the full forty-five minutes and twenty-seven seconds long video. From the looks of it, he'd positioned the phone up high on what must have been his bookshelf to get the full view. I watched as Brad dragged her into his room by her hair. Watched as her cuffed her, hit her, and strung her up like a toy to dissect as she hung from his punching bag hook. My mouth dropped open in shock as I witnessed the cruelty of his actions.

I was in agony as he cut off her clothes. Screamed when he touched her and wanted to punch his lights out when his fingers disappeared inside of her. And then there was the gag. I almost threw up when he forced the gag into her mouth.

I had to stop watching for several minutes. How could he have hurt her that much? How could a human being do that to someone? But also, I couldn't help but wonder why Sarah never told me. Did she not trust me?

No. It was worse than that...she didn't say anything because she cared. She wanted to spare me the hell I was in now. There was no doubt about the sort of woman she thought she was, the self-imposed sacrificial lamb.

Steeling my resolve, I hit play again. If she had to endure this hell, then I would too. However, when he held the lighter to her breasts and she flinched away in legitimate fear, I almost lost my shit. Brad was whispering something to her, but all I could focus on was Sarah as she fought to get out of her restraints. She fought so hard that blood began to trickle down her wrists. I went pale remembering an earlier conversation I'd had with her. I had accused her of trying to kill herself. I stood up and paced, remembering it like it was yesterday.

"I like it rough," she had told me that night. And I had believed her. I'd thought less of her. I was disappointed in her, while at the same time, jealous of her relationship with Brad. She had been protecting me the whole time. Protecting me from having to know what my brother was capable of.

Without any forethought, my fist hit the wall, splintering the freshly painted drywall.

"Damn you straight to Hell!" I screamed at the wall, envisioning Brad's face there instead.

I pulled my hand out, which had a few scrapes on it but was otherwise fine. The wall, however, had seen better days. My head spun with everything I'd seen. How could he have done this?

My eyes blinked away a few tears when a third voice came onto my screen—mine. "Brad?" I heard myself say.

I walked back over to the screen. Brad's eyes grew wide in excitement while Sarah's froze with fear. She started shaking her head, pleading with him to be quiet with her eyes. She was begging him to spare me from hearing.

Brad's eyes positively glinted. He grabbed her by the neck and forced himself into her. "Yeah, baby, that's it! Scream for me, Sarah! Ride my cock. Ride me, bitch, ride me!"

My eyes were locked on Sarah's as silent tears rolled down her face. Bile rose in my throat.

This was hell. Positively the worst thing I'd ever seen...until it wasn't. When she heard my truck peel away, her eyes turned to the window. Her eyes...her eyes went positively dead. I saw all hope drain from her body as she went slack against the restraints. She no longer had the will to resist. She had resigned herself to her fate. The truth of the moment came flooding in. I had let her down. I hadn't helped her when she needed me the most.

That's when I threw up.

I felt so disgusted by it all. By what he did to her, by how broken she looked, but worst of all, how I had failed to save her from any of it. I had been right there...one thin door away from helping her, and instead, I had allowed myself to believe that she liked Brad more than me. I had allowed myself to believe whatever bond Sarah and I had made was all in my head. I had assumed the worst about myself, that she didn't like me. Brad knew I liked her, he knew that seeing him with Sarah killed me, and he did it anyway.

My fingers closed around the phone, ready to toss it across the room so it would shatter into a million pieces, and I'd never have to watch it again. I almost did too. But something buzzed in my head to watch the video again. "You're missing something."

Gritting my teeth, I backed up the feed, and when I hit play, it was right there, almost as though it wanted to be found.

Brad's voice came across loud and clear. "You know, it's a pity that the rain smothered the fire last night. Having this place go up in smoke would have saved a lot of problems for Dad. With the insurance money, he could have moved out of state to that facility to be with Mom." I stopped the video again.

He admitted that he had wanted the place to burn... Could he have started the second one and blamed Sarah because she was such an easy target?

I closed my eyes. Yes. Yes, he could have.

Maybe there was more he fessed up to? After all, there were still two more videos to watch. I honestly wasn't sure how much more of this I could take.

Letting out a deep breath, I played the next one. From the looks of it, he had placed the phone on Molly's dresser to capture his next conquest. My nostrils flared.

Mercifully, it was short, only about five minutes. It began with Brad starting the recording then lying comfortably on her bed, waiting. The focus was off center, though. I could only see a small bit of him. The frame was mostly on the window.

When Sarah entered the room, she blocked the shot for a bit

so all I could see was her back. The audio was mumbled until he came toward her and started to play with her hair. "The dots are all there, Sarah. The 'truth' doesn't matter. In the end, people just want someone to blame." My gut twisted. It was true. That's what I'd wanted. At the trial, I had desperately wanted a person to point the finger at for destroying our lives. I just had no idea it had been pointed in the wrong direction.

I refocused my eyes as he moved her to the window. This was where he knew the real action would be. At the window, not the bed. My hands clenched into fists.

"Pull your pants down," he told her.

I fought back the bile as she obeyed him.

"I want you to think about him," Brad said as he lowered himself over her back. Her eyes stared back at him in horror.

"Kyle," Brad practically purred. "I want you to think of my brother as I screw you."

I had to stop watching. This was beyond sick. I couldn't watch any more of it. It was too much. I couldn't handle it.

I needed to talk to Sarah. I had to apologize to her. I had to let her know how utterly sorry I was. But how was I supposed to find her? Then I remembered the package she'd sent me. It had a return address. Dad had said something about a rehab center in Lincoln. Scrambling off the floor, I quickly called Dad back.

"Dad!" I shouted the second he picked up.

"Kyle? What is it? What's wrong?"

"That package. From Sarah. Do you still have it?"

There was a slight muffling noise on the phone. "Yeah, I held on to it for you, just in case."

I sighed in relief.

"Want me to open it?"

My eyes widened. I had no idea what was in there. If it was anything like what I'd just seen, I did not want my Dad to look at it. It would kill him.

"No! I—it's addressed to me for a reason. I'm coming back to get it."

"What?" Dad asked. "Now? You just got there. Have you finished with Brad's things already?"

I looked around at the discombobulated mess in his room—the laptop in the center of it.

"Yeah, I'm done here."

I hung up my cell, and shoved the laptop, Brad's phone, the memory sticks, and Mom's jewelry box into my bag. The footage might be enough to lighten her sentence. I mean, after everything he did to her, she was justified in pulling that trigger. I know I would have if she hadn't. She didn't deserve to be locked up like some animal after what he did to her. She deserved more, so much more.

REVELATIONS

The drive back passed in a haze. I barely slept or ate during the twenty-six hour drive. I needed to know what was in that package. Was it another memory stick? Was she coming clean about what happened? So many ideas about what could be waiting kept my brain awake enough to drive the long stretch of highway back to Nebraska.

At the very least, the package would have a return address so I'd know where she was. That seemed the most important part of all. In fact, I almost called Dad back just to get the address and head directly there, but something told me I needed to see what she had sent me first. That it would be vital to understanding the larger puzzle.

When I finally got back to the apartment Dad and I were sharing, I practically broke down the door, anxious to get in and find out what she'd left.

There it was. Sitting on the table along with a note from Dad saying he was out visiting Mom. I glanced at the clock. It was past noon. He'd be gone until at least 7:30.

I grabbed the package. Dad was right. It was big, but it didn't feel like a memory stick. It felt like paper. The postmark showed that it was mailed weeks ago. The yellow forwarding labels —first

Annabel's sister's house where we had moved right after the fire, and then, finally, to the apartment here. Eager to see what she sent, I ripped off the top and pulled out a stack of paper about an inch thick.

A slow, measured breath escaped my lips when I saw the handwriting, instinctively knowing it was hers. I collapsed onto the chair.

"Everyone always wants to know about the first fire I lit. I honestly don't remember it. I was four."

My heart began to race as I read the first lines of her words. This was her story. Her truth, the one she tried to hide from me... from everyone.

Her first impression of me had me laughing, but then, through her own words, I saw how that opinion shifted into something deeper, something, perhaps, on the same level as what I felt for her. I found myself wishing I would have kissed her so many of the times that I had wanted to, but I'd chickened out. Maybe if I had, she would have confessed sooner about the hell she was living in right under my nose.

For the next several hours I sat and read, transfixed by her pain. The passages about what Brad did to her had me in tears, even though I had seen it all with my own eyes. Somehow reading it was a thousand times worse. How had I not seen the fear in her eyes? How had I not seen the hunger in Brad's? And then, how could I make it right? She, more than anyone I'd ever met, needed a chance at redemption, and I needed to help her find it.

There was one passage from the last page of the letter that almost killed me. *The romantic in me hopes you get this, read it, and come rushing to tell me that you forgive me. But the realist in me knows that even if this somehow makes it to you, you'll never bother to read it.*

She thought she needed to be forgiven. She actually felt *guilty* about what my brother did to her. She accepted his treatment of her as something she deserved. I swallowed down the anger. She needed to know, without a doubt, that she didn't deserve anything that happened to her, and most important, she needed to know that I didn't hate her. In fact, it was quite the opposite.

It sounds ridiculous, but I had known she'd be in my life from the moment I saw her get out of Dad's truck. That maze of dark hair blowing around her face had captivated me beyond comprehension. Dad had said that's how it was with him and Mom. Just one look and he knew. I had always thought he was exaggerating when he talked about love at first sight, but after I saw Sarah, I was a believer.

Hidden deep within the shadows of her dark eyes, she held a world of secrets. I wanted to be the one she shared them with. With her letter to me, she had done just that. She had shared the most gruesome and intimate details of a life I had no clue about. There was so much about her that I didn't know. Yet...

After reading the letter I had to see her. She had to know that I didn't blame her for any of it. I had to make it right. She didn't start that fire, just as I'd suspected. Her letter had revealed the truth. Brad had set her up. His death was an accident. She wasn't guilty of anything, and I was going to prove it. I was going to get her out of there.

I vaguely heard a door open. "Kyle, you home?" It was Dad. I glanced at the clock. The day had slipped away. Shoving the pages back into the envelope, I stood up to meet him. I had no idea what I was going to say about this horrifying discovery.

"Yeah. I'm here. But not for long."

Dad walked into the room, his hat in his hands. One look at me and he knew something was wrong.

"What is it, Kyle?"

I stood, the package tucked under my arm. "It's Sarah, Dad. She didn't do it. She didn't start the fire."

"What?"

I held up the package. "It was Brad. He set it. For the insurance money, and he blamed it on her."

Dad frowned. "Now Kyle, just because she says it, doesn't mean it's true. A court convicted her. The evidence proves—"

"The evidence is wrong!" I yelled.

Dad took a step back from me. I didn't often lose my temper. That was Brad's thing. I had to calm down.

"Dad," I said, trying to reign in my anger, "Brad did some horrible things to the runaways." I swallowed. I had wanted to protect him from this, but at the same time, I didn't see any other way to convince him of Sarah's innocence. I hated having to reveal the dark nature of his own son, but he was leaving me little choice.

"The runaways? What are you talking about?" he asked.

I let out a deep breath. "Sexual things," I said, glancing at the ground.

"Our Brad?" Dad scoffed. "No, you can't listen to that girl. She's trying to ruin our lives, even from prison! She's filling your head with lies. I should have thrown that envelope out, just like you asked."

"I found video footage, Dad!" That shut him up. "Of him with the runaways. He tortured them, Dad. At our farm...right under our noses!"

Dad's face drained of color. "What? But, how..." He was at a loss for words. Having seen the footage myself, I could relate. It was hard to swallow.

"He found out stuff about them and then blackmailed them into being his sex slaves." I flinched at the term. It was so vile, so degrading, and yet that was exactly what they had become to him — something to use for his own gain. They had ceased to be people anymore. They were simply his play things. I still couldn't wrap my head around it. "When he was through with them, he kicked them out."

Dad sank into a chair. "No. No, that can't be. You must have seen it wrong." His voice was weak from disbelief.

I reached into my bag and pulled out Mom's jewelry box.

Dad's eyes widened. "Where did you get that?"

"It was at Brad's apartment. Claire never stole this stuff. He did, to make her look guilty." I fished out the memory sticks.

"There are over a dozen videos of him, Dad. Each one shows what he did to them. Each one is as plain as day."

I let him sit with that for a moment before I moved on.

"The runaways didn't try to commit suicide. The marks we saw on them were made by Brad. Beth was choked, Michelle was hit. A lot." I shoved down nausea, remembering each blow he made. "Claire and Sarah were handcuffed."

Dad looked up at me, shock on his face.

"He enjoyed hurting them. He got off on their pain." Dad kept staring at me, horror-stricken. I tried to let it sink in as I sat next to him. "It was true. We were living with a monster. But the monster wasn't Sarah...it was Brad."

Neither of us spoke for a minute.

"But, if she's innocent, why did they convict her?" Dad ventured.

"She never told the police the truth. Part of her thinks she deserves this punishment for having pyromania in the first place, but mostly, she was protecting us. She didn't want us to know how vile Brad had become. She's in there because she cared about us. We were the family she never had." Tears formed in my eyes. I let them fall without shame. "I abandoned her, Dad."

"We all did, son." His face buckled with emotion. "What do we do?"

"We get her out." I rose, held up the envelope, and pointed to the return address. "I'm going here. I'm going to find her. I'm going to make this right." How I was going to do that, I had no idea, but I was sure as hell going to try.

What made this whole thing worse was the fact that the rehab facility was only two hours from our apartment. It made my head reel. She had been so close to me, suffering all this time, and I hadn't known it. I would never be able to forgive myself for that. Could she?

I hated that I had to pull over at some point to eat, but I hadn't eaten since last night, and the lack of food was starting to affect my driving. I didn't even taste the burger as it went down my throat. My mind was still an hour away.

When I finally got there, I practically ran from the parking lot to the entrance. Tall shrubs did little to mask a gate that ran the length of the ward. The guard at the entrance was the only sign that betrayed the truth of what was hidden beyond.

"Hi, I'm here to see Sarah Brickle," I said to the guard. His badge glinted ominously in the fading sun.

"I need to see some I.D.," he said in a bored tone.

I dug out my wallet and handed it to him.

He clicked a few keys on his monitor and handed me my card back. "I need to check you for weapons."

"Weapons?"

He patted me down without answering. "Have a nice day," he said and hit a buzzer to let me into the complex.

"Um, you too."

I stuck my hands in my pockets and followed a small stone path that was surrounded by greenery. It was rather pleasant, all things considered.

The lobby was painted in muted creams and olives. Earth-toned furniture finished off a seating area. There were plants everywhere, and the sun beamed in from a massive skylight. From far off, I heard the sound of water bubbling gently. It was very serene.

"Can I help you, sir?" a large woman behind the reception desk asked. She seemed kind.

"I sure hope so," I said, walking up to the desk.

"Are you seeking help today?"

"What? Oh, no. Not for me. I'm actually here to see a patient."

"And your name?"

"Kyle. Kyle King."

Her fingers clicked my name onto a screen.

"Okay," she said, clicking a few more buttons, "and what's your relationship to the patient?" Finally, I was getting somewhere.

"I'm not family, just a friend."

Her fingers stopped moving. She folded her hands over her lap and smiled politely up at me.

"In that case, I'm afraid I can't help you. Visitation needs to be with family only, and even then, only after patient consent. As you can imagine, some of our patients want nothing to do with their families."

I could sense the *I'm sorry, I'm going to have to ask you to leave* coming.

"Look, I drove two hours to see her. Please, it's important. I just need five minutes," I begged.

"I'm sorry." There it was. The hard refusal I had been fearing landed like a weight in my gut. "I'm afraid I can't help you." Her face grew a bit tense as though sensing I was not the type who was going to go quietly.

"Just five minutes, that's all I need. Then, I promise I'll leave." I was raising my voice, but I couldn't help it. I had to see her. I just had to.

"Is there a problem here?" A woman in her mid-forties, maybe early fifties, was suddenly beside me. Her gold nametag said: Jennifer Mills, Director of Operations.

"There's no problem," I said, bringing my voice down to normal. "I just need to see a patient. Her name is Sarah. Sarah Brickle."

The director exchanged a small glance with her receptionist.

"He's not family, nor is his name on any of our patients' visitation allowances," the receptionist said, raising her eyebrows at me.

"I see," Ms. Mills said. "Perhaps we could step into my office." She gestured towards a hall.

Not wanting to make a further scene, I let her lead me down the hall and into her office. I thought maybe I would be able to talk some sense into this woman. Thirty minutes later, however, I was no closer to seeing Sarah.

"Look, I know she's here. She sent me a letter with this return address label," I said, verging on hysteria.

"Patients move from facility to facility all the time based on their treatment needs," she said, revealing nothing. "I'm sorry, Mr. King. As I tried to tell you earlier, we can't reveal the identity of our patients."

"But you could have if I was her brother?"

She blinked at me. "Correct."

My hands clenched into fists. "Ms. Mills, with all due respect, I'm the only family she has."

I could see that she was trying to hold her smile in place. I wanted to roll my eyes. Everyone here was so damned polite in their refusal for me to have access to Sarah that it was maddening.

She folded her hands neatly in front of her, just as her receptionist had done. A strand of her graying, upswept hair fell loose, but she didn't make a move to fix it.

"You have to understand I can't tell you anything about any of our patients. Confidentiality, while in treatment, is vital to their success."

"But I'm telling you, she's not guilty. She doesn't belong here!"

"With all due respect, Mr. King, if someone ends up in here they have a physiological need to be here. Criminal history notwithstanding." She blinked her eyes at me, clearly beginning to lose her temper.

I sighed. "Fine, yes, she is a pyromaniac, but she didn't do the crime she's convicted of! The crime to land her here!"

"I can assure you everyone that is placed in my facility is here so that we may help them become a productive member of society again. It's therapy, Mr. King. Not a jail cell. We're here to help them recover from an illness."

I rubbed my hands over my eyes. "Can you just tell me if she's still here?"

"I'm afraid I can't." Her lips pressed together.

"Fine. Can I, at least, give you a message for her?" She opened her mouth to protest. "On the off chance you should ever see her? Please. It's important."

Ms. Miller let out a breath and raised her hands. "I can offer you no promises."

"Understood."

She reached into her desk and gave me a small pad of paper and a pen to compose my note.

Sarah,

I got your letter and I don't hate you. I believe you. I found the video footage of you...and the other runaways in Brad's apartment. What he did to you—I just—there are no words. I was wrong to ignore my gut when they convicted you. I knew you were innocent. I was just so mad I couldn't think straight. I had no idea I was angry at the wrong person, Sarah. I'm so sorry. I'm going to make it right. I'm going to get you out of there. I'm going to make this better. I promise.

Please forgive me,

Kyle

I folded the note over a few times and then slid it across the table. "Thank you."

"I told you I make no promises."

I stood. "I know, but at least I can hope."

Ms. Miller rose from her chair and walked me to the lobby. "What will you do now?"

"I have to go see the D.A. He and I need to have a nice long chat." I shook the envelope in my hand. The memory sticks and Brad's phone were still tucked neatly inside with Sarah's letter. "I have some things I think he'd be interested in seeing."

"Well, I wish you luck. This is a long road you have ahead. I hope it will be worth it."

I smiled. "There are things in this life worth waiting for. Sarah is one of them."

Her strict demeanor softened for a fraction of a second. "It was nice to meet you, Mr. King."

With that, I shook her hand and headed to the parking lot.

Next stop, the D.A.'s office.

REDEMPTION

The D.A.'s office wanted nothing to do with Sarah's letter.

"She's already confessed." He sighed, clearly exasperated by my persistence. He was likely regretting taking the time to see me. I told him I had new evidence, so he'd reluctantly let me into his office. "Mr. King, I understand your concern, but she admitted to setting the fire and to pulling the trigger. The gun was in her hand. The prints on a match at the scene were hers. She's guilty."

"No! She's not. I'm telling you. I have proof."

He crossed his arms, bored.

"Yes. Of course," he said, leaning back in his chair. "Her letter to you. I've already told you that won't hold up in court. Criminals have lots of time to think while in prison, or in her case the loony bin. They have loads of time to think up cover stories, excuses for what they've done. I see it every day."

I dug inside the envelope and brought out the memory sticks and Brad's phone.

"I have videos. Would that be enough?" I spat.

He looked at my hand then back at me, one eyebrow raised. "It depends on what's on them."

A few minutes later, he had a laptop ready. He turned the screen around then sat down beside me. He plugged in the memory stick and the videos came to life. Instinctively, I looked away. I knew what was there and had no desire to see them again, but if it meant helping Sarah...

The D.A. sat there, a pen in his hand, occasionally scribbling notes but seemed otherwise unaffected by the vulgarity on the screen. I couldn't watch most of it, but I could hear it—hear the pleading, the tears, the begging for him to stop.

When he switched over to the footage on the phone, I was spared much of the visuals as the D.A. watched the screen. My body felt like it was trying to crawl out of its own skin, watching Sarah's torment again. It was hard to understand how the D.A. could be so calm, but then he probably saw worse stuff like this on a daily basis. I found myself thankful that I had never wanted to get into law enforcement. I couldn't see this sort of thing day in and day out and still function in society.

"Is this last video more of the same?" he asked.

I blinked, realizing he'd asked me a question. He'd said nothing while watching them.

"Um, honestly, I don't know. I didn't have the stomach to watch any more at the time. "Does any of this help her case?"

The D.A. shifted in his chair. "Actually, it may hurt her case. It gives her the motive to kill him. It appears premeditated. She could have turned him in, but instead she took the law into her own hands." He gave me a sad smile.

He started to play the final video. It was of Brad's truck again. I recognized his shirt. Remembered it covered in blood. It was the shirt he had worn the day he came for Sarah at the carnival. I felt the color run out of my face.

"This is the day he died," I whispered.

The D.A. sat up and leaned in to hear.

"He had a gun on her. He threatened to kill her if she didn't come with him," I said, the words tumbling out.

Across from him, the D.A. folded his hands, trying to remain calm with my erratic behavior. "Your brother was a trained officer. Having a gun is part of that job. He was bringing in a person with a warrant out on her. Now, granted, that charge has since been dropped as they found the guy who actually set the church on fire, but even so, he was just doing his job by bringing her in for questioning. So why don't we just wait and see what really happened?" he said, unconvinced.

I gritted my teeth. "Fine."

We both turned to watch as Sarah sat next to Brad, half visible in the shot, but the dried up blood running down her face from a cut over her eyebrow was clear.

"I didn't start a fire in your room," Sarah said, looking at Brad, clearly confused.

"Oh, I know. You *tried* to start it in the barn, but your failed attempt gave me the idea."

"Bingo," said the D.A.

I started to say something, but he waved for me to be quiet.

Brad prattled on and on about his entire plan. *His* entire plan, not Sarah's.

"That proves it, doesn't it?" I said, unable to stop myself. "That proves she's innocent."

He didn't turn to look at me. "It only proves she didn't light the fire, not that she didn't kill him."

We watched in silence as they turned into a parking lot.

"I must admit, of all the girls I've had the pleasure of experimenting on, you have been my favorite by far." Hatred for my brother built in my gut. When he pulled out his gun, we both stopped breathing. Even though I knew the outcome, I panted heavily as he placed the barrel of the gun against her head and traced it menacingly along her jaw. My own clenched in anger.

"Screw you," she said to him. There was no trace of fear on her face. It was almost as though she was taunting him, wanting him to pull the trigger.

"I will screw you one last time, and this time it won't be part of our arrangement. I'll do it without your consent. This time, it will be rape."

I pounded my fist on the table. It was happening just as Sarah had written. Brad's shoulder hit the camera he'd mounted on his rearview mirror a bit as he moved in on her, which actually gave us a clearer shot of his cab.

We could easily see that he forced himself on top of her and her protesting beneath him. It made my stomach roll. My jaw hardened as I watched him press the gun to her chest while his other hand fumbled with the buckle of his pants. *If he wasn't already dead I would have killed him myself for what he put her through.*

Just then, something shifted in Sarah's eyes. She grabbed the gun and began tugging it away from her. I knew from her letter that she had wanted him to shoot her in the head and end her own life, but on the screen, it just looked like self-defense.

"Get off her!" I heard myself scream.

The D.A. said nothing. His eyes were locked on the screen.

They struggled, and then the gun went off, making me jump. His body collapsed on top of Sarah's, obscuring our view of her face.

Sarah laid there, his body draped in a heap over hers.

"It was an accident," I said, just as she'd written. She was trying to get the gun away from her head."

The D.A. turned to me. His dark brown suit was slightly wrinkled from a long day at the office. His face was clean shaven and showed the dark circles and worry lines his job carved into his skin.

"I'll do you one better. It was self-defense. Involuntary manslaughter."

"What does that mean?"

The D.A. shifted in his chair. He opened up her file. "Looks like she's being treated for pyromania at present," he said, reading. "After her treatment, she was headed to County for the manslaughter charge. I can get that dropped, but I'll leave the medical treatment in place. When they release her from there, she'll be a free woman."

"But she's innocent! She shouldn't be in that place!" I fumed.

The D.A. placed a hand on my shoulder.

"Mr. King, after what you've told me, after what I've seen, I've never seen anyone more in need of some therapy. She's sick. I won't deny her the treatment. On that, I won't budge."

I swallowed hard but knew he was right. I was being selfish. I just wanted her back with me. I had to come to terms with the fact that in order for her to return to me whole, she needed time to piece herself back together first.

"We'll be in touch," he said, taking away his hand from my shoulder. He gestured politely to the door, signaling the end of his time with me. I had done what I needed to do. Now it was in their hands to clear her name.

Now what?

Back in the parking lot, I sat in my car for several minutes, just sitting there. I tried to figure out what my next move should be. There was no telling how long her treatment would last. It could be months; years for all I knew. My nostrils flared in determination. It wouldn't matter how long it took. I'd wait for her. No matter how long they kept her away from me. I wasn't going to leave her. I made her a promise back at the farm, and I kept my promises.

I pulled out my phone and opened the notepad app on my phone. Speaking into the mic, I listed the things I needed: paper, pens, envelopes, and a local newspaper.

My path was in motion. I was going to write to her, every day if I had to. I was going to prove to her that she could believe in me. She could count on me. She could be assured that I wasn't going to forget about her, like so many people in her life had. Of all the horrific things that happened to her, our connection was the one thing that might heal some of the damage. She deserved more than the life she was given.

That just left the last pesky part of the plan. That's where the newspaper came in. I needed a job and a place to live, right here in Lincoln with her. If Sarah was going to be stuck here until her treatment was finished, then I would be too.

LETTERS

It was surprising how many jobs were posted in the newspaper. I wasn't in the small town of Mullen anymore. I was in Lincoln. It was a bustling mid-size city. I felt like a fish out of water, but I was determined to stay close to her. Two hours away, back at Dad's apartment, was too far. I now understood why Dad went to visit Mom every day. The thought of being away from Mom, even though most days she had no idea who he was, was too painful. It felt the same with Sarah. I couldn't bear being that far away from her. Somehow being in the same town made my heart hurt less. And yes, I realized how crazy that sounded.

I commuted back and forth to Dad's apartment until I could find a place that was willing to rent week to week. Until I landed a job no one wanted to let me sign a lease. That was the hardest part. I wasn't really qualified to *do* anything, except work on a farm. That left stocking shelves at Super Saver Foods as my best option. It was nights and weekends, but I was desperate and didn't know anyone here anyway, so I didn't need to work a typical shift. I just needed to pay my rent.

Before my first shift, I sat and wrote my fifth letter to Sarah. So far, she hadn't returned any of my letters, but I wasn't deterred. The way I figured it, she may not have been given them yet, or maybe she was still struggling with what to say. I knew she might not even be at the rehab facility that I was mailing them to. They might have moved her. Her getting them really didn't matter anyway. The letters were more for me. It was the ritual of it. I had convinced myself that in some small way, I was helping to fix some of the destruction I had left her to face alone. I had to believe that. I had to believe I was helping.

After I finished the letter, I decided to try dropping it off in person instead of mailing it. Maybe I had the address wrong? Maybe I'd catch a glimpse of Sarah? It was a long shot, but it was worth a try.

When I got to the security checkpoint, however, I wasn't allowed in.

"What? Why not?" I asked.

The security guard placed his hand on his holster and peered at me from his perch.

"Do we have a problem here?" His lips pressed into a tight line.

I raised my hands up. "No, I just, I don't understand. I was here a few days ago. Why can't I go in now?"

"Because now you are on my Do Not Allow Access list."

I stared at him in disbelief.

"What? What are you talking about?" I shouted.

At my raised voice, the officer's demeanor changed. His shoulders pushed back as he stood taller. "Sir, I'm going to have to ask you to leave."

I raised my hands higher in surrender, lowering my voice. "Can I just ask who didn't want me here? Ms. Mills? Let me talk to her. This has to be some kind of mistake."

The guard stepped out of his booth. "Sir, the only way a person is placed on this list is if the patient doesn't want to see them," he said, raising his eyebrows as though letting me in on a secret. Unknowingly, he had confirmed that Sarah *was* at this facility, which should have been a relief, but instead it was a kick in the gut. She was here, and she didn't want to see me. "Now, I'm going to have to ask you to leave."

I just kept staring at him. "She doesn't want me?" I whispered, more to myself than him.

"Seems not, lover boy." He gestured towards the parking lot again, and I felt my feet finding their way back to the truck. "Don't let me see you here again," he called out after me.

For a moment, I couldn't think straight. Why didn't she want to see me? Did she not get my letters? Did she not know how much I cared? That I didn't blame her? Had I said something in them to set her off?

Or worse, did she not care for me the way I did for her?

On the drive back to my apartment, I had all of these questions running through my mind. How could I have mucked this up so royally?

Once I got home, I barely noticed the mailman at the boxes until he handed me a flyer for Super Saver with a letter tucked inside it. I froze. It was from Sarah.

I raced up the two flights to my apartment and tore into the letter, hoping for answers.

Kyle,

I have a favor to ask of you. I need you to please stop sending me letters. It hurts too much to read them. I am writing to you because I need to be clear with you. I don't want you to wait for me. I know how this story plays out. The days will pass, the memory of me will fade, and then someone real and sane and beautiful will come into your life, and the letters will stop coming. I'm not angry about that. It's what I want for you more than anything. You deserve it, you and your parents.

Please understand that this is going to be a long road ahead for me, but one I need to make alone. I need to know I can get better on my own because I want it, not because someone wants it for me. Pyromania is an addiction, just like a drug, and I'm the only one that can do this work, and I work better alone.

You need to let go of me. I won't allow myself to hold you back. I'm used to being alone. I thrive on it. You aren't. You are the type of person who needs and deserves someone beside them. Go. Look for that girl, the one you want to grow old with. She's out there. I just know it.

Thank you for everything you've done for me, despite the hell I put you and your family through. I wish nothing but the best for you.

-Sarah

I gaped at the letter. She was trying to blow me off. She didn't think she was worth waiting for. She had no idea how wrong she was. It became clear to me then that she still had a lot of work left to do on her own self-worth. She was right. She did have a long road ahead, but I'd be damned if she was going to walk it alone. I wouldn't give up on her. I couldn't. We deserved a chance together, a better one than we were first given. My letters to her would prove it to her. I was not to be deterred. I'd keep writing every damn day.

After a month of Sarah's returned letters, however, my mailman started to get annoyed with me.

"How long do I have to keep bringing you these refused letters?" he asked me one day. The silver in his hair darkened along the edges where the sweat of the afternoon heat had gathered.

"Until she stops refusing them," I said simply, taking the latest bundle.

He muttered something under his breath, which compelled me to ask him something.

"Have you ever been in love?"

He turned to look at me, holding up his left hand. A worn gold ring was there. "Twenty-seven years. To my high school sweetheart."

I cocked my head and tapped the letters against my chin for a moment before I spoke. "Would you stop writing her letters if she sent them back to you?"

He paused to consider my question. "No. No, I guess I wouldn't."

I gave him a solemn nod of shared understanding.

"Good luck, kid."

"Thanks," I said and headed upstairs. Inside, I dropped my

keys onto an overturned box I'd converted into a table and placed the latest batch of letters into a milk crate to lay in wait with all the others. One day...one day I knew she'd open each and every one of those and know for sure how much I cared for her, but until she was ready to hear it, to accept my love for her, I kept them safe and in the order of when I wrote them. Just their existence gave me hope that all was not lost. They provided a visual reminder to stay strong, for Sarah.

I won't lie and say getting the letters returned week after week was easy. A part of me wondered if my theory about being persistent would pay off. I wondered if Sarah was right, that over time I'd learn to forget about her—that I'd move on without her. It was when those dark thoughts entered my mind that I wrote another letter. It was the only thing I could do. Writing them helped me feel close to her. I wouldn't let her go. Not without the fight of my life.

As the weeks turned into months, I sort of lost myself in the routine I'd created. I'd wake up at 4 P.M., shower, have breakfast, pack my lunch and go to work from 7 P.M. to 4 A.M., and then I'd come home, eat, write Sarah's letter, call Dad, and fall asleep in front of the TV. It was sort of pathetic. I didn't go out, except to get essentials. Life felt empty, all except the hour I sat to write to Sarah. I wrote to her about all of the boring, monotonous stuff like stocking shelves and what I had for dinner, but I also wrote about the highlights. The night crew was a colorful bunch. They made going to work at least bearable. I always closed the letter with something from the heart, a confession of sorts of how deeply I was falling for her. It didn't matter that the conversation was one sided. Somehow it felt good to put it out into the universe.

On the weekends, I went to visit Mom and Dad at the nursing home. Mom was getting a bit worse, more confused, but otherwise seemed in good spirits. It was a nice place. Dad had become a close friend to all of the nurses who worked there. They even recruited him to dress up as Santa for the upcoming Holiday Bazaar.

I'd help him set up the decorations in the halls. First came the pumpkins and cute black cats at Halloween, then the cornucopias and turkeys. Now, paper snowflakes and wreaths that some of the more coherent patients had cut out, were hung from the ceiling tiles with paperclips. We had put up a Christmas tree with ugly decorations, a Menorah, and about a thousand stuffed holiday toys in the windows. Dad was always humming when he worked on those sorts of projects. He liked feeling useful. I guess I got that trait from him.

"All done with your Christmas shopping?" Dad asked.

We sat in the recreation hall, the sun pouring in from the many skylights. He had taken out the cribbage board while Mom napped in a nearby chair.

"Almost. Still searching for one thing."

"Only two weeks left..." Dad warned with a smile.

I nodded. "I know, I know. I just haven't found the right thing yet." It was probably foolish to look for a Christmas present for Sarah, but I did. Every day. Nothing seemed right. "Oh, I got Mom a—"

"Shhh! Don't say it out loud. She might hear you," Dad hissed.

I glanced at mom who was still snoozing. "Dad, she's asleep." Although it wouldn't matter if she was awake. She wouldn't have a clue what I was saying or even remember it two minutes later.

Dad looked at me, as though reading my thoughts. "You'd be surprised what she hears and understands."

"You still think she's in there somewhere?" I asked, staring at the bit of drool coming down her face. Dad noticed and wiped it lovingly away.

"I know she is."

"How?"

Dad beamed. "I can feel her. Even though her eyes are looking somewhere else, I can feel her heart in tune with mine. And it always will be, until the day we die."

He wasn't trying to wax poetic. He believed what he was saying. So did I. Their bond had always been special.

.

"Has she written back yet?" Dad asked in such a way as to suggest he already knew what the answer would be but thought it still polite to ask.

"You know I'd tell you if she had," I said, counting my points. I dealt out the cards and glanced at the cribbage board. If my hand was decent, I could skunk him. Dad took his cards and shuffled their order around a bit before he slid his two cards over to me. He cut the deck and revealed a six. It went nicely with my seven, eight, and two nines, though probably did little good for my crib, but I knew I had at least my two points in that.

"Son," Dad started.

I closed my eyes. I'd been waiting for this conversation for weeks now.

"Yes, Dad," I said, the annoyance on my tongue was thick, but I couldn't help it.

"Nothing," he said.

I put my hand down. "No. Something's on your mind, so I want you to say it."

"It's not important. Let's just play cards."

I crossed my arms over my chest. "You think I should give up on Sarah, don't you?" I practically hissed. So far he'd said nothing against my determination, but he hadn't outwardly supported it either.

Dad sat back in his chair. "It's been three months, son."

"When she gets released, I'll see her then." My teeth clenched together.

"And if she doesn't want to see you?" he asked carefully. It was a simple question, one I'd asked myself a hundred times, but still didn't have an answer for.

"I don't know," I said, standing up. "Look, I gotta go."

"Kyle, I didn't mean—"

"It's okay. I have a long drive back. And I still haven't written to Sarah yet." My lips pressed into a hard line.

I started to walk off and then turned around. "You know how you said you think Mom is still here with you? Mentally, I mean?"

He nodded, taking Mom's hand.

"That's the way it is with Sarah. She'll come back to me, Dad. I can feel it."

Dad's eyes glossed over a bit.

"I hope so," he said taking my shoulder. "I hope so."

CHRISTMAS

Well, the romantic, happy ending to this story would have been that on the day Sarah got released from rehab, she came rushing back to me, apologizing for being so stubborn and falling effortlessly into my waiting arms. We'd kiss, maybe shed a few tears, and then share Christmas Day together, surrounded by people who cared for her and would love her despite her past. It would have been a great-made-for-TV sort of movie ending.

However, on December fifteenth, I got a letter from the rehab center telling me to "Cease and Desist" writing her letters. It went on to say that Sarah had been discharged two weeks prior and had left no forwarding information.

Two weeks.

She'd been out of rehab for two weeks, and she hadn't come to find me. I knew she had my address. It was on every single letter. I made sure the clinic had me in their records too. But she hadn't reached out. She didn't want to find me. She was just...gone.

I felt so utterly betrayed. Although I knew her instinct was to run, to be alone, I had hoped...prayed, that maybe I had convinced her that she could lay down roots with me. Then again, maybe she didn't want that. Maybe I had made a huge mistake in thinking she had cared about me the way I cared for her. Maybe I reminded her too much of my brother. Maybe the memories were too painful.

I wandered the streets aimlessly the day I got the letter from the clinic. It was completely illogical, but I started searching for her. Convinced I'd spot her in the crowd. For weeks, I searched. I stopped going to work, stopped showering and shaving. I barely ate. All my time was spent wandering the streets looking for a ghost. I was, quite literally, losing my mind. Eventually I lost the will to keep searching. I just stayed in bed, trying to find the answers to what to do with my life now, praying for answers in the shadows of the popcorn ceiling.

I didn't want to leave my bed ever again. I didn't want to go out. I didn't want to see anyone. Mostly because I didn't want to fake being happy. Smiling hurt. Pretty much everything hurt. It didn't even matter that it was Christmas, in fact, that sort of made it worse.

That's when there was a knock on my door. My heart lifted for a split second.

"Kyle? You in there?" It was my dad.

You fool. She isn't going to show up. Ever.

"Go away, Dad," I grumbled from under my covers.

"Kyle, you open this door, or I'll wake the whole complex up on Christmas morning."

Not that I cared what my neighbors thought of me, but I pulled back the sheets because I knew he wasn't going to leave until he'd had his say. Might as well get it over with.

I opened the door, but then walked right back to my bed, not even saying hello in the process.

I heard my father's footsteps following behind me.

"All right," he said. "That's enough." A second later, I felt the blankets being ripped off me.

"Hey!"

"Don't you 'Hey' me, boy. This moping around has gone on long enough. It's Christmas Day, and you will get your butt out of this bed and visit your mother, or I'll drag you out of it myself!"

I looked up at my dad in shock. I'd never heard him raise his voice before. As though he realized this same thing, he took a breath and sat on the bed next to me.

"I know what you're feeling, son."

I sat up and rubbed at my eyes. "No, you don't." It came out all "Woe is me" sounding, but I didn't care. He had no idea what I was going through.

When I looked over at him, I was surprised to see anger there.

"You think I don't know what it's like to love someone who isn't there?" his voice shook with barely contained rage. "You think you are the only person in the world to love someone who can't love you back, no matter how hard she may want to?"

The truth of his words hit me like a brick. While it was true, it was also different with them.

"Dad, it's not the same. Not really. Mom loves you. She can't seem to communicate it, but the love you have for each other never went away." I felt emotion flood into my eyes. "It's not like that with me and Sarah. She doesn't care about me at all."

"You don't know that," he said, trying to cheer me up.

I let out a breath before I spoke. "Yes, I do." I pulled myself out of the bed and walked over to the window, too ashamed to face my father. "She got out of rehab at the beginning of the month. She didn't tell me. She didn't text me. She didn't come find me. She just left, Dad. She ran away again. Clearly she never wanted me, okay? I was an idiot." I turned to face him. "Happy?"

"Of course I'm not happy, boy." Dad sighed. "When you wouldn't return my calls, I guess I figured something like that must've happened."

Zombie-like, I walked back to the bed and collapsed onto it. "I don't know what to do with myself anymore, Dad. I don't know why I feel so lost without her."

"Because you loved her."

I nodded, my lips pressed tight together, holding back the emotions. "I still do."

Dad put his arm around me as I wept for the past memories we'd shared and for the future I had to let go of.

"God, Dad. What am I supposed to do?" I sat up, running my hands through my dirty hair. I had never felt more lonely in my entire life.

"Well, son, you're gonna wake up each day. You're going to get out of bed. You're going to put one foot in front of the other. You are going to keep living. You have to keep going, Kyle, or the pain will consume you."

"What if I want it to?" I asked, pulling a pillow over my face.

"I know this isn't easy," Dad said. "You've hit your rock bottom. It's hard to move when the climb back up is so damn high."

This whole thing was so irrational if you thought about it. We'd only shared a handful of days together. Nowhere near long enough to make me feel so strongly for her, and yet, I couldn't deny that I did. I loved her. And I hated myself for it at the same time.

"How long did it take you? To come out of the funk of mom's illness? To finally let go of what you thought your life was going to be?" I asked, suddenly curious.

He smiled and patted my knee. "I'm still climbing."

I nodded in understanding.

"Come on. You get in the shower. I'll make you some coffee. I'll take these first few steps with you. They're the hardest. I promise."

"Dad?" I asked, catching him before he left the room. I had a question I'd been wrestling with since the fire. There was never going to be a good time to ask it, so... "Do you ever wonder why he did it? Why Brad..." I couldn't even finish the thought.

My father's face fell. Although neither of us talked about what had happened since the day I found the tapes, I knew it had been weighing on his mind as hard as it had on mine, maybe more so.

He hovered in the doorframe a moment, hanging onto the molding, probably more for emotional support than anything. I could tell it hurt to think about what his son had done.

"When your mother was first diagnosed, I didn't want to

believe it. They didn't know my Annabel. She's one tough cookie. They didn't know how strong our love was. Nothing could touch the strength of that." Dad's eyes glazed over. "Of course, over time, she became a different person. Not because she wanted to, but because there was a sickness eating at her. I think that Brad had a sickness too. I think that the Brad we knew and loved wasn't in his right mind when he took advantage of those girls." He struggled to say the words. "I have to believe he was sick. I have to, because I know for damn sure your mother and I didn't raise him to treat women that way."

I nodded slowly. Maybe he was right. Maybe it wasn't that Brad was a monster so much as the thing that possessed him was. Maybe what happened to Molly was a breaking point in his mind. Maybe it all started with her death, and not before. The mystery surrounding Molly would probably never be solved. Nothing else had been uncovered in his belongings, and there was no one left alive to ask.

"It's time to get ready, son. Your mother is waiting for us. We have to be there. For her."

With that, he left me to my thoughts. As much as I hated to admit it, he was right. It was time I moved on and left the memory of Sarah far behind me. It was time to start over, to begin anew, like she must be.

By the time I was shaved and dressed, there were two coffee cups steaming on the table. I flinched when I saw Dad. He had the crate of my letters to Sarah in front of him.

"You wrote her all of these?" he asked, astonished. He knew I wrote to her, but clearly he had no idea how often.

"Um. Yeah," I said, grabbing the cup.

"And she only wrote back that one time?"

"Yep. All the rest were returned to me," I said, before taking a huge sip of my coffee. It burned like hell going down, so I took another sip to feel something other than emptiness. "Actually, can you take those back to your place? Maybe toss them for me?" I heard myself ask. "I don't want to see them anymore."

"Of course I can. I'm sure I can find room somewhere in the truck." He liked to complain about how small his new truck was after selling his rig, but in truth, I think he preferred it to the monster he used to drive. "Why don't we go see your mother now?"

I nodded once. "Good idea."

Dad grabbed the crate while I snatched the large gift bag that held the presents I'd bought and wrapped back in November—back when I still cared about such things.

The nursing home was decked out to the nines. Decorations and well-wishing cards were hung on just about any surface that would hold them. The staff seemed to be genuinely having a good time and not angry that they were stuck there on a holiday. It was odd to see that, someone happy in their job. Maybe that's what I needed, a career shift. Maybe it was time to find something that I was passionate about, besides her.

Stop thinking about Sarah.

"Good morning." I waved at the residents as we passed by. Those that still had their memories waved back, or wished me "Happy Holidays." Those like Mom just blinked at me.

We went to find Mom in the recreation room. There were a few others about, sharing their holiday with family, but not many yet. It was still early. We found Mom sitting peacefully in the chair she liked best, a plaid wingback. One of the nurses had positioned it in front of the tree for her to watch the lights as they twinkled.

"Merry Christmas, Annabel," Dad said, kissing her on the head.

She surprised us both by looking at us dead in the eyes and asking, "Where's Sarah?"

Dad looked at me with a mix of sadness and apology. Of all the days for her to have one of her dementia spells. Hearing that name was like a kick to the gut.

"Honey, Sarah doesn't live with us anymore. She left over the summer," Dad said, taking her hand.

Annabel shook her head adamantly. "No. She was just here. She went to get me some eggnog."

"Mom," I said, exasperated. I was so tired of this same song and dance with her memory. "She's not here. She never was here. She's never coming back either because she doesn't give two shits about us!"

But then, out of nowhere, there she was, standing by Mom's chair, a small paper cup of eggnog in her hands.

My jaw dropped. It was her. It was really her.

Her hair was cut shorter and her skin seemed healthier somehow, but it was her. Her hands tightened around the cup as her eyes darted from Mom to me.

"Sorry, they had to make a new batch," Sarah said, before she quickly handed Mom the cup.

"What are you doing here?" I blurted out.

She swallowed and then shoved her hands into her pockets. "I was just leaving. Sorry."

She started to turn away, but I grabbed her by the elbow.

"No, please. Don't go." My heart was racing, trying to reconcile that she was here, standing in front of me. Now that I was touching her, there was no way I was letting her go without a fight.

"I should have checked with you all before coming. It's just, well, it's Christmas," she said simply. "This town was the closest thing I ever had to a family. I knew she wouldn't remember me enough to hate me so..." She bit her bottom lip and then looked at the floor. "I didn't mean to upset you. I'll go."

"No!" I said louder than I meant to. She wasn't going to leave. Not again. Not until we talked at the very least. There were things to say. "I'm glad you're here. We all are."

She glanced up at me. "You are?" There was no hiding the hope that laced her question.

Without thinking, I pulled her into my arms and held her. My nose buried in the crook of her neck as I held onto her for dear life. At first, she just stood there, almost robotic, as though too afraid to return the embrace, but then, slowly, I felt her hands press timidly against my back. I let out a sob of relief at the feel of her body against mine, and suddenly, her grip grew tighter. Soon, she clung to me as hard I was to her.

In that one embrace, weeks of sorrow had been lifted.

"I can't believe you're here," I whispered into her hair. My fingers felt as though they had anchored themselves into her flesh, too afraid to let go.

It was only when Dad coughed that I realized we might be making a bit of a scene.

"Maybe you two should go talk somewhere in private," he suggested.

Reluctantly, I pulled away. I was surprised to see that tears had cascaded down her face as well. I wiped her tears away with the back of my thumb. It broke my heart to see her upset, but maybe, just maybe, they were tears of joy?

"Wanna take a walk?" I asked, My voice was thick with emotion. She nodded quickly, which made me feel encouraged.

"Good to see you, Sarah," Dad said.

"Good to see you too." Her voice cracked with nerves. She had no idea how we felt about her, so naturally, she was intimidated.

I latched onto her hand. She looked down at our intertwined fingers, but made no movement to withdraw.

Neither one of us spoke until we found a quiet bench outside.

It was a little chilly. The thermometer posted to the fence read forty-nine degrees. I was comfortable in the light sweater I wore but wondered if Sarah would be okay in the thin jacket she had on.

"You warm enough?" I asked, gesturing to a bench in the sun.

"I'm fine," she whispered, letting me guide her towards the seat.

At first, neither one of us spoke as we let the Christmas sun warm us up.

"Look, Kyle," Sarah began.

"No. It's okay," I said. "You don't need to explain. You're here now. That's enough."

She smiled but shook her head. "No, it isn't. I owe you the truth." At that, she tugged her hand out of mine and stood up.

She walked a few steps and cradled her mid-section with her arms.

"In time," I said. I could tell she was nervous, and I didn't want her to feel that way with me. "So are you still in the area or..." I trailed off, trying not to sound accusatory.

She seemed to relax a bit. "Um, yeah. My place is pretty small, not much to look at, but it's mine, and that's the most empowering feeling I've had in a long time. I finally feel like I'm in the driver's seat of my own destiny, you know? I'm even working toward my GED." A determined look fell across her face.

I smiled. I was happy for her. I really was. As much as I wished she'd been able to take that journey with me, I could see now how important it had been for her to take those first few steps alone, if only to prove to herself that she could.

"Is that really what you wanted to ask me? About where I was living?" she asked with a cautious laugh.

I gave a short chuckle. "Well, no. I do have a few more, but only when you're ready. I don't want to rush you."

She smiled at me. "You were always so kind to me. Until I met you, I didn't really believe that sort of compassion was real." She let out a slow breath. "It's okay. I want you to ask your questions. I owe you that much."

"Okay," I said, deliberating on what I wanted to ask her first. "Can we start with why you returned my letters?" I braced for her answer. Maybe I'd read this visit all wrong. Maybe she had just come to see my mom and was now stuck having to talk to the one person she was trying to avoid. Maybe I'd twisted this whole thing around.

She turned around to look at me. "Honestly? I didn't want them."

She didn't want them. My stomach rolled. If she didn't want the letters, then she didn't want me. My mouth went dry.

Seeming to understand what a blow that was, she came back over and sat again. "You have to understand. I was in a very dark place when you wrote to me. I had convinced myself that I didn't deserve your forgiveness, especially after what I'd done to your family. I didn't want you to forgive me. I *wanted* the guilt." She shook her head as though ashamed for admitting her feelings. "That's why I finally wrote back to you. I needed you to move on. I wanted you to forget about me. At the time, I didn't feel like I was worth anything to anyone, and I knew you deserved so much more than I could hope to give you."

I reached out and took her hand again. I couldn't help it. I couldn't be this close to her and not touch her. I just couldn't. Instead of pulling away, she squeezed my hand back.

"And now?" I asked.

"I'm still working on that." She laughed lightly. "I'm back on medicine for the pyromania, which has its own lovely side effects I won't bore you with, but they seem to be controlling the urges. My therapist and I still meet once a week to monitor my progress, and I'll probably need to see her for several more years before they'll consider me cured." She pursed her lips together as though holding back her emotions. "The pyromania wasn't the only thing that was broken about me, Kyle. It was just a manifestation of a much larger beast that was my childhood. I was a mess during rehab. Like in a bad way. I didn't want anyone to see that, least of all you."

I wanted to tell her how I would have understood. That I would have given her all the space she needed, but I could tell she had more to say.

"I wasn't a very nice person back then, Kyle. I was angry for so long. So very long...until I wrote you my story. That's when things in my head became a bit calmer. It was actually an assignment from my therapist," she said. "She told me to write down the truth, or the truth as I remembered it, as objectively as I could. Tell the story to her, the good, bad, and the horrible. She said it would help me come to terms with what happened. Of course, at the time, I thought she was full of shit, but as I wrote, I could feel some of the weight being lifted off of me. It was as if once it was out on paper, my brain didn't have to hold onto it anymore. It was the opposite of what I thought would happen. I thought that if I wrote it down, I would be haunted by the memories, but I wasn't. It was cathartic, actually." She laughed softly. "Each day I'd bring her what I'd written about and our therapy session would revolve around whatever memory surfaced. Naturally, some days were harder to share than others." She swallowed. "But eventually we got through it all."

She rubbed her face to compose herself. I wanted to pull her into my arms, but I respected her need to hold herself up.

"It was my idea to mail the whole thing to you. I felt like I owed you the truth. Even if you never got around to reading, I knew that I had at least tried to tell you my side."

"I'm glad you did," I said.

She smiled a tight smile, as though holding back a damn of emotion. "My therapist thought it would bring you some closure too. Of course, she had no idea that you'd become a letter-writing-lunatic after." She laughed again. It made her whole face light up.

"I had no idea, Sarah. No idea about your past, about what my brother had done to you," I said, my body going tense with anger. "If I had..."

She squeezed my hand gently. "I know. But you can't blame yourself. I hid it from you. I could have easily said something. I knew you would have believed me too." A tear fell free, unable to stay still.

"Why didn't you?"

"I guess...I wanted to spare you the shame of knowing your brother was capable of, well..." She looked down at her hands. "Mostly I didn't tell you so I could spare myself from getting that look."

"What look?" I asked.

She glanced up at me through her lashes. "The one you're giving me now. The one that can never look at me the same way again now that you know the truth."

I opened my mouth but closed it.

"You were the one person I didn't want to let down." She

sniffed. "And I did anyway." A great sob escaped her lips before she pulled herself back together.

"No. No, you didn't," I said, taking her other hand in mind. "You could never let me down."

She stared at me with her dark chocolate eyes. "Yes, I could," she said. "That's something I learned in rehab. I *will* hurt people, I *will* feel shame, I *will* let people down, but that's only because I'm human. My emotions aren't bad. They are simply a response to a situation. I know this now. I don't have to let those emotions consume me. I don't have to live with the labels people put on me. I don't have to become the things I hate about myself."

I didn't say anything. It wasn't the time to. She was building herself up for something.

"That's why I couldn't accept your letters, Kyle. I had to focus on healing myself. I had to learn to love who I was before I ever had any hopes of loving someone else."

I stroked the back of her hand with my thumb, trying to convey, just by my touch, how much I cared about her.

"There's still a lot of work left to do, Kyle, but at least, I'm working on the idea of being loved by someone, not just used by them." She let out a breath. "Wow. My therapist would be thrilled to hear me say that."

"You are, Sarah. You are worthy of love."

Her bottom lip trembled.

"Why didn't you come find me, Sarah? Why didn't you let me know you were out of rehab. I would have come for you. I would have taken care of you—"

"I know." She sat up straighter. "I know you would have. Which is exactly why I didn't contact you."

I started to speak, but she held up her hand.

"You were supposed to leave town when I didn't return your letters. Hell, I just assumed you did. I had blocked you from my mind, as best I could. I convinced myself that you had packed up and headed somewhere off into the sunset. I needed to believe that." Her voice caught in her throat. "But then I saw you one day in town. I was on my way to a therapy session, and I saw you. You hadn't left. You were still here...you had a beard, but I knew it was you." There was a level of disbelief as she spoke. "You didn't see me, of course, because I ducked behind a corner and hid. I know it was foolish of me, but I was so scared you might see me. Terrified you might see the emotions that came flooding in. Ones I thought I had pushed away."

"You saw me?"

She nodded. "You looked like you'd lost your best friend."

"I had. I was looking for you," I confessed.

"You were?" she asked, confused. Clearly she didn't understand how enthralled I'd become with her. I squeezed her hand.

"I was looking everywhere for you from the moment I knew you'd been released. I kind of lost it for a while there," I said, remembering my aimlessness. "I was a mess, right up until I saw you walk in this morning."

She blinked a few times.

"Really?"

"Really," I said.

"Why?"

I shook my head. "You have no idea, do you?"

She looked at me, her pink lips parted. "No idea about what?"

I stood up suddenly. "Come with me. I want to show you something."

She cocked her head, but she followed me. Our footfalls synced seamlessly together as we walked, as though we were one body walking instead of two.

I led her out to the parking lot where Dad's new truck was and opened the tailgate. I slid the crate of letters Dad had stored there out a bit so she could see them.

"These are for you," I said. "Merry Christmas."

She looked at the crate, then at me, seemingly bewildered. She took a tentative step forward to glance at the contents. "Oh, my God," she whispered, leafing through the stack. "These are all addressed to me."

"And each one of them got returned," I confessed as she continued to stare at the letters.

In that moment, I realized this was the reason I couldn't find the perfect gift for Sarah. What she wanted couldn't be bought in a store. She wanted someone to love her, to care about what happened to her.

"You kept writing to me?" she asked, pausing to look up at me. Tears were forming as she spoke. "Even after I asked you to stop?"

"Every day," I said, swallowing down some emotion.

She held one of the letters to her chest. Tears welled. "They never told me..." She brushed at her eyes with the sleeve of her jacket. "Why?"

I shrugged. "Because I refused to give up on you."

"Why?" she repeated.

I took a step closer to her. "Because I love you, Sarah." Her bottom lip quivered. I reached out and held both of her arms steady, locking her eyes with mine. "I've loved you since the first day we met. From the very second I saw you." I smirked. "Just like Dad said it would happen, like lightning."

"But you hated me when we first met. You spit at me."

I flinched at the memory. "Oh, I was mad all right, but not with you. I was pissed at myself." I noticed the confusion she wore. "I don't know what it was about you, but damn it all if you didn't intrigue me. You were unlike any girl I had ever met, and it bothered me that you had such an effect on me. I was angry because I couldn't figure you out. I was angry that my dad had been right. That love would hit me just when I wasn't looking for it."

A single tear slipped down her face as she struggled to believe my words. I took her by the shoulders again. "Do you remember the day I removed that tick?"

"Oh, I do." She shivered at the memory.

I blushed knowing what I was about to say. "I remember it too, but for a very different reason. I wanted to kiss you so badly that day and, since we're being honest, I've wanted to kiss you every day since.

She sucked in her bottom lip and took a small step back.

"But you didn't," she said, sounding wounded.

"No, I didn't. I didn't think *I* was a person *you* could love."

Her eyebrows shot up in disbelief. "Why not?"

I hopped onto the truck bed, my feet dangling off the edge. "Because I was just some hick farmboy. I didn't have any of the real-life experiences you had. I wasn't edgy or street-smart. I was boring compared to the life I had imagined you had, and then when Brad came along..."

Sarah flinched at his name.

"I guess when I saw him with you, I sort of convinced myself I was right. That someone like you could never have fallen for someone like me."

Sarah stepped carefully between my legs. My heart began to quicken at her closeness. Her hands knotted themselves in front of her as she fought with the words she wanted to say.

"You know about my history with men...it's left me sort of hating them, you know?"

"Sarah, I wouldn't blame you if you hated our kind for the rest of your life," I said, tucking a strand of her dark hair around her face that was blowing in the breeze.

"Even still...even with the hellish history I have had with guys, you were the only one I have ever actually *wanted* to kiss."

"Were? Like, as in used to?" My eyebrows shot up in anticipation of her answer.

She took my hand, pressed it against her cheek and closed her eyes. "No." She sighed. "Somehow I don't think I'll ever stop wanting to kiss you."

I searched her face, waiting for the invitation.

"Will you kiss me?" she asked in a whisper.

My lips parted into a smile. "Everyday, if you'll let me."

Brushing the sides of her face with my thumbs, I looked deep into her eyes to make sure this was really what she wanted and not just what she thought I wanted.

"I think I'd like that." She smiled coyly. With my heart in my throat, I brought my face closer to hers, going as slow as my body would allow until I finally lowered my lips to hers.

The kiss was soft, passionate, and filled with so much emotion I thought my heart might shatter. This was the girl I was meant to love. She was the missing piece of my life that I didn't know I needed. With just this one taste of her, I knew my hunger for her would never be sated.

My legs circled around her waist, pulling our bodies closer. I was gentle with her, trying to make sure she didn't feel like she was being caged in; yet at the same time, I longed to feel her closer to me. A soft moan escaped her lips, and I had to stop kissing her.

"Jesus," I gasped. I was panting. *Panting.* "That was—"

"Yeah," she finished. "It was." Her fingers went to her lips, as though trying to remember the feeling.

I wanted to kiss her again, but I had to respect her. I had to go slow. I had to let this happen on her terms. I never wanted her to feel afraid of me. Ever.

For a long moment, we just held each other, oblivious to those milling about in the parking lot around us. Holding her was enough.

"Sarah, I know you have a lot on your plate now, but can you please not shut me out anymore? Can you let me be there for you? Can you trust me enough to know that I will never intentionally hurt you and that I won't leave you, no matter how hard you try to push me away?"

She pulled back a little and looked up at me. There was no fear there. No trace of hesitation on her face.

"I'm starting to sense that." Her eyes welled with tears, as though still doubting she could be loved that much. I took the edge of her jacket and I pulled her in for another kiss as a light dusting of snow began falling from the sky.

"You should know that I'm stubborn." I smirked.

Her beautiful smile graced her lips and my heart swelled. "Good. Cause I can be pretty bull-headed sometimes."

"Sounds like a match made in heaven then," I said playfully.

She stared at me, all trace of humor gone. "You know, I think you just may be right."

I pulled her into another embrace, knowing now that everything would be all right, for both of us.

***

Thank you for reading! Did you enjoy? Please add your **review** because nothing helps an author more and encourages readers to take a chance on a book than a review.

And don't miss more from **Danielle Bannister**. Stay up to date on all of her release information, cover reveals, sales, and giveaways by joining her **newsletter.**

Until then read RED TEA by City Owl Author, Meg Mezeske. Turn the page for a sneak peek!

You can also sign up for the City Owl Press newsletter to receive notice of all book releases!

SNEAK PEEK OF RED TEA

By Meg Mezeske

Jordan always talked to taxi drivers. Something about such a brief, anonymous encounter made them eager to talk about anything. Even things they wouldn't, or shouldn't, share otherwise.

Still, she was taken aback. Perhaps she had just misunderstood. Her Japanese was imperfect, after all.

"Pardon?" Jordan leaned forward to better catch the driver's response above the breeze whipping in the window, which was already sultry despite the early morning.

"It's too bad about that boy dying," he repeated loudly, then swiveled to look at her when she didn't reply. A puff of cigarette smoke and a surprised grunt burst from his lips when he saw her confused expression. "You didn't know?"

"No, I didn't... Who died?" Jordan asked with careful enunciation, swallowing her discomfort.

"One of the students at your school." He said "your school" so matter-of-factly. As though she weren't about to arrive for her very first day of work. As though she were already a fixture there. "He died just the other week. Everyone around here is pretty broken up about it."

"Can I ask what happened?"

This time, the driver didn't turn to look at her, peering at her through the rear-view mirror instead. His eyes narrowed with thought before they returned to the road.

"Word is he killed himself." The driver's voice didn't betray any emotion, but he shook his head and exhaled a long sigh of smoke.

"I—I'm sorry," Jordan said, both with sympathy and regret for asking. Like a reflex, thoughts of her brother surfaced, and she felt a familiar pang deep in her stomach. She tried to push his face from her mind, focusing intently out the window for something else to latch onto.

Jordan watched the homes and shops of Ogawa roll by. Most were either streaked with green algae or mottled with rust. She wondered if all of Japan's little riverside hamlets were like this: crumbling, wet, oppressively muggy. Even the air felt thick and heavy, and the other cars trudged past as though suspended in gelatin.

The driver spoke up again, his affable tone restored. "There it is!" he said and pointed out the window.

Jordan saw a three-story building rise into view and was glad for the distraction. The school looked more recently built and its floor-to-ceiling windows were spotless. It shone in the yolky morning light like a soap bubble. As the taxi slowed to a stop, Jordan watched students file in its huge front doors, greeting each other as they entered.

Only when the driver politely cleared his throat did Jordan realize she had been staring, rooted to her seat. She handed over her fare and grabbed up her jacket and bag as she scrambled out of the taxi.

The students around her stopped and looked on with interest as she neared. They tried to hide their excitement, shielding their whispers and smiles behind their hands, yet none mustered up the courage to approach her.

Nervous, Jordan patted her hair and skirt. She had taken a taxi instead of bicycling the short distance from her apartment so that she'd look impeccable for her first appearance. It had been a good idea, but now that she had arrived, it did little to boost her confidence. Between the conversation with the driver and the students' penetrating looks, anxiousness clutched at her.

With a deep breath, Jordan straightened and marched toward

the school. A gangly girl standing at the door finally let out a squeak of a greeting.

"Good morning, *sensei*."

"Good morning," Jordan said a little too quickly and tried to make up for it with a broad smile. She brushed past the girl and her friend as they dissolved into titters.

Jordan walked into a wide entryway that held rows of shoe compartments and an umbrella bin housing a few torn and rusting occupants. She found an empty cubby for her shoes, which she slipped off and replaced with a pair of indoor slippers from a nearby shelf. At least she had been in Japan long enough not to embarrass herself with improper shoe etiquette. But, she realized with a sinking feeling, she had no idea where to report to. She cast her gaze about until a student finally took pity and pointed her to the stairs.

As she walked up, the teenagers made way and fanned out like frightened sparrows. Jordan tried to smile at whoever would catch her eye, feeling like a new student herself instead of an instructor.

The stairs ended outside of a large room that bore a helpful sign marking it as the teachers' lounge. With a shaky breath, Jordan grabbed the handle of its sliding door and bowed at the waist as she entered.

"Excuse me," she said as formally as she knew how. She straightened from the bow and announced herself to no one in particular. "My name is Jordan Howard, and I'm your new assistant language instructor." She could've kicked herself for her voice rising in question.

From some desks near the door, a handful of people stood up smoothly and bowed in return. Among them was a middle-aged man with wings of dark hair encircling his bald head.

"Jordan-*sensei*, good morning!" he said with enthusiasm and straightened his glasses to get a better look at her. "I'm Principal Kikuchi. We're so pleased to have you join Ogawa High School."

"Nice to meet you," Jordan said and bowed again for good

measure. The principal offered another formal pleasantry she didn't quite catch before he gestured to an older woman. If Jordan had to guess, she was nearing seventy.

"This is Vice Principal Umiko Nakamura."

Jordan was surprised at how tall the vice principal stood. Ms. Nakamura gave only the barest indication of a bow, remaining at almost her full height. Her mouth was small and pinched, emphasized by her unsmiling, tight-lipped expression. The only cheery thing about the woman was her incongruously pink jacket and skirt.

"Nice to meet you," Ms. Nakamura said as flatly as if she were giving the time, and she looked Jordan up and down. Jordan swallowed and listened attentively as the introductions continued from teacher to teacher, bowing and nodding like a marionette, until at last, a bell rang.

Jordan drained her second cup of green tea, rolled the glass between her palms, and surveyed the teachers' room. Besides her, only the frail lunch lady remained. All the other teachers had filed out to their homerooms and the principal had retired to his office when the first bell of the day had sounded.

As she waited for the other teachers to return, she organized her stack of three textbooks, one for each grade level. "First grade" was the equivalent of an American high school sophomore class, and so on.

Jordan tapped her foot against the floor, unsure of how to occupy herself. She stared out the large window in front of her, which framed a corner of the baseball diamond, a wing of the school that mirrored where Jordan sat, and low, green hills in the distance.

The entire length of Ogawa trickled along and abutted such hills. The small town was bound on one side by these stubby, broccoli-like trees and by a long, twisting river on the other.

Though not yet nine o'clock, the air was stifling. Not a single cloud smudged the sky, and Jordan felt herself sweat more with every passing minute. Already, she could feel her blouse sticking between her shoulder blades, and a bead of sweat snaked from the back of her knee down her calf.

She stood to find a washroom for freshening up and jumped when a loud chime lanced through the intercom. A moment later, students began to file through the halls, filling the recent silence with muffled conversations and footsteps.

Ms. Nakamura slid open the door and moved to her desk without even a glance in Jordan's direction, soon followed by a trickle of teachers. A short woman with round, close-cropped hair made a beeline from the door toward Jordan. She smiled broadly and held out her hand.

"Good morning! I'm Chiaki Okubo, the English instructor," she said in brisk, near-perfect English as she shook Jordan's hand. "I'm sorry I didn't introduce myself earlier but I was already late for homeroom announcements. Are you ready? We only have a few minutes."

Jordan was pleased and surprised by such an informal introduction. Mrs. Okubo merely seemed anxious for an answer.

"I'm as ready as I'll ever be," Jordan said with a smile.

"Okay! Bring your third-grade textbook. I'll be back in a moment." Without waiting for a response, she strode off. Jordan grabbed the top textbook from the stack and stood patiently for no more than a minute. When Mrs. Okubo returned, she cradled a tower of books, sheaves of loose assignments, and a pencil case in her short arms. "Let's go."

Jordan had to hurry to keep pace with the small woman as she exited the teachers' lounge and made her way up a staircase. Mrs. Okubo spoke again after a few steps, unfazed by her burden and quick pace.

"So, what do you think about Japan? It must be very different from your home."

"It's very different, yes, but I like it so far," Jordan said.

"Think you can handle a whole year? How long have you been here?"

"This is only my third day." Jordan raised her voice to be heard over the slapping of her shoes against the echoing stairs. "I spent the first day getting from Tokyo to here and yesterday sorting out my paperwork. My alien registration card, bank card, all that."

"So, this is your first time at Ogawa High School?" She seemed curious but pushed ahead without waiting for details from Jordan. "Well, the students are very excited to meet you."

As if on cue, Jordan saw necks craning as she passed each classroom. Heads turned in concert with her passing steps, as though the students' noses were connected to her by long threads. She smiled and nodded, assuming someone would notice, and returned her attention to the petite English instructor.

"I'm eager to meet them, too."

"You'll meet the first- and third-grade classes today. Second-graders tomorrow. But don't worry about that too much. You can give the same introduction for each class." An odd grin quirked her lips. "You're our first female assistant language instructor. You may even be the first foreign woman some of these students have met."

Jordan's stomach was already painfully tight, and Mrs. Okubo's words settled in her gut like burrs. Unsure of anything to say that didn't reveal her nervousness, Jordan simply nodded.

"Well, here we are." Mrs. Okubo stepped in front of a closed door underneath a placard that read *san-nensei, ni-gumi*: third grade, second class. There was a porthole window on the door, and Jordan could see the dark silhouettes of at least three students crowding behind the frosted glass. The sun at their backs made their faces indistinguishable. She heard low laughter and shushing as Mrs. Okubo continued.

"Introduce yourself—tell them a little about your hometown, your family—and we'll take it from there. Okay!" She said the last bit more loudly, probably as a warning to the students, and slid open the door. Jordan stepped inside and took a deep breath.

All the students sat at their desks, giving no indication of having spied against the window only moments before. Most had their hands clasped on their desks or in their laps, some grinning or leaning toward their friends with whispers on their lips. Jordan overheard hushed remarks between a pair of girls and couldn't help but smile.

"She's so pretty—and tall!"

"I'm jealous! I want her blond hair."

They jumped and returned their attention to the front of the classroom when Mrs. Okubo dropped her stack of books against her desk.

"Good morning, class."

"Good morning, Okubo-*sensei*," the class intoned with practiced unison. Mrs. Okubo looked at Jordan, and she took that as her cue.

"Good morning, everyone." Jordan scanned the room, meeting the eyes of whoever would catch her gaze for more than a moment.

"Good morning, Jordan-*sensei*." Many students stammered and tripped over her name. Some laughed at their friends or repeated her name to themselves to get a feel for the sounds on their tongues.

"Everyone, as you know, this is our new assistant language instructor, Ms. Jordan Howard," Mrs. Okubo said with slow, clear precision. "Now it's time to introduce yourselves—the American way!" She grabbed Jordan's hand and shook it to demonstrate, which lead to another round of murmurings. "Kenji, please come here to introduce yourself."

A handsome boy at the front of a row—hair styled to look tousled—pointed at himself incredulously then looked behind him, as though searching for another Kenji. This earned a few laughs, especially from a tall classmate who gave him a friendly shove out of his seat. Kenji sauntered to the front of the room and took Jordan's outstretched hand.

"My name is Kenji." His handshake was firm but hurried and he smiled with warmth. "Nice to meet you."

"Nice to meet you too."

As Kenji returned to his desk, a few boys gave him teasing congratulations. Even some calls of "teacher's pet" could be heard as the next student rose from her seat.

This continued for a few minutes, some students were hesitant and timid. Others laughed and made a show of the handshake. Jordan struggled to remember each student's name but soon became lost. She looked to their nametags pinned to their shirts for assistance, but they were written in the Chinese-based *kanji* character system, of which Jordan only knew a scant few.

The girls all wore white short-sleeved shirts with maroon ascots. Their long skirts were grey-and-maroon plaid, paired with knee-high black socks. At least, most of them were dressed to uniform.

One sullen girl who mumbled through her greeting—Emi—had unbuttoned the top of her shirt, exposing a hint of cleavage, and hiked up her skirt to the middle of her pale thighs. Her friends tried to emulate her style but introduced themselves far more politely. These girls began to chat among themselves as soon as they returned to their seats.

The boys wore similarly conservative uniforms: black slacks and white button-down shirts. Their neckties bore the same grey-and-maroon plaid as the girls' skirts. Some had loosened their ties because of the heat or removed them altogether; whether this was a breach of school conduct, Jordan couldn't be sure.

Finally, only one student remained—the tall boy who had been joshing with Kenji. All long limbs and lanky movements, he shuffled toward Jordan with a lopsided grin. Standing so close, she was even more surprised by his height, though she supposed he was one of the oldest students. She held out her hand.

"My name is Ryusuke," he said haltingly and bowed. "Nice to meet you."

"Nice to meet you, Ryusuke," Jordan said and bobbed her outstretched hand, which he failed to take. He bowed again after a moment of hesitation. A few students laughed.

"Shake her hand," Mrs. Okubo said in English, but her instructions only further confused him and he looked anxious.

"*Akushu!*" Kenji supplied.

Ryusuke smiled with relief, his face flushing. He sheepishly looked toward the class, and with great emphasis, wiped his palms on his slacks. Everyone laughed at this, Jordan included, and he enveloped her hand in his. He shook it firmly and turned away.

"He was very excited to meet you," Mrs. Okubo said to Jordan as the boy returned to his seat, then she addressed the whole class. "Well done, everyone. Now let's all listen as Jordan-*sensei* tells us about herself and where she's from."

"Well, for starters, I'm twenty-two years old and just graduated from college. I have a very big family," Jordan said and made a sweeping motion with her arms to indicate a long line. "I have two sisters and two...uh, one brother. I'm the youngest." She forced a smile to gloss over the fumble and looked at the floor, allowing herself a moment to recover. Mrs. Okubo glanced in Jordan's direction when she didn't continue right away.

"I heard you're from Las Vegas. Is that right?" Mrs. Okubo prompted.

"Yes, I am," Jordan said quickly and raised her head, taking care to project her voice.

"Oh! Like in James Bond," one boy said and mimed shooting a gun with his hands clasped together. Others nodded in sudden understanding.

"Um, something like that," Jordan said gamely and continued. As she spoke, she tried to take in each student. Some nodded with excitement, while others listened politely as the sun climbed up the window.

"You survived your first class," Mrs. Okubo said when they arrived at the teachers' room.

"Barely." Jordan smirked to show she was joking. Actually, she felt remarkably at ease. If every student was so open and friendly, she imagined her time in Ogawa High School wouldn't be as intimidating as she had feared.

"We have about ten minutes before the next class, so please take your seat for a moment," Mrs. Okubo said but had no intention of taking a break herself. She scurried off and disappeared among the other teachers milling near their desks and filing in and out of the copier room.

As Jordan took her seat, she was happy to find a cold glass of green tea placed on her desk. She drank the tea gratefully in a few gulps, parched by the heat and from speaking throughout the entire class.

A female teacher seated close by glanced in Jordan's direction at the sound of her chair scraping the floor, but she returned her attention to a student instead of greeting Jordan.

The student was a gawky boy. He looked younger than the students Jordan had just met—a second-grader, judging by the color of his nametag—and he seemed upset. His eyes were red, and his voice quavered as he spoke. Jordan knew it would be impolite to eavesdrop, yet she couldn't help but train her ears on him.

"...he keeps insisting that Yuki didn't do it," the boy said between hiccuping gulps of breath. "I just—I wonder if he's right."

"He's upset. After all, he lost his brother." The teacher didn't sound sure of her own words, and her voice wasn't much steadier than his. "Denial is common after a death. I know it's hard to understand, but..."

Jordan shifted her focus elsewhere and reprimanded herself for listening in on such a private conversation. Selfishly, she also regretted that her snooping had poked at her own deep, gnawing aches.

Before long, the boy excused himself and left, his head drooping with the weight of his thoughts.

With a sigh, the teacher shook her head and stared at her clasped hands. A minute passed before she remembered Jordan's presence, but once she did, she perked up and turned in her chair to face her.

"You must be Jordan-*sensei*," she said in Japanese. "My name is Reiko Tatsuya."

"Nice to meet you," Jordan said and bowed as best she could while seated. Ms. Tatsuya also bowed her small frame, thin and bird-like, and readjusted her glasses after they slipped down her sharp nose. "What subject do you teach, Tatsuya-*sensei*?"

"Mathematics," she said. Her lips stretched over her jutting teeth in an odd sort of smile. Then she lowered her eyes. "It's not as exciting as English, I'm sure."

"I wouldn't say that. Your students must like you very much if they come to visit you in the teachers' room."

"Oh, you mean that boy just now? Akira?" Ms. Tatsuya's large glasses made her look bewildered and wide-eyed. "Akira was Yuki's best friend. I asked him to see me since he's having such a hard time of it."

"I'm sorry, but I don't know who you're talking about," Jordan said, feeling discouraged. She tried to piece together the bits of conversation she had just overheard but couldn't place them in some larger picture.

"Yuki? He died about a week ago." Ms. Tatsuya's eyes teared up behind her glasses. "I'm sorry. I thought you knew."

"Oh! I had heard something... I just didn't know the student's name. I'm sorry." Jordan could tell the diminutive woman was upset, and she didn't relish wading into others' personal tragedies. She would have let the matter lie, but Ms. Tatsuya picked it up after a beat.

"He committed suicide," she said, her voice becoming a pitiful wail.

"I'm so sorry." Jordan felt her throat constrict around the words.

"Yuki wasn't just Akira's best friend. He was probably his only friend. They were both in my homeroom class." She sniffled but restrained herself from crying, eyes shining and red. "I can't believe Yuki would kill himself. He had so many plans. He never..."

Jordan nodded and waited for Ms. Tatsuya to continue, but the other woman stared at the handkerchief she had pulled from her pocket and turned away. Mumbling to herself, Ms. Tatsuya picked up and set down a handful of papers, only to grab at them again a moment later, forgetting all about their conversation.

"Ready?"

Jordan jumped at the brusque voice behind her, not hearing Mrs. Okubo approach. "Yes!" Jordan grabbed her textbook and darted out of her seat, grateful for the excuse to leave. "I'll see you soon, Tatsuya-*sensei*. Umm, it was nice to meet you."

"Hmm? Oh, yes, the pleasure's all mine," Ms. Tatsuya said as though she were just waking up, her distracted gaze never leaving her desk.

"She's an odd duck, that one," Mrs. Okubo whispered once they were out of earshot of Ms. Tatsuya. "Just come to me if you have any questions, okay?"

Jordan nodded and followed Mrs. Okubo out of the teachers' room. As she slid the door shut behind them, she spared one last glance at the mathematics teacher, who stared out the window silently.

Jordan exchanged her indoor slippers for the flats in her cubby, purse and jacket in hand. Jordan was alone in the entryway at the foot of the stairs. Either most students had returned home at the close of the school day or they were attending their many after-school clubs.

Jordan felt a bit uncomfortable heading home when the faculty room was still packed with teachers poring over assignments. But as far as she knew, she had no further duties for the day and would only be wasting time by pretending to look busy at her desk.

She decided it was best not to concern herself with the other teachers' responsibilities as she stepped out the door. She was tired and had had a long day, after all.

Her apartment was a short distance away, and she planned to walk home instead of calling a cab. It was still bright out, and the oppressive midday heat had mellowed.

As she passed the covered bicycle port and made for the road, she heard a voice calling her name. Turning back, Jordan saw two figures loping toward her at a brisk pace. A moment later, she recognized the boys from her first class that morning: Kenji and Ryusuke.

"Jordan-*sensei*," Kenji said with gusto. Despite Kenji's youthful features, Jordan could tell he would grow up to be quite handsome. He was favored with a straight, bright smile and eyelashes so dark they seemed painted on. "Would you like to watch our baseball team practice?"

A quick glance showed he was dressed for it, wearing a nondescript jersey with the sleeves rolled up, baseball pants, and high socks paired with cleats.

His tall friend was dressed the same, glove in hand, and stood beside him, smiling. Jordan could feel beads of sweat stippling her neck after only a few moments outdoors, and she longed for some rest after an exhausting first day. But she suspected the boys would be disappointed if she declined, and she was flattered.

"I'd love to, Kenji," she said in English. At the confused expression that crossed Ryusuke's face, she added in Japanese, "Sure, let's go."

"Please follow me," Kenji said, and Ryusuke's smile broadened.

Jordan took a seat on the concrete risers as Kenji and Ryusuke returned to the field. A few of the other boys looked to the stands and waved. Jordan waved back. She glanced around for an instructor, but it appeared as though the students had organized themselves.

They formed small clusters in the fields, tossing balls in

practiced drills. Jordan watched attentively for a few minutes, but the warm sun still hanging high above began to lull her.

Kenji left his group and barked an order to the rest of his teammates. Some of the players trotted to the diamond. One began to don catcher's gear, and three took places in the outfield. Jordan decided Kenji must be team captain, if he was leading the group.

Kenji spoke to Ryusuke as he passed, prompting the tall boy to stop and say something playful back. Kenji pushed him and grinned. From her place in the risers, Jordan heard Kenji say, "You are such an idiot."

Ryusuke ambled to the pitcher's mound, and Kenji joined the line near the batter's box. Soon, Ryusuke began pitching to his teammates—rather expertly, Jordan noticed. He had seemed oafish before, a little too tall for his own skin, but on the mound, he was fluid and imposing. He threw each pitch with obvious force and power, and very few balls floated past him to the outfield. Kenji came to the plate and was struck out in three pitches.

"Home run!" Ryusuke teased. "We'll never win with that swing, Captain."

Kenji handed off his bat and headed for the mound.

"Yeah, well, pitchers don't have to be good hitters, right?" Kenji said and motioned to Ryusuke, who gave him his glove before jogging toward the plate.

The drill continued at a steady but relaxed pace. Kenji and Ryusuke took turns on the pitcher's mound with two other boys, and the outfielders switched out to bat. Jordan watched the balls arc through the air, as though plowing furrows through the humid dampness. They skirted the sky like tiny sails at sea, and the trees' shadows barred the field as the sun drew to the horizon.

It was dusk by the time baseball practice ended. After saying goodbye to the team, Jordan began to make her way home. She walked the same narrow road her taxi had followed that morning, passing a fire station with an almost comically large statue of a fire extinguisher out front. This was followed by rows of houses with yellow lights in their windows.

After a few minutes, she came to the largest, and only, major roadway through town. The north-south highway ran the entire length of Ogawa, primarily used by commuter vehicles and shipping trucks passing through on their way to larger cities. Jordan had yet to explore all of Ogawa, but of what she had seen, she could count every stoplight on one hand, and all of them along this single roadway.

Jordan crossed the highway via an underpass and made her way toward a Lawson store just off the road. The convenience store's blue-and-white sign cast a pale light across its parking lot. Jordan pushed open the door and felt a sweep of conditioned air across her flushed face.

Though she had done little but stand and shake hands all day, Jordan was exhausted and hungry, now that the nervous tension began to loosen its grip on her stomach. She passed aisles of snack foods on her way to the refrigerators along the back wall.

Jordan skipped over the sandwiches, from egg salad to *yaki soba* noodles piled in torpedo rolls. She selected two *onigiri*: triangular mounds of rice the size of her fist. One was filled with flaked bonito and the other with cod roe, both wrapped in sheaths of seaweed.

She also grabbed bottled oolong tea and melon *pan*, a sweet roll crowned with a lattice of sugary crystals. The store was empty, so Jordan went straight to the register, which was manned by a teenage girl.

The girl smiled politely from behind sleek, dark hair that draped her face, but she showed no other sign of recognition. Not one of her students, then. Jordan offered a greeting and placed a handful of yen and her point card in a tray near the register.

As she waited for the girl to complete her transaction, Jordan's eyes fell on a stand of newspapers. The shelf contained the national *Mainichi Shimbun* newspaper and a local publication bearing Ogawa's symbol in the header.

The front page's lead story featured a record-breaking strawberry grown by a local farmer in his greenhouse. Jordan took another glance at the photo of the grinning man, holding a huge fleshy strawberry the size of an apple, and added the newspaper to her purchase. Though she knew she'd be unable to read many of the *kanji* characters, she hoped she could glean enough information to make small talk around the school.

She thanked the young clerk and stepped outside. The sky had become inky with only a shrinking swath of blushed light along the horizon. The path to Jordan's apartment was sparsely lit, so she quickened her pace while she could still make out the deep, treacherous gutters that lined each sidewalk.

She passed a pharmacy and a grocery store before walking down a narrow side street that hedged in a few dozen houses. When Jordan emerged onto a larger road, she could see her apartment building.

Beside the building was a fallow rice paddy that sprouted with thin, pale weeds. Jordan skirted the edge of the dry paddy and walked in its soft dirt to avoid the shoulder of the dark road. The soft chirping of frogs emanated from the vacant paddy and the lush, water-drenched fields that stretched along the opposite side of the road.

Jordan entered the apartment building's stairwell and climbed the steps to its second floor. Her apartment was flanked by two identical spaces that mirrored those below. She had yet to meet any of the building's other occupants, who either kept to themselves or held different schedules than hers. Jordan saw only two cars in the parking lot and could barely make out the sounds of a television behind her neighbor's door.

As she entered her own apartment, she took off her shoes in the recessed entryway and placed them in her shoe shelf. She had no indoor slippers, enjoying instead the feel of the warm wooden floor beneath her bare feet. The entryway opened up into the kitchen, which was connected to the living room past sliding glass doors.

Jordan had been more than pleasantly surprised by the amount of space when she had moved in just the day before. She had imagined she might have to live like a sardine in a tin or squeeze into a pod-like room, as popularized by hotels in Tokyo.

Instead, she had a furnished kitchen with a small table and two chairs, a living space with a television, a three-tatami bedroom, and separate toilet and bath rooms. It wasn't much smaller than the loft in Las Vegas she had just moved from.

Jordan was still getting used to calling the apartment "home," and its interior gave little indication of who lived there. The furnishings had accumulated over the last decade, as the assistant language instructors before her had come and gone. They had created a hodgepodge of personal aesthetics, from a vintage bookshelf to zebra-striped couch cushions.

Advised by her Japanese Exchange and Teaching Program counselor to bring just two large suitcases' worth of belongings, Jordan had packed only clothes, personal necessities, and a few teaching aids—nothing to distinguish the place as her own yet.

She dropped her purse and jacket in a pile on the kitchen table and fished a bonito *onigiri* and the oolong tea out of their plastic bag. Jordan sat down with a sigh and nibbled the crisp, salty seaweed on the *onigiri*, unfolding the newspaper with her other hand.

The publication was thin, especially for a weekly edition, and she thumbed through the local and national news sections in no time, only understanding a portion of the content. Jordan turned to the recreation section and saw a photo of Ogawa High School's baseball and *kendo* teams posed in solemn groups. She recognized Kenji, Ryusuke, and most of the other boys from that afternoon, though it was odd to see them so unsmiling.

The article was positive, either boasting of the baseball team's record or their promise for the season. She couldn't be sure without consulting a dictionary, so she flipped to the next section. Birth announcements and obituaries.

Below the photos of plump, soft-cheeked babies, an image in the obituaries caught Jordan's eye: a serious teenage boy with wire-thin glasses. A *kanji* character below the photo read "Yuki," and Jordan's pulse tripped as she scrambled for her phone to bring up Google Translate.

Yuki Watanabe, age 15. Survived by his mother and father, Shiori and Hiroshi Watanabe, and younger brother, Shun. Yuki loved science and hoped to one day become a chemist. He will be sorrowfully missed by his family and his friends at Ogawa High School. Memorial services will be held on September 4 at the Yamashita Funeral Home.

Jordan remembered Akira from that morning, Yuki's best friend, and she felt a pang. Familiar feelings of grief began to curl their cold fingers around her neck, her wrists.

Jordan closed the paper quickly and finished the second *onigiri*. Minutes passed with her doing nothing but staring at a few grains of rice that had fallen on the table. Finally, she heaved herself from the chair and went to the writing desk in the corner of the living room. Only an unadorned photo album sat on the desk—the single nonessential Jordan had allowed in her overstuffed suitcases.

She touched the cover of the album, hesitating for a moment before letting it fall back to expose its glossy leaves. From the book, her own face looked back, her mouth open with laughter and cheeks blushed by the sun. On either side of her stood her four siblings with their arms thrown over one another's shoulders. Both of her sisters and one brother were dark brunets—the other brother fair-haired like Jordan—but the upturned noses and high cheekbones they all shared gave them away as family.

Jordan's brief smile crumbled as she touched a finger to the photograph of her brother Aiden. The young man was grinning just as widely as Jordan, straw-blond hair shining with imbued sunlight. They weren't the closest in age, but they were most alike in personality. Or had been, she corrected herself.

Jordan admitted that she had envied Aiden and his willingness to act on his urge to roam, whereas she had so recently pulled up anchor that she could still see the shore. When she was just beginning high school, Aiden had forgone college and instead hopped across the country. He had lived on friends' couches and worked odd jobs before finally alighting in a studio apartment in Brooklyn. Though he said he didn't plan to stay long, he had remained for several years, and it was ultimately the last place he'd lived.

The previous summer, Jordan and her brother and sisters had spent a week in New York to be with Aiden. The photograph before her was the last of all the siblings together, taken at Coney Island one sultry afternoon. Like always, whenever she and Aiden were together, she had wondered how they could ever stand to be apart—both joking and laughing and perfectly understanding each other.

Eight months later, Aiden was dead. Overdosed on prescription pain medication. Pills that no one knew he was taking. Some questioned whether he had taken his own life, Jordan included, until she felt sick from her attempts to rationalize his death. Aiden had debts, but he never seemed to give them a second thought, and he quickly recovered from any bouts of melancholy. He always shrugged off despondency like an ill-fitting jacket.

Jordan sighed as worn feelings of doubt and regret began to pool around her. She had already waded through such waters countless times over recent months, so much so that her emotions felt too muddied to ever settle and clear. She thought moving to Japan would place enough distance between her and the memory of Aiden, as though the hurt would dull with each mile.

His beaming face in the photograph began to blur, and Jordan wiped away a tear with the cuff of her blouse. She closed the album and sank into the couch, listening to the frogs and crickets mutter outside the open window.

Don't stop now. Keep reading with your copy of <u>RED TEA</u> by City Owl Author, Meg Mezeske.

And find more from Danielle Bannister at daniellebannister.wordpress.com

Don't miss more more from Danielle Bannister at
daniellebannister.wordpress.com

Until then, grab your copy of RED TEA
by City Owl Author, Meg Mezeske.

A mystery unfolds in rural Japan. "Mezeske's debut is
quietly ominous, the tension rising like steam off a freshly
made cup of tea." — Heidi Lang, author of *Rules of the Ruff*

Jordan Howard moves to the Japanese countryside to become a high school English teacher, not an amateur detective. But when Jordan's students are murdered one after another, she resolves to find the culprit, fueled by lingering guilt over her own brother's death.

Toshihiko Sakurai, the ambitious police detective investigating the murders, warns Jordan against getting too involved, both with the case and with him. Yet, the two of them cannot seem to disentangle.

As Jordan gets closer to uncovering buried secrets surrounding the deaths, the murderer closes in on her too. And she just may be the next victim of the serial killer's deadly brew . . .

Please sign up for the City Owl Press newsletter for chances to win special subscriber-only contests and giveaways as well as receiving information on upcoming releases and special excerpts.

All reviews are **welcome** and **appreciated**. Please consider leaving one on your favorite social media and book buying sites.

Escape Your World. Get Lost in Ours! www.cityowlpress.com

ACKNOWLEDGMENTS

Now that you've finished the book, I can make a confession: it almost didn't see the light of day. It was *way* out of my comfort zone and so much darker than I had ever written before that I wasn't sure I could go through with it. I showed my early drafts to a very small handful of people asking them to tell me if it was too much to put out there. It is because of the feedback I got from those small few, that I had the courage to see it out to the end. For these brave women who saw the story, despite the many first draft flaws, I thank you:

My mother, Sharon Estes, who read my book despite my pleas for her to skip this one.

My dear friend and author, Amy Miles who nagged me daily to publish this book.

My first draft beta reading team: Kari Suderley, Stephanie Philbrook, and Jenn Tenney who gave me the courage to hit the 'publish' button despite my fears.

And finally to City Owl Press for taking a chance on such a dark story.

ABOUT THE AUTHOR

DANIELLE BANNISTER lives with her two teenagers in Midcoast Maine along with her precious coffee pot and peppermint mocha creamer. She holds a BA in Theatre from the University of Southern Maine and her master's in Literary Education from the University of Orono. When she's not on the stage, or on the page, you'll find her binge-watching all the Netflix. As one does.

danniellebannister.wordpress.com

 facebook.com/DanielleBannisterBooks
 twitter.com/dbannisterbooks
 instagram.com/daniellebannisterbooks
 pinterest.com/bannisterbooks
 bookbub.com/authors/danielle-bannister

ABOUT THE PUBLISHER

City Owl Press is a cutting edge indie publishing company, bringing the world of romance and speculative fiction to discerning readers.

Escape Your World. Get Lost in Ours!

www.cityowlpress.com

facebook.com/YourCityOwlPress

twitter.com/cityowlpress

instagram.com/cityowlbooks

pinterest.com/cityowlpress

Made in the USA
Monee, IL
09 May 2023

33375154R00146